THE RIPPEROLOGISTS

JOHN GASPARD

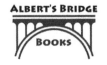

ALBERT'S BRIDGE
BOOKS

Published by Albert's Bridge Books, Minneapolis, MN

Although real places and institutions are depicted in this book, they are used in the service of fiction. No character in this book is based on any person, living or dead, and the world presented is completely fictitious.

Manufactured in the United States of America

Library of Congress Cataloging-in-Publication Data Gaspard, John, 1958-

The Ripperologists / John Gaspard

ISBN: 1449519253

EAN-13: 9781449519254

For Jim, who took me on my first Ripper walk.
And for Amy, who has accompanied me on every
walk since.

Special thanks to Tom Wescott for helping me get the
facts right.

And to Joe Gaspard for many, many things, but mostly the anagram.

"I discerned, among the youths, a young man, passing through the street near her corner ... in the twilight, in the evening ... in the time of night and darkness."

The Wiles of the Harlot
　　Proverbs 7

CHAPTER ONE

The first one was easy.

There were several reasons for that. To begin with, there were more people named Nichols in the greater New York City metro area than he would have predicted. As it turned out, a lot more. And within that group, a subset of nearly a half-dozen named Mary Ann. Once Jack generated that list, it became a simple exercise in elimination. First, because he was after all a purist, he removed any of the potential candidates who spelled their middle name "A-n-n-e." Next, he needed a Mary Ann Nichols who lived alone. Preferably in a house and not an apartment. No dogs. Neighbors at a comfortable distance. And, if possible, an attached garage.

It was quite simple: Go down the list, check your preferences, and the process of elimination does the work for you. And it did, resulting in a short list of three women in the city and surrounding boroughs named Mary Ann Nichols who fit his criteria.

The first was in her eighties. She was, of course, too old; someone of that age would muddle the investigation and get things off on the wrong foot.

The second one was in the midst of what appeared to be a messy divorce. Her soon-to-be ex-husband turned up at all hours, apparently hoping to catch her with her new boyfriend. Jack rejected that one as well. There was too much room for surprise there.

And that's why Jack – or, at least, a man who was currently calling himself Jack – found himself waiting patiently in the living room of Mary Ann Nichols of 2331 Park Lane Circle in Queens. It was a cheerful bungalow (with an attached garage! Score!) which, he discovered upon entering, had been decorated in the country style within an inch of its life.

In the kitchen alone he counted twenty-one chickens in various guises – chicken potholders, chicken salt and pepper shakers, a chicken cookie jar, chicken coffee mugs, chicken place mats and a chicken clock that crowed at fifteen-minute intervals and laid an egg on the hour. This Mary Ann Nichols certainly liked chickens, you had to give her that, he thought as he took it all in.

The living room was equally over-stuffed, but in this instance chickens had been abandoned in favor of a country Christmas theme. The level and degree of decoration was phenomenal. It would have been grotesque in December; in August, it looked pathological, like a nightmare holiday from hell.

Upon entering the living room, your eyes were drawn to the too-tall-for-the-room white-flocked Christmas tree. Next, your gaze fell on the miniature Dickens ceramic village that monopolized easily one-third of the room, including a working toy train that circled the snowy village before venturing west and circumnavigating the Christmas tree.

Stockings were hung by the chimney with what appeared to be care bordering on OCD. And next to the garland-wrapped rocking chair sat a small wooden table with a perfect, ceramic version of milk and cookies, just waiting for Santa to come down the chimney and break his teeth on.

Jack realized as he looked the room over, trying to take it all in, that he had no fear of leaving fingerprints. There was nothing in the room that invited human touch.

And, of course, he was wearing gloves.

Mary Ann Nichols followed her typical schedule, arriving home a few minutes after six. Jack heard the garage door opener grind into action and was in the closet off the kitchen before the overhead door had completed its opening process. A moment later he heard the

2

muffled sound of a car door open and slam shut, and then the sound of the heavy overhead garage door as it reversed its course and started to close.

She came into the kitchen, this Mary Ann Nichols, weighed down with a paper sack of groceries, a clear plastic bag of dry cleaning and a large, bumpy purse bulging at its seams.

She was plump like her purse, with brown frazzled hair that went in several directions simultaneously. She had a look of being persistently stressed, as if she were consistently out of sorts regardless of the time or situation. She'd look crabby even if she weren't at the end of her day and loaded down with stuff, he concluded as he peered at her through a gap between the door and the door jamb.

The groceries found a home on the one chicken-free spot on the kitchen counter, while the purse was tossed haphazardly on the floor near the door to the garage. It would probably remain there, untouched, until she picked it up on her way to work the next day.

Except, of course, Mary Ann wouldn't be going to work the next day.

The dry cleaning, Jack realized, was problematic. The small crack of light that came through the barely-opened closet door gave him a dim view of the contents of his confined hiding space. There were coats hung on hangers and what appeared to be a few kitchen towels and linens on the shelf above his head. Although he didn't have enough light to prove it, he was willing to bet that he'd find a few more chickens embroidered on those linens.

After taking in his environment, Jack felt reasonably certain that she wouldn't put the dry cleaning in this closet. Odds were that she had picked up some freshly-cleaned business attire on the way home and that she would be taking those items to their proper hanging place in the bedroom.

And he was right; she disappeared out of sight, taking the dry cleaning with her, heading in the direction of the bedroom. The room grew quiet. His heart began to beat noticeably faster.

She was home. He was ready. Now it was just a matter of picking the right moment. This jostled his memory and he remembered a joke from late night TV – was it Kimmel? Seth Myers? No, it felt like Johnny Carson, remembered from one of the old 'Best of' VHS tape collections his mother treasured so dearly. Carson's stuff was always memorable and his delivery better than anyone else, before or since.

"Anything is legal between two consenting adults," the joke went, "but not necessarily between one consenting adult and one very surprised adult." Carson would have clucked his tongue at the end of the joke and shook his head, playing the laugh and drawing it out, like the pro he was.

A few moments later she came back into the kitchen and began to unpack the groceries. Jack could see glimpses of her, just flashes, as he peered through the small crack between the door and the doorframe. But he remembered what she looked like. Small and round. Dark hair. Fair, almost pale skin. Big eyes.

He wondered why she was living alone. By choice or circumstance? Was she between relationships, or recovering from something, or just one of those lonely people who never quite find a way to make it work?

Now was not the time to puzzle that one out, of course. Not just now.

* * *

He was about to step out of the closet, ready to both start and finish the job, when the phone rang, changing the course of Mary Ann Nichols' life, if only for a few, scant moments.

"Hello? Oh, hi, mom. No, I just got home."

She cradled the cordless phone with her shoulder while she continued to unpack the groceries, setting some items aside – a pound of ground turkey, a can of stewed tomatoes, some tomato paste, a box of organic brown rice pasta – and putting other items up on the cupboard shelves.

"Later in the week is good. Sunday, maybe. Okay, Sunday definitely. We'll drive down, make a day of it." She stopped her work and listened intently for a moment. "No, Saturday's no good. It's just not, that's all."

Mary Ann Nichols stopped unpacking the groceries, her voice becoming higher, a bit more shrill, as she focused entirely on the phone conversation. "Well, I'm sure Gordon would be thrilled to drop everything and take you on Saturday. Why don't you ask him? I'm just saying Sunday works better for me. No, it's not all about me, Mother. You asked when it would be convenient and I said Sunday, that's all."

He could see that the wind was getting sucked out of her by this conversation. It had only taken moments – thirty seconds, maybe – and the color was rising up her neck, flushing her face. Mothers and daughters could do that, he knew. Go from zero to sixty in five seconds flat.

"Mother, I can't get into this now. I've got company."

This gave him a momentary start, but she gave no indication of knowing he was there. And then he realized what she was doing. She was lying. To her mother. He clucked his tongue silently, thinking, *She's breaking not one but two commandments: Not honoring her mother and bearing false witness. That's bad.* He shook his head sadly.

A pause while she listened to the phone, preparing to embellish the lie. "No, it's no one you know, but I've got food on the stove and some-one's here and I've got to go. Yes, that's right, it's a date. We can talk about it later. Yes, fine, we'll talk about it tomorrow. Good-bye."

She pushed the END button on the phone with a defiant punch, which didn't provide the same emotional satisfaction of slamming the receiver down onto the phone cradle, but it was the best she could do. Unsatisfied with that, she tossed the phone across the counter, toward its charger.

At that very moment, the chicken in the clock above the stove popped its head out of its hutch and started to loudly cluck the quarter hour.

Before the chicken had finished its work, Jack was out of the closet and behind Mary Ann, grabbing her around the neck with his gloved hands. He came at her from behind, because that's the way it had to be done, the way it needed to happen. She gasped as his fingers tightened around her chubby, fleshy throat, pinching her windpipe, cutting off her breathing.

She was so surprised she didn't even struggle, much, just waved her arms helplessly at her sides. Her fingers splayed, reflexively. Her mouth moved, with no sound coming out.

And then, after several long moments, she stopped moving alto-gether and became limp. He let her fall to the floor. She lay there, not moving, the color in her face slowly starting to shift, from red to violet on its way to purple.

The room was quiet. The eyes of a hundred chickens, in plastic, cloth and ceramic, stared at him silently. Jack opened his black case and got down to work, carefully taking out the knife.

The first one was easy, he thought. Nice and easy.

One down. Four to go.

CHAPTER TWO

"I never saw a man I so disliked, and yet I scarce know why. There is something wrong with his appearance; something displeasing, something down-right detestable. That child of hell had nothing human. He walked fast, hunted by his fears, skulking through the less frequented thoroughfares, counting the minutes that still divided him from midnight.'"

Barbara looked up from her notes, sneaking another look at the crowd. This was not a typical literary crowd, she thought. But then, this was not a typical book reading, either.

"These were the words of Robert Louis Stevenson," she continued, "introducing the world of the 1880s to a new form of evil. He called this character Mr. Hyde. But, in reality, this monster came from the darkest recesses of Stevenson's own soul, and is better known by an entirely different, albeit just as well-known, moniker: we know him as Jack the Ripper."

She closed her soft leather notebook, beginning her wrap-up. She'd given this talk several times before; however, doing it in front of this particular audience was generating a greater degree of stress and nervousness than she'd experienced in the past. But she was almost done. Then she could sit down and maybe start to relax. She focused on that image and continued.

"The truth is this," she said. "Beloved author Robert Louis Stevenson not only predicted the actions of the first modern serial killer, but he also took a more personal interest in the crimes. For as my research bears out, it was in fact *his* hand that held the knife in each of the Whitechapel murders. *His* hand that cut down the five innocent and unwary prostitutes. And *his* hand that created the character of Mr. Hyde as a hidden confession for the crimes.

"The truth can be found at the final crime scene, at 13 Miller's Court, with the death of the unfortunate Mary Kelly. That's where I found the solution to the Jack the Ripper murders and unmasked the first serial killer of modern times – aka, Robert Louis Stevenson."

She paused, in an attempt to make her conclusion a tad more dramatic. "Thank you."

Barbara stepped away from the lectern, heading back to her seat at the dais. The audience began to applaud. And they kept applauding. They were still applauding after she made it back to her chair and settled into her seat.

It was, she thought again as she looked out over the room, a mixed crowd. The room was full of men and women of all ages. There were housewives, teenagers, senior citizens. Some looked like academics, teachers or students. All were crammed into a too-small ballroom in a midtown hotel, seated ten to a round. Some were taking notes while others paged through books – including hers – they'd bought that afternoon in the book room.

As she pulled her chair in closer to the long, linen-covered table that ran the length of the dais, she was finally able to get a better look at a man in the front row who had been snapping photos throughout her talk. While she was speaking, she had wondered why he hadn't stood up to take the photos, but from this new vantage point she realized that he had, in fact, been standing the entire time. He wasn't a midget, she realized, or a dwarf. He was just remarkably short in stature. His hair was slicked back and he was dressed in what looked to be a tailored bowling shirt, with the name "Billy" stitched over the left breast pocket.

Although tiny, he was surprisingly dapper, in some ways resembling a well-dressed doll more than an adult man. He took a few more photos of her before turning his attention back to the podium, where he continued to snap away contentedly.

Barbara looked away and let her gaze settle on the entire ballroom. She understood book fairs and book signings and book readings. She'd been there and done that hundreds of times. But a Jack the Ripper conference and the people it attracted was a world away from what she knew and understood. She relaxed back into her chair and took a much-needed sip of water. The worst was over, she thought. She hoped.

The applause finally died down as the session's host, Grace Marquardt, made her way to the microphone. She was, Barbara thought, an unlikely person to host a seminar on "The Many Moods and Murders of Jack the Ripper."

Well past middle age and spreading in all directions, Grace Marquardt was as jolly as the topic she loved was morbid. Her hair was an unnatural shade of gray/blue, matching her eyes. A string of pearls hung around her neck. Her ever-present reading glasses rested upon her head. Grace's wide, happy face lit up as she turned to Barbara.

"Thank you, thank you so much, Barbara Thomas, for reading a selection from your new, fascinating book, *13 Miller's Court: Robert Louis Stevenson and the Solution to The Jack The Ripper Case.* Many of us are fans of all of your wonderful mystery books and you can imagine how excited we were to hear that your very first non-fiction book would be on a subject we all find so near and dear to our dark little hearts, so to speak."

She laughed at her own joke, then continued. "Thank you again for taking the time out of your busy schedule to be with us here today."

While the audience applauded again, Grace glanced quickly at the small pendant watch that hung around her neck, deftly cross- checking it with her ever-present agenda card.

Grace Marquardt knew how to keep an event running smoothly and, more importantly, on time. She had no problem giving a verbose speaker the hook, particularly when he or she threatened to play havoc with her well-planned schedule. God help the speaker who threw Grace Marquardt's agenda out of whack. Barbara had finished a few minutes short of her allotted time, which boosted her up even higher in Grace's estimation.

"We have a few minutes left in this session," she said, "so if there are any questions for this afternoon's panel of experts, we'd be happy to take them now."

That opened the floodgates and hands shot up around the room. Grace scanned the faces, looking for a worthy candidate for the first question. Her gaze settled on a tall, too-thin man in his twenties with dark circles under his eyes, wearing a worn and torn "9th Annual Jack The Ripper Conference" T-shirt, with that year's theme – "Get Ripped!" – still legible on the front. As the hostess for all fifteen of these events, Grace had always felt that alumni deserved preferential treatment, so he got the nod.

"My question is about Barbara Thomas' book."

All heads turned to Barbara as she leaned forward to see her questioner. Yes, definitely not a typical book signing. "Yes?"

She was surprised to see the thin, nervous man merely glance her way, and then turn his attention toward the other end of the dais.

"Well, I'd love to hear what Mr. McHugh thinks of her book and her Robert Louis Stevenson theory and evidence, such as it is."

He clearly wasn't alone in this wish; his request started a rumble of assent throughout the room. The short, greasy-haired photographer moved down the front row and started taking photos of the far end of the dais. Barbara leaned forward, only to find that everyone else on the panel had made the same move. She scooted her chair back and craned her neck to see down to the other end of the long table.

Henry McHugh looked up, raising one gray eyebrow at the sound of his name. He had settled comfortably into his thoughts and although he hadn't technically dozed off, he had come close. He could have blamed it on jet lag, if he wished. Or age. Or the sheer torpor of another Ripper conference. He suspected that it was, truth be told, a combination of the three.

Grace Marquardt leaned into the microphone. "I'll repeat the question for those of you in the back," she said. "This attendee would like to know what Henry thinks of Miss Thomas' book and her theory. Is that right?"

The tall, too-thin man nodded, never taking his eyes off McHugh, for fear that he might miss a telling look or damning wink. McHugh leaned forward, adjusting the glass of water in front of him, feeling the cool condensation on the glass as it wet his hand. He looked at the glass. He looked at the crowd. He didn't look at Barbara as he moved closer to the microphone in front of him.

"Having not yet had the pleasure of reading Miss Thomas' book," he said, his soothing British accent nearly a whisper in the sound system, "for me to comment on its contents or her ... let's say, unique and original theory, would be, I feel, ungallant."

This produced some laughter from the crowd as McHugh settled back in his chair. The audience turned to Barbara, to see if she would rise to the bait. The short photographer turned as well, continuing to snap photo after photo.

"It's all right, Mr. McHugh," Barbara said, leaning toward her own microphone. "I've read your book. I know what you've said about other theories. I'm a big girl. I can take it."

McHugh turned and looked down the panel toward her, past Wilson with his Druitt theory, past Lockhart with his Cohen theory, past Borrup with his Masonic nonsense, past Grace Marquardt with her on-again, off-again Tumblety theory, to this new – what was the American expression? – flavor of the month.

"Well, Miss Thomas, you'll have to pardon me, but I'm at an age where I'm not quite so sure I can still dish it out."

Another laugh from the crowd. Before Grace Marquardt could regain control, Barbara pressed forward.

"All evidence to the contrary, Mr. McHugh. But since the topic has come up, let me ask you a question," she said. "The $64,000 question. And it's one that you never answered in your book: who do _you_ think was Jack the Ripper?"

McHugh looked up and smiled, thinking back on the hundreds – perhaps thousands – of times he had been asked this very question. The crowd hushed, their eyes moving from Barbara to McHugh in anticipation of his response.

"Well, that's our Fermat's Theorem, isn't it?" he said, settling into his response. "The Ripperologist's Holy Grail. Our _raison d'etre_, so to speak." He smiled, looking out at their faces, then turning to Barbara.

All the other panelists leaned back in unison, to allow them to face each other, eye to eye. Attractive woman, he thought. Better looking than her photo in the conference brochure. And how often did that happen?

"Based on the facts," he said, "in my estimation the answer has always been quite simple."

If an audience can hold their breath in unison, this one was doing it. McHugh turned his gaze from Barbara to the crowd, then back to Barbara.

"I'd say he was a local man," he said, letting his words sink in. "And that he didn't like prostitutes."

* * *

"Would you like a day pass or are you here for the whole conference?"

"I'm sorry?" Ben edged closer to the registration table, trying to hear the soft-spoken girl over the din of the crowded hotel lobby.

She was at most twenty, pale and thin with big eyes and straight, jet-black hair that looked like she had cut it herself. She wore a faded black t-shirt and tight black pants, with dark black mascara around her eyes. Her blood-red lips were the only spot of color she seemed to be permitting. Even the small ring piercing the side of her nose was black.

"A day pass," she repeated, pointing to a hand-printed rate sheet taped on the front of the registration table. "A day pass is twenty-five dollars and includes admittance to all of today's seminars, the book room, and this afternoon's book signing. Tonight's movie screening is an extra fee, as is tomorrow night's banquet. Five dollars for the movie, twenty dollars for the banquet, which has a cash bar and some great door prizes."

"Door prizes?" Ben had moved in close enough now to hear her, but he wasn't really sure what she was talking about.

"Oh yeah, we have some cool stuff this year. Some signed books, an autographed print by Jason Beam, and even a trip for two to Whitechapel, which includes a personal tour of the five murder sites by Henry McHugh himself. That's our big prize this year. All of that is also part of the conference package, which covers admittance to all the seminars for all three days, all the meal functions, including the awards banquet and the late-night movies. Tonight we're showing

From Hell, and tomorrow we've got *Time After Time*. Malcolm McDowell is really cute in that one, although for my money David Warner is the coolest Jack the Ripper going."

"Cooler than Johnny Depp?" Ben asked, finally beginning to track with what she was saying.

She sighed. "Johnny Depp didn't play The Ripper in *From Hell*. Common newbie mistake. Plus, that movie strayed so far from reality it's not even funny. Anyway, you ever see *Time After Time*?"

Ben shook his head, deciding that silence was the best defense.

"Too bad. David Warner's got all the best lines. You see, the story is, H.G. Wells builds this time machine and his friend – who turns out to be Jack the Ripper – uses it to jump into the future and get away from the cops. So H.G. Wells follows him and he has to deal with our modern society when in fact he thought he was traveling to a future utopia. And when I say modern society, I mean, like, 1979."

"Uh huh." Ben nodded, politely.

"So H.G. tracks the Ripper down to this hotel room and they're just sitting around, shooting the shit, and the Ripper points out all the violence on the TV and he says to H.G., 'Ninety years ago I was a freak. Today I'm an amateur.'" She laughed, her pale face beaming at the memory. "Best line in that movie. Maybe in any Ripper movie."

Ben waited a long moment, to be sure that she was finished with her recitation. "So, how much is the conference package?" he asked.

Ben realized at that moment that he could probably just show his police badge and walk in for free, but her sales pitch, with her flat delivery and monotonous speech patterns, had become surprisingly hypnotic.

"Normally it's a hundred and twenty-five dollars, but since the first morning's pretty much over and you've missed lunch, I'm allowed to sell it to you for a hundred bucks. I suppose I could cut the rate on the day pass as well since it's nearly two. Let's say twenty instead of twenty-five."

Ben opened his wallet and wasn't particularly surprised to find it nearly empty, holding just a couple crumbled singles, his Metro card, and an old dry-cleaning receipt that he kept forgetting about. The girl peered over the table at the meager contents of his wallet and then looked up.

"We take plastic, too," she said helpfully. "MasterCard, VISA, American Express."

"I'll just take a one-day pass," he said, handing her a VISA card. "Do you have a reduced rate for the police?" he added, flashing his badge.

"Yeah, but only if you're with Scotland Yard," she said, sliding the plastic card through a reader and handing it back to him.

Ben chuckled as he took the card. She looked up at him again, a blank expression on her pale face.

"No, I'm serious," she said. "We have a special rate for Scotland Yard. We've had it for years. No one's ever used it, at least not while I've been working the desk. But we still offer it."

"How long have you been working this conference?" Ben signed the receipt that she had torn off the small printer and handed it back to her.

"This is my sixth year as a volunteer, but I've been coming here forever," she said, taking the receipt as she deftly stuffed a small packet of materials inside the Conference Guide brochure, and handed him a thin, black lanyard with a nametag hanging from it.

"Really? How many years has this conference been going on?" Ben asked, taking the packet of materials and his copy of the receipt.

He stuck the packet under his arm while he put the receipt in his wallet, making a mental note to do an expense report as soon as he got back to the station. Even as he made this mental note, he knew he was as likely to remember that as he was to pick up his laundry from the cleaners.

"This conference has been around, officially, for about fifteen years. We're not the only one, of course. They've got one in England, and there are other, smaller events that turn up from time to time, but we're definitely the biggest. Of course, we weren't always this big. When I went to my first one with my mom, it was only about fifty people in a Holiday Inn conference room that we shared with a square-dancing group on our last night. That was fun."

"I guess it's grown quite a bit," Ben said, looking around at the hotel lobby as it bustled with people.

The girl shook her head. "Well, yeah, but all these people aren't part of our conference. I mean, there are other guests in the hotel who have nothing to do with us and are glad of it, believe me. But we've got nearly two hundred people registered this year, which is a record. And whenever you get two hundred Jack the Ripper fans in one place, you're bound to have a good time."

"How could you not?" Ben agreed.

Another customer had stepped in line behind him, so Ben thanked the girl and moved aside, studying the large poster next to the registration desk that listed that day's agenda of events.

The girl was right, he noted. He had missed the morning session and that day's luncheon, with a special guest speaker who – according to the printed agenda – spoke on the topic "The Veracity of George Hutchinson and Other Myths."

He checked his watch and realized that he had also missed an author panel discussion, but was still in time for most of the afternoon sessions including the author book signing at 3:00 p.m.

Ben looked at the options laid out on the agenda poster for a few more moments, and then started wandering toward the hotel's conference center, following directional signs that pointed him to the various concurrent sessions.

If not for the magic of Google and the Internet, he thought, he'd still be sitting at his desk at the precinct, going over the written reports and photos from the Mary Ann Nichols crime scene. But he'd punched the victim's name into the search engine, just to see what – if anything – popped up. He didn't expect much, as this was usually a dead end, so to speak. As a result, he was surprised to see the words "Jack the Ripper" turn up in the vast majority of the Google results for "Mary Ann Nichols."

He spent a couple hours sifting through the listings and a couple more hours in the public library at Fifth Avenue and Forty-Second Street, and then a couple more hours on-line again. Among other things, he was surprised to discover that an annual Jack the Ripper Conference was taking place this week a mere twenty blocks from where he was sitting.

Ben moved down the conference center's long main hallway, which smelled of roast beef and mustard. Gaudy mirrors lined the walls, placed strategically, he guessed, to make the hall seem larger than it actually was. He passed a set of restrooms and a row of payphones and then came upon another corridor filled with a line of small meeting rooms, each with its own name: Jefferson, Washington, Lincoln, Roosevelt.

This presidential theme seemed to come out of nowhere, but Ben figured that they had to identify the rooms in some way and dead presidents was as good a method as any. Personally, if the choice had been up to him, he would have gone with something more interesting, like Groucho, Chico, Harpo and Zeppo. But the hotel industry had never looked in Ben's direction for nomenclature advice and he guessed they never would.

He slowed and surveyed the signs posted on the wall outside each of the small meeting rooms. The first two signs made little sense to him (one session, in the Washington room, was called "Magic, Meanings and Mysteries in the Macnaghten Memorandum" and the one in the Jefferson room was listed as "New Analysis of The Swanson Marginalia"). As far as Ben was concerned, the signs could just as easily have been in Swahili.

The posting for the Lincoln meeting room listed that session's topic as "An Authentic English Victorian Tea." Intrigued, Ben cracked the door a bit and peered in. A proper and dignified woman in what appeared to be an authentic Victorian gown was addressing the crowd of about twenty, some of whom were similarly dressed in period costumes.

"Now, before we begin the tea service, who among you can tell me who Tom Twining was and what he did in 1717 at his London Coffee House that drastically changed the world as we know it?"

She cast a stern and steady gaze around the room where only one or two hands were meekly raised. The Victorian woman surveyed the room unhappily. "Now, let's not always see the same hands," she said, shaking her head slowly from side to side.

She glanced over and saw Ben peering through the crack in the doorway. Their eyes met and he stepped backward, quietly shutting the door.

Ben quickly moved to the session across the hall, opening the door to the Roosevelt room without bothering to read the sign on the wall. Once inside, he stopped dead in his tracks and as a consequence the door whacked him sharply in the back as it swung shut.

For a moment, Ben was certain that he'd somehow stepped out of the Jack the Ripper conference and into a *Star Trek* convention. Seated throughout the room, among the normally dressed attendees and those wearing Victorian frock coats, were people costumed in the traditional red and blue shirts of the *Star Trek* crew.

In addition to the crew members, he recognized several Vulcans, a handful of Klingons, and what looked to be a Romulan princess. Some costumed audience members wore phasers as side arms. More than one held a furry, purring Tribble in their laps.

All eyes were on the panel seated at the front of the room. Three of the people on the panel were dressed in *Star Trek* gear. They ranged in age from late teens to late forties and all were male. At the other end of the table were two middle-aged men dressed in Victorian suits; one wore a Sherlock Holmes coat, half cape and deerstalker cap; the other gentleman wore a plain gray suit and bowler hat.

Between them was a handsome black man, in his thirties, who was leaning back in his chair with his arms folded, looking at the other panelists with a bemused smile. He had short-cropped hair, an angular face, and was dressed in a contemporary tailored blue suit, easily making him the best-dressed person in the room.

In contrast, at the far end of the table was the moderator, a heavyset kid in his early twenties dressed in jeans and a t-shirt, with an unruly mop of red hair cascading off his head. He was in the midst of riffling through a stack of index cards as one of the *Star Trek* panelists was just wrapping up his response to a question from the audience.

"Well, even Gene Roddenberry himself admitted that the creation of the transporter, as a dramatic device, was a mistake," said the middle *Star Trek* panelist, a pasty-faced man in his twenties, "because it removed any element of jeopardy from the storylines. How suspenseful is it if, every time your characters are faced with danger, you can just beam them back to the ship?"

"That's right," added the panelist to his left, the youngest of the three and the only one of them who looked as if he'd been in the sun any time in the last few months. "I mean, the writers were always having to come up with reasons for the transporter to break down, just so the characters wouldn't have an easy means of escape. It's not an issue so much in *Wolf in the Fold,* but I did a statistical analysis of the original series that delineates all the equipment malfunctions on the Enterprise and their dramatic consequences. Based on my research, when something goes wrong on the Enterprise, it's most likely going to be the transporter. Nine out of fourteen times, statistically."

The door opened behind Ben and he stepped aside as the girl from the registration entered soundlessly. She had a clipboard in one hand and with the other she quickly counted the number of attendees in the room, making a note of the figure on her clipboard. She looked up at Ben and smiled in recognition.

"Hey. How's it going?" she whispered.

"Great, I think," he whispered back. "But what's going on in here?" he asked, gesturing to the panel and the audience.

She nodded, understanding his confusion. "Yeah, a little weird, isn't it? There's a big *Star Trek* convention over at the Javits Center this weekend. They bring in huge numbers, I mean, like thousands of fans. Anyway, Jack the Ripper appears in an old *Star Trek* episode – one called *"Wolf in the Fold"* – so we decided to sponsor an inter- conference roundtable in the hopes of siphoning off some of their numbers." She consulted her clipboard. "Looks like we did okay."

She gave him another smile as she slipped out of the room. Ben turned his attention back to the panel, where the moderator had selected another question from his stack of index cards.

"We have time for one more question, which concerns the title of the episode, *"Wolf in the Fold,"* he said, wiping his nose quickly with the back of his hand. "The question is: 'Can any of the panelists shed some light on the derivation of the title of this classic episode?'"

The three *Star Trek*-clad panelists exchanged looks, as did the two men in Victorian dress. No one jumped at the opportunity. The moderator looked at his panelists expectantly. "Anyone have any thoughts on the title?" he asked with a tone suggesting that one of them had better start talking, and soon.

"Well," the oldest of the *Star Trek* panelists finally said, haltingly, "you know, when a wolf dresses up in sheep's clothing ..."

"Yeah, he's right," said another. "A wolf, dressed as a sheep, would, you know, be able to infiltrate the flock more efficiently and, um, you know ..."

"That's right," said the first, "because, you know, the sheep would think that the wolf was one of them or something. And that's what Redjac is doing in this episode when he takes over Scotty's consciousness. He's the wolf. In the fold. Essentially."

There was an awkward pause while the audience considered this response. The moment of quiet was broken by the black man, who leaned back even further in his chair and spoke to the ceiling, loudly reciting a poem.

"'The Assyrian came down like the wolf in the fold. / And his cohorts were gleaming in purple and gold; / And the sheen of their spears was like stars on the sea, / When the blue wave rolls nightly on deep Galilee.'"

He straightened up in his chair and continued his recitation, focusing his gaze on the audience members in the front row, his deep, sonorous voice reverberating through the high-ceilinged room.

"'For the Angel of Death spread his wings on the blast, / And breathed in the face of the foe as he pass'd, / And the eyes of the sleepers wax'd deadly and chill, / And their hearts but once heaved, and forever grew still!'"

He finished his reading, letting the final syllables echo in the room before speaking again. "For those of you who didn't recognize those classic lines, they are from the first two stanzas of *The Destruction of Sennacherib*," he said. "By George Gordon Byron, better known to most as Lord Byron," he added as an afterthought.

The rest of the panel nodded and grunted in agreement, each trying to give the impression that they had also known that answer. The moderator straightened up the index cards and turned to the audience, but before he could say anything, the black man continued.

"Some scholars have conjectured that the wolf in the fold was Byron himself, in a sly reference to his relationship with his lover, Lady Caroline Lamb." He emphasized the word "Lamb" with a quick smile. "And who knows," he added. "Byron was something of a wolf and his sexual conquests were legend. Even Lady Lamb had famously referred to him as 'mad, bad, and dangerous to know.'"

"Which is also," the moderator interjected, trying to regain control of the panel, "a fairly apt description of our friend, Jack the Ripper. I want to thank all of our panelists for their thoughts and insights this afternoon, and I've been asked to remind everyone that the author book signing – which starts in about ten minutes – has been moved out of the book room and into the foyer outside the main ballroom. Thanks everyone and have a great rest of the conference."

There was a smattering of applause as the panel members and the audience stood and began to make their way towards the door.

Ben, seeing the costumed crowd moving toward him, opened the door and stepped back into the hall, feeling for just a moment that he was leading the crew of the Enterprise into a brave, new adventure where no man had gone before.

CHAPTER THREE

Barbara discovered, as she was preparing to leave the ballroom, that her obligation wasn't complete at the end of her presentation. Grace Marquardt informed her, gently but persistently, that she still needed to sit through the requisite book signing.

In the past, these had been more elegant affairs, if sitting at a wobbly folding table in a Barnes & Noble in a suburban mall could be considered elegant. But those signings had an ease and a calmness to them, with an orderly line of fans patiently waiting to get her latest mystery novel signed, ask a quick question, and inquire about when the next mystery would be available. It wasn't exactly a tea party, but it was civilized.

Consequently, Barbara was surprised to find that a book signing at a Jack the Ripper Conference had a much more frenetic quality to it. To begin with, she was just one of many authors with books to sell and sign. They were all lined against one wall in the foyer outside the main ballroom, seated at a long line of rectangular tables, each surrounded by stacks of books. The fans moved from author to author in a disorderly jumble, seeking out their favorites and quickly brushing by the rest.

It didn't take Barbara long to realize that the authors were just as eclectic as the audience. Seated on one side of her was a twenty-something writer, a large, bushy-haired man with a thick red beard and an air of intensity that seemed to hang over him like a dense fog. He was dressed in a worn t-shirt and jeans, old work boots and suspenders.

He was selling a self-published book that appeared to go into great depth about the social conditions of the East End of London in the 1880s and put the blame for the Jack the Ripper crimes clearly on the government and their treatment of the poor. He had very few customers, although Barbara couldn't be sure whether it was the subject matter of the book or the intensity of its author that was keeping buyers at bay.

Barbara's neighbors on her other side were two young men, Mike and Dave, the writer and illustrator, respectively, of a series of extremely lurid comic books that told variations on the Jack the Ripper story – Jack the Ripper meets Dracula, Jack the Ripper meets Franken-stein, Jack the Ripper on the Titanic, Jack the Ripper in space. Every cover included a busty young woman, with torn clothes and ample cleavage, in a struggle with Jack or one of the issue's guest monsters.

The two men ignored Barbara in favor of leering at and commenting on many of the young women who passed their spot in the hall. She couldn't hear the comments they exchanged with each other, due to the constant din in the foyer, and she was glad of it.

Although her line wasn't the longest in the room, there was a steady stream of visitors to her spot. She signed autograph after auto-graph, trying to take a moment with each fan to exchange a few words about the book, their theories, or anything else that might be on their minds.

She finished up signing a copy of her book for one customer, a severe-looking woman in her twenties.

"Thanks," Barbara said, handing her the book. "I hope you enjoy it."

"Do you have any other books coming out?"

"Yes, I have a new mystery called *Jack Sprat, DOA*."

The fan was puzzled. That name didn't ring any bells in the Ripper world. "Is it about Jack the Ripper?"

Barbara smiled and shook her head. "No, it's part of a series of nursery rhyme murder mysteries, based on my first book, 'The Mother Goose Murders.'"

Her voice trailed off. She was speaking to no one. Once the fan had heard that Jack the Ripper wasn't involved, she had moved onto exploring the comic books to her right. Barbara looked at the next person in line as he handed her a book.

"And who should I make it out to?" she asked, uncapping her pen and turning to the title page of the book.

"It's not for me. The book is for you," he said. Barbara looked up to see that it was the very tall, thin man who had asked the question at the end of her session. Barbara smiled and looked at the book, surprised to see that it was a copy of her book, *13 Miller's Court: Robert Louis Stevenson and the Solution to The Jack The Ripper Case.*

"For me?" she said, not completely understanding the intention of the transaction.

"Yeah," he said. He spoke in a flat, soft monotone and only occasionally made eye contact with her. Most of the time his gaze darted around the room, never quite settling in any one spot. His hair, which was dark and borderline greasy, hung in long, thick strands from his head. "I've made some notes for you, corrected mistakes, disabused some of the faultier notions, you know."

Barbara nodded and held the book up, for the first time noticing that a colorful rainbow of Post-It notes stuck out from nearly every page.

"Well, thank you, I guess," she said, casually flipping through the book. She saw immediately that, in addition to the Post-It notes, he had also made copious notations in many of the margins, all written in amazingly small, neat handwriting. "Looks like you think I've made a few mistakes here," she said, trying to add a bit of a laugh to the end of her sentence and coming up short.

He snorted, still not quite making eye contact. "More than most, I guess, but about par for a newbie. Schoolboy mistakes, really."

He looked around the room, his dull eyes moving smoothly from point to point without ever settling on any one thing. "I color- coded the notes to make it easier for you – red for errors in fact, blue for misquotes, yellow for unsupported conclusions and green for misspellings of names and locations."

She nodded politely, still paging through the book. "Thank you," she said. "And the notes in the margins?"

23

He nodded in unison with her. "Yeah," he said, "I almost forgot. Those notes are on your theory. You know, points where you made leaps in logic or ignored known facts in order to support your theory."

"Oh," Barbara said. "I hadn't realized that I did that."

"Oh yeah, you do that a lot," he said, almost making eye contact with her for a split second, and then looking away again. "But a lot of authors who are trying to shoehorn a particular suspect into the case make that same mistake."

He stood silently in front of her for a long moment. Barbara closed the book and set it aside on the table. "Well," she said, not sure of the proper etiquette in this situation. "Thanks again."

"No problem," he said as he turned and moved off into the crowd. Barbara watched him go for a moment, and then looked up as another copy of her book was handed to her.

"Autograph?" she asked tentatively. She was greatly relieved to receive a nod of assent in response from this fan as she uncapped her pen and quickly flipped to the title page.

* * *

Henry McHugh wasn't selling books.

It's not that he didn't have any to sell. He was standing next to two stacks of his book, *The Jack the Ripper Omnibus*. And it wasn't that he didn't have customers; his was probably the longest line in the foyer. The reason he wasn't selling any books was that all of his customers – really, all of the *attendees* – already owned his book.

For most of them, it was the first book you bought when you caught the Ripper bug. It was certainly the first book you turned to when you had a question or needed to track down a fact. And it was considered by most to be the final word. If you wanted to settle an argument or win a bet, McHugh's book was the accepted final arbiter.

Fans had quickly learned that there was only one thing better than reading McHugh's book, and that was talking to him face-to- face. He was endlessly patient with all of them, from newbie to old hand, as they asked their questions and offered up their latest theories.

This was currently evidenced by the two teenage boys who were excitedly offering him their own ideas on the case. He nodded intently and listened thoughtfully to their ideas – many of which, he could tell, were a combination of several theories currently popular due to a recent movie on cable.

"Well, that's splendid in theory, my boys," he said gently. "But as is so often the case, it doesn't hold water when you put it against the facts, does it? I don't doubt that Dr. Cream was a murderer. And a vile one at that. But at the time of the Ripper murders, he was in prison. And not just any prison – a prison in Joliet, Illinois, which as you know is quite a jaunt from Whitechapel."

"No shit?" said one fan.

"I hadn't heard that part," said the other.

McHugh smiled at the teenagers. "Many authors choose to leave out those sorts of annoying little facts when they're trying to sell books. But facts are facts, aren't they? And they do have a tendency of getting in the way of a good story."

He could see that the wind had gone out of their sails, so he leaned in and spoke in a conspiratorial tone. "Do you want to know what a wiser, more fruitful line of investigation might be?"

Both boys perked up, looking around first to make sure no one else was in on this.

"What?" they asked in a hushed dual whisper.

McHugh lowered his voice to match their level. "Read up on an asylum inmate named 'Cohen.' He will lead you up some interesting avenues. And, if I'm not mistaken, my colleague down at the end there – the curious man with the gray beard and unkempt hair – has a new book on that very topic."

"So, you think this guy Cohen was Jack the Ripper?"

"Follow Cohen. That's all I'm going to say on the topic."

The boys nodded conspiratorially and headed down the row of tables to the gentleman McHugh had indicated.

McHugh smiled as he watched them wend their way down to the empty space in front of Lockhart, who looked up, surprised to have any attention given to his book or himself. He listened to the boys for a few seconds and then threw a glance toward McHugh, who nodded and smiled in return.

McHugh could have sent them in the other direction, to Connelly-Smith and his book on Druitt. It was a horse apiece, really. If they followed Cohen, they wouldn't find Jack the Ripper, but they would learn a great deal about the treatment of mental illness in the 1880s, and they'd pick up some sobering facts about poverty in London's East End.

On the other hand, he reasoned, if he'd sent them toward Druitt, they'd learn about the public-school system of the day and possibly develop an interest in cricket.

Those were just two of many available choices. For example, he could have sent them toward the artist Walter Sickert, where they'd learn all about either – depending on which author he recommended – the art world in London at the end of the nineteenth century ... or the history and impact of the British Monarchy. In the world of Jack the Ripper, he mused, there was no shortage of options.

McHugh turned his attention to the next fan in line, a bookish chap in his thirties who was wearing a button on his lapel which read, "Did Druitt Do It?"

"I've done some research," the man said excitedly, "and I want to run an idea past you – a highly-original idea!"

Highly unlikely, thought McHugh, but he smiled at the man, clapped him on the shoulder and pulled him close, saying, "This I must hear. Out with it, man. Out with it."

* * *

"Are you the gentleman who was looking for me? I'm Grace Marquardt."

Ben looked down at the small, round woman in front of him. She looked like his grandmother. That is, of course, if his grandmother were the main contact for a Jack the Ripper conference. Which, of course, she wasn't.

"Yes, thank you," Ben said, smiling down at her. "I'm Ben Black. Detective Ben Black, with the NYPD."

"The police? Oh dear," Grace said, visibly flustered, taking his arm and pulling him out of the flow of traffic in the hallway. "I hope there's nothing wrong. We applied for and received all of the necessary permits, I can assure you."

"No, ma'am, it's not that."

She pushed him toward a corner and lowered her voice, looking around as she spoke. "It's those men from the union, isn't it? I told the hotel staff, I will not pay for people who do not work. They said union 'shadows' are a common occurrence at an event like ours, where we do a lot of the work ourselves. I mean, this is a volunteer organization and I will not pay for people who just sit and read the newspaper. I made them leave and I will not pay for them. And that's final," she said, stepping back and attempting to fold her arms defiantly across her massive chest.

Ben held up his hand and shook his head, trying to calm her. "No, ma'am, it's not that. I'm sure everything is in order. And it's not about the union."

"So you don't believe in these 'shadow' workers either, do you? It's an outrage, I tell you."

Ben held up his hand again, trying to remember the three key steps to disarming a potentially violent assailant and coming up empty.

"Yes, ma'am, I agree. Union shadows are the worst. A terrible injustice. However, I'm working on a case – unrelated to the union and their shadows – and I was hoping you could help me get a few minutes with one of your people." He pointed at the line of authors signing books and chatting with fans. "One of your Jack the Ripper experts."

Grace relaxed and instantly shifted into her hostess-with-the-mostest mode.

"Oh, oh, certainly, Detective, certainly," she said, taking him by the arm and barreling her way through the crowd. "By all means, my pleasure."

Ben, in tow, did his best to limit collisions and crashes as she pulled him across the lobby, through the clusters of attendees, all animatedly discussing the books they'd just purchased.

Barbara looked up to see Grace alternately yanking and pushing a slightly flustered-looking man in his thirties toward her, positioning him ahead of the long line of book buyers who were patiently waiting their turn with the best-selling author.

He was the most normal person she'd seen all day, she thought. And certainly the best looking, with dark hair, a neat blue suit that matched his eyes, and – unless it was a trick of the light – actual dimples, which made him look younger than he probably was.

"Barbara, Barbara," Grace said, breathlessly, "A quick moment please. This man needs to speak with you."

She planted Ben awkwardly in front of Barbara. He smiled down at her, then looked away, seemingly scanning the room for something or someone.

"He's a police officer, Barbara, and he needs to talk to you about The Ripper."

Barbara looked up at Ben, who was looking a bit pained, turning his gaze from her to Grace and then across the room. "How can I help you, Detective ...?"

"Black. Ben Black. Actually, Miss ..."

"Thomas. Barbara Thomas."

"Miss Thomas, actually, when I said I needed to talk to a Jack the Ripper expert, I was referring to a, a, another Jack the Ripper expert, who I now see over there. Mr. McHugh. Over there."

He gestured in McHugh's direction, then turned back to Barbara, adding quickly, "But I would love to get your opinion, as well."

"Would you?" Barbara was enjoying his embarrassment. "Would you really?"

* * *

"Sorry to drag you two away from your convention."

"One more rubber chicken entrée, more or less, will be of no great loss, my boy. Don't you agree, Miss Thomas?"

Ben, McHugh and Barbara were making their way down the crowded hotel hallway, past weary conventioneers headed toward dinner in the opposite direction.

Barbara struggled to keep pace with the two men, thinking that they looked like an odd trio as they headed down the hall. Ben looked more like an insurance adjuster than a cop.

And McHugh, who she thought must be well into his seventies, resembled an oversized leprechaun with his tweed coat and matching tweed hat. And did he ever take that hat off?

"Pardon me?" she asked as the crowd thinned for a brief moment and she was able to move alongside Ben and McHugh. She was surprised how quickly McHugh moved for a man of his age. He noticed her attempt to keep up and gallantly slowed his pace, which forced Ben to do the same. McHugh made room for Barbara alongside them as they maneuvered through the crowd making their way down the crowded hallway.

"Perhaps this is how salmon feel, negotiating upstream," McHugh said, navigating around the short photographer Barbara had noticed earlier, who was looking at the monitor on his digital camera and not where he was going.

As they deftly made their way around the photographer, McHugh turned to Barbara. "I was only just commenting to Detective Black here that missing a dinner on the conference circuit would not be considered a large sacrifice. Hotel cuisine, when it's served in scores, is, as I believe the saying goes, nothing to write home about."

"This is my first Ripper conference," Barbara said, "so I haven't had the pleasure of sampling the food yet."

"Well, the brochure promised food for thought, and I believe that is as far as they go." McHugh looked at Barbara and smiled, adding, "Your presentation this afternoon was particularly enlightening."

Barbara couldn't tell from his tone if he was being complimentary, condescending or simply polite. The British were brilliant at that, mixing mockery with puffery so expertly that you never knew if you were being celebrated or crucified.

"Thank you." She felt she needed to return the volley in some fashion. "Will you be presenting this weekend?"

"No, no, I won't be presenting this year. I'm just here for ... what's the term they use at sporting events on the telly?" He thought for a moment, and then it came to him. "Color. I'm here to provide a bit of color."

They rounded another corner and passed The Book Room, which was merely another meeting room which had been filled wall-to-wall with tables, on which sat displays of all sorts of Ripper books, magazines, video games and DVDs. A steady stream of people made their way in and out of the room.

Standing near the door was a street performer, a mime portraying a statue, covered in white from head to toe. Barbara actually did a double take as they passed him because he looked so much like a real statue, standing frozen in the center of the hall.

The mime statue was costumed as a British newsboy, circa 1888. He wore a white cap over hair that been slicked down and colored white. His face and hands were slathered in white make-up and his clothes had also been painted white, with gray highlights to provide depth. At his feet were a bundle of newspapers, also completely white, wrapped tightly with several thick strands of white twine.

He held up a newspaper and the headline was the only thing on him that wasn't white. In bold, black type it declared, "Jack the Ripper Strikes! Claims First Victim!"

Barbara looked at the mime and the headline as they passed. She found the white figure unnerving and was further chilled by his eyes – black spots in a sea of white – which stared intently at the trio as they made their way down the hall, away from The Book Room.

"What is it about mimes that's so unnerving?" Barbara asked in a low voice. Both McHugh and Ben turned in unison as they walked, looking back at the mime, who still appeared to be watching them steadily from his frozen position.

"Mimes and clowns," Ben said, looking away and back at Barbara. "Nothing creepier to me than mimes and clowns."

Ben stopped at one of the meeting rooms, called The Presidential Board Room, and held the door open for them. McHugh gestured for Barbara to go ahead of him. Ben followed, closing the door behind them, taking one last look at the mime statue as the door silently closed.

The mime continued to watch the door for many moments after it had closed. And then, in an uncharacteristic move for a statue, he bent down and picked up his stack of newspapers, then turned and walked away.

* * *

"I should warn you that some of these photos are quite, well, graphic."

Ben held up a large manila envelope. The front of the envelope had several numbers on it, written with a thick, black marker. A red stamped seal declared that the envelope was the property of the New York City Police Department.

Ben started to undo the red string that tied the envelope shut, while

30

he looked across the dark oak table at McHugh and Barbara. "A little over a week ago, there was a murder of a young woman. A very violent crime, even by today's standards."

Ben opened the envelope and took out a file folder, setting it on the large table that nearly filled the small conference room. McHugh reached into his breast pocket and pulled out a pair of weathered reading glasses. He slipped them on and held out his hand for the file. Ben handed it to him.

"The specifics of her injuries were that she was strangled and her throat was cut, nearly ear-to-ear, almost back to the spinal cord. The abdomen was mutilated and cut open."

McHugh glanced over at Ben and then flipped through the photos quickly. From her vantage point next to him at the table, Barbara could only see glimpses of the images, quick flashes of flesh and blood. She made no move to take the photos that McHugh set, face down, on the table as he finished with each one.

"Remarkable ..." McHugh said as he made quick work of the dozen or so photos, giving each a well-practiced glance before moving on to the next.

Ben watched him, and then opened a burgeoning file of papers. "It gets better," he said. "Or worse. The victim's name was Mary Ann Nichols."

Barbara let out an involuntary gasp, turning her attention from McHugh to Ben. McHugh lowered the photos and looked at Ben over his glasses.

"Mary Ann Nichols," Barbara said. "That's the name of the Ripper's first victim."

Ben nodded. "Yes, it is. I looked that up. There was good information in your book, Mr. McHugh." Ben turned back to Barbara, realizing that he had once again slighted her. "Although I'm sure yours is rich in detail as well."

"Yes," Barbara said. "I mean, it's in all the books. Of course, there's some disagreement as to whether or not she was the first. But most experts think of her as the first. Right?" She looked to McHugh for confirmation.

"Yes. Many do." McHugh leaned across the table, gesturing to Ben's paper file. "May I?"

Ben slid it across the table to him, and McHugh began confidently flipping through the pages. He evidently knew what he was looking for, Barbara thought. Feeling like she wasn't adding much to the occasion, she picked up one of the photos in the stack and turned it over, instantly wishing she hadn't.

Although she had looked through the autopsy and crime scene photos of Jack the Ripper's victims while researching her book, all of them had been in black and white and from a comfortable distance of more than a hundred years.

They were murky and out of focus and even though you knew, in your gut, that these were real photos of real women, there was always a patina of unreality to them. Even the most gruesome of the images – such as Mary Kelly on her bed in Number 13 Miller's Court, her skin peeled back, her face a mask of desecration – never seemed quite real to Barbara, although she knew instinctively that they were very real.

The same was not true of the pictures Ben had provided. The photo Barbara picked up was in living color and though the body and its placement resembled one of the historical photos, the sharpness of the image and the richness of the color immediately tagged it as current. She forced herself to examine the photo, trying to match McHugh's level of interest and authority.

"I'll be honest with you both," Ben said, sitting across from them. "I'm not getting a lot of support for this downtown, but it seems like too much of a coincidence. The woman's name as well as the injuries so closely resemble the injuries of the Ripper's first victim."

Barbara looked up, glad for the opportunity to look away from the photo. "There's more than a resemblance," she said. "I saw the original autopsy photos, read the files. This is exact. He's reproduced the murder."

Next to her, McHugh clicked his tongue. "More than that, I fear." He pushed the file across the table to Ben, pointing to one line in the report. "Is this the correct date of the murder?"

Ben glanced down at the file. "Yes. August 31st."

McHugh exchanged a look with Barbara, who nodded, seeing the significance. Ben looked from one to the other. "Why is that date important?"

Before they could answer, Ben's cell phone buzzed to life.

"Sorry," he said. He stood and pulled the phone from his inside jacket pocket, answering it as he stepped away from the table, his voice becoming a low hum as he crossed the small room.

Barbara took the file folder back and started to page through the report, while McHugh sat back in his chair, contemplating what they'd heard. He took a pipe from his pocket and absentmindedly tapped it on the underside of the wooden table. Barbara, processing what the date suggested, spoke while she looked through the file.

"He not only copied the details of the murder," she said, "with a victim who has the same name, but he's committed the murder on the same date as the original. August 31st."

McHugh nodded. "Which means," he said, "If his intent is to be true to form, the next murder would take place –"

Barbara finished his thought. "Today. September 8th."

McHugh nodded. "Annie Chapman."

They both looked at Ben, who was listening intently to the voice on his cell phone.

Ben closed his eyes and nodded, repeating the name he was hearing on the phone.

"Annie Chapman," Ben said with a sad shake of his head.

CHAPTER FOUR

T he second time had been surprisingly fun.

It was different than the first murder; Jack sensed that immediately. Of course, it took just as much planning and carried the same dangers, but with the first killing under his belt, Jack was able to approach the second one the way a new bowler approaches his next turn after rolling his first strike: with confidence and pride for a job well done.

At the same time, he was careful not to get cocky. He knew that cockiness was the downfall of many. "Pride goeth before a fall" was the common expression, but Jack knew it better from its original wording in Proverbs: *"Pride goeth before destruction, and an haughty spirit before a fall. Better it is to be of an humble spirit with the lowly, than to divide the spoil with the proud."*

As soon as one pithy quote occurred to him, he was instantly aware of another popping to the surface of his consciousness, like bubbles in a glass of cola. This one was from Seneca and was picked up during his first and only year of Latin: *"Success consecrates the foulest crimes."* Yes, he thought, that was very true.

So he approached the second murder with confidence and humility and in very short order, Annie Chapman – the one he had picked out of the veritable slew of Annie Chapmans who called the New York metro area their home – discovered a stranger in her living room.

He took her by surprise and he took her quickly and, he felt, in his own way, he took her humanely. Cutting someone's throat was a messy business, but it was done quickly and it was done efficiently.

She went from being alive one moment to being quite dead the next. And as he looked down at her body on the floor of her apartment, the blood beginning to pool around her and seep into the thick, colorful braided rug that covered the wooden floor, Jack was proud. He had done a good job on this one, just like the first.

He took a second to savor the feeling, but before he allowed himself to be overcome with pride, he got down on one knee and continued his work.

Two down.

So far, so good.

CHAPTER FIVE

She's over there," the young patrolman said, pointing toward a nearby alley. "Two kids found the body."

"Kids? Really? How are they doing?" Ben asked. He peered past the officer, at the crowd of official types surrounding what was, he assumed, the body of Annie Chapman.

A squad car, its light bar flashing, blocked the entrance to the alley. Ben recognized a police photographer entering the narrow space, and noticed Isobel, a woman he knew from the Medical Examiner's office, just headed out of the alley.

"The kids? Oh, they're fine. You know kids." The patrolman returned to his duties, shooing gawkers away from the yellow police tape that cordoned off the area.

"Yeah," Ben said. "Probably won't surface until they're thirty." But by then the patrolman was out of earshot of Ben's comment.

Ben continued toward the alley, passing Isobel from the Medical Examiner's office as she stopped to make some notes on the small pad she always carried.

"How's it look in there?"

She looked up sternly, prepared to face down any outsider who had strayed too close to the crime scene, and then smiled when she recognized Ben. "It's a mess, my friend," she said in her lilting Jamaican accent. "Someone's gone and made a real mess of that poor girl. You going to see for yourself?"

Ben nodded. "I've brought a couple of, well, experts I guess." He gestured toward McHugh and Barbara as they approached. "I thought I'd see what they could add."

Ben's authority had cut a swath through the crowd, creating a gap that quickly disappeared as McHugh and Barbara attempted to follow him the short distance from the police car to the crime scene. After a bit of pushing and shoving, McHugh and Barbara had finally caught up to him.

Isobel glanced at the two and continued on her way. "We'll chat later," she said, and then stopped again, turning back to him, flashing him a smile. "Oh, here's one for you to ponder: Gregory Peck to Andre Gregory, with two people."

"Gregory Peck to Andre Gregory in two?" Ben repeated. "Could be a stretch."

"We'll see how you do," she said, her smile broadening as she pushed her way through the crowd and out of sight.

"How's that?" McHugh asked, as he and Barbara made their way toward him.

"Oh … nothing," Ben said. "We're back here."

He held the yellow tape up high enough for McHugh and Barbara to duck under, and then followed them toward the crime scene, which was halfway down the alley and surrounded on both sides by squat, weathered warehouse buildings. The police Crime Scene Unit had erected several portable lights, which cut through the darkness in the space while strangely adding to the location's overall feeling of dread and gloom.

To Barbara's surprise, suddenly and with no real warning, they were almost on top of the body. Several working officials blocked most of her view, but before she could look away she saw a bloody, bare leg and a flash of the woman's face, the eyes open and vacant.

Barbara stopped quickly and McHugh nearly collided with her as he followed her down the alley. He saw what had caused her to stop so suddenly and put a comforting hand on her shoulder, gently turning her away from the scene.

"Bit more difficult than looking at the old autopsy photos, isn't it, dear?"

"It's not ... not what I expected."

McHugh nodded in agreement. "It something we often neglect to remember on the Ripper circuit. The girls. The aptly named 'unfortunates.' Ghastly business. Always was."

Ben looked around for a familiar face, finally recognizing Dale Harkness, at the same moment that Harkness noticed Ben. Harkness made his way toward the trio.

He was younger and shorter than Ben but, as he was quick to point out, he was Ben's superior. He had a cocky swagger that was evident even when he wasn't walking. A former Marine, he operated his division on a strictly Need to Know basis, and right now he felt Black didn't need to know any of this.

"Black, this isn't a museum tour."

"I just want them to look for a moment, to see what you've found."

Before Harkness could refuse the request, McHugh spoke up. He was lighting his pipe, his gaze turned away from the crime scene as he studied the walls of the surrounding warehouses.

"She'll be disemboweled, her entrails pulled out and placed over her shoulder. Her right shoulder, as a matter of fact."

Dale Harkness looked over at the older man, and then his attention was turned to Barbara, who added her own prediction.

"You'll also find two brass rings at her feet," Barbara said. "A couple of pennies. And two new farthings." Her voice lacked the confidence of McHugh's, and she was still trying to shake the emotion of the reality of the situation. The blood. The alley. The unfortunate.

Harkness was unsure what to make of this pair. "Oh, will we?" he asked, putting his hands on his hips and rocking back on his heels.

McHugh turned. "That's unlikely," he said, glancing from Harkness to Barbara and back again.

Harkness nodded at the older man. "You've got that right."

McHugh continued, turning back to Barbara. "Those items were reported in the papers of the day, but never substantiated." He looked back at Harkness. "No, I'm guessing you've found two combs – a small-tooth comb and a pocket comb in a paper case. There would also be a piece of muslin, and a bit of a torn envelope, with only a portion of the address still intact – the letter 'M.'"

Harkness looked at McHugh for a long moment and then deliberately held up a clear plastic evidence bag.

Through the plastic they could plainly see two combs, a piece of what looked like torn linen, and a bit of a weathered envelope. On the envelope was the letter "M."

McHugh glanced at the contents of the bag before returning to the work of lighting his pipe. "Well, there you are. Good for you."

* * *

The Precinct station house was one of many faceless glass buildings built in the mid-fifties. Perhaps it had once been a traditional office building, but now it housed offices for law enforcement, the Medical Examiner, the coroner, and related community services.

Once they made it past security on the first floor, Ben ushered Barbara and McHugh into a large, fluorescent-lit squad room on the second floor. While Ben went to retrieve their beverage order (coffee, black, for Barbara; tea, Lipton, for McHugh), the room filled up with plainclothesmen and some uniformed officers, all of whom ignored Barbara and McHugh, who had taken seats away from the large, worn conference table that filled the center of the room.

Dale Harkness burst into the room talking loudly, and quickly drowned out the quiet rumble of conversation in the room.

"All right," he said to no one and everyone. "So, we've determined that clearly there's more than a passing resemblance to the Jack the Ripper case. Two victims, with the same names as the original victims, killed in the same manner as the original victims, and on the same dates."

McHugh, who had been studying his watch, looked up. "He also may be re-creating the times of the murders, taking into account the time difference from London to New York ..."

McHugh let his sentence trail off when he saw the expression on Harkness' face. At that moment, Ben re-entered, his hands balancing three full and presumably hot paper cups. Harkness turned from McHugh to glare at Ben.

"Black, what are these two here for again?"

Ben looked around and realized that he'd missed something, but a look at McHugh and Barbara, and the tone of Harkness' voice, quickly brought him up to speed.

"Mr. McHugh – and Miss Thomas – are experts in the study of the Jack the Ripper murders," he said, handing them their coffee and tea. "In fact, Mr. McHugh's book on the subject is considered the definitive text on the topic."

Harkness turned to Barbara. "And you?"

Barbara looked up from her coffee, not sure what Harkness was asking. "I have a background in crime fiction, and a new book on the Ripper murders," she replied, hoping that was the answer he was looking for.

Harkness turned away from the two and found a place to perch on the edge of the conference table. He looked at the staff around the room, some sitting, some standing, and then turned his attention back to the two outsiders.

"All right," he said. "We've got experts. Give us the short version."

Barbara and McHugh exchanged looks. McHugh, in the midst of sipping his tea, nodded to her politely.

Barbara looked at the assembled group, and then decided it was best to just jump in.

"Well, um, the short version," she said, trying to think of a quick way to condense the story. "In the fall of 1888, five prostitutes were murdered in the East End of London. Brutally murdered. Throats cut. Disemboweled. The killer, who some think called himself Jack the Ripper, was never apprehended."

Harkness waited for a long moment, to be sure that she was finished. "And who was he?" he asked harshly.

Barbara hesitated for a moment. "You mean, Jack the Ripper?" she asked.

"Isn't that who we're talking about?"

Barbara looked to McHugh for help, but he was occupied with a stray speck of something he'd found floating in his tea.

"Well," Barbara continued, "The killer was never identified. There are lots of theories as to who he might have been. That's part of the continuing appeal of the story."

Harkness made a noise that sounded a lot like a stifled snort, because that's what it was. "The continuing appeal?"

Ben decided it was time to throw his guests a bit of a lifeline. "Maybe you could give us a recap of the suspects," he said to McHugh. "That might be a good place for us to start."

McHugh had found and disposed of the offending speck in his tea. "Suspects? Excellent thought. No shortage of suspects, that's the beauty of the case," he said, immediately sparking to the topic. "Let's see, in no particular order and adding very few judgments, there's Prince Eddie, the Duke of Clarence. He's a popular favorite, royal conspiracies of any ilk always being most difficult to resist."

"Speaking of royal conspiracies, the Queen's physician, Dr. Gull, is also high on the list," Barbara added.

"Klingbile!" Harkness gestured to a young officer, who scrambled for a black marking pen and started to jot down the names on a large, erasable white board that hung somewhat tenuously on one wall of the room.

"There was a local butcher, Jack Pizer," McHugh continued.

"He was also known as Leather Apron," Barbara added. "When there was talk of a leather apron being found near the body of one of the victims, he became an obvious suspect."

"Obviously," McHugh agreed. "But the fellow had a solid alibi and so he's not considered a serious suspect. Ah, shame on me, I promised no judgments. Oh, well, it comes with the territory, I'm afraid."

Klingbile froze in mid-stroke, not sure if he should finish writing "Leather Apron" or not. He decided to forge ahead and finished writing, capped the pen, set it down and returned to his seat.

McHugh, however, was just getting rolling. "Next ... there's the artist, Walter Sickert – I promised no comments and none there shall be. And, let's see, the Duke of Salisbury."

"And Montague John Druitt, of course."

Klingbile jumped up, snatched up the marker and quickly resumed his listing chore, trying hard to catch up with the two as they volleyed names back and forth.

McHugh nodded at Barbara. "Ah, yes, can't forget old Druitt. Threw himself in the Thames soon after the final murder and for some reason that makes him a major suspect. Makes bloody little sense to me, but there I go again adding commentary."

He smiled and shook his head, and then continued. "There's also, oddly enough, a plethora of doctors – the mysterious American doctor, Dr. Francis Tumblety ... the Russian doctor, Dr. Ostrog ... Dr. Neill Cream, Dr. Stanley. And, lest we forget, if you really want to open the conspiracy can of worms, so to speak, the Freemasons."

"Yes. And let's not forget James Maybrick," Barbara said. "He of the fake diary."

"Utterly fake," McHugh grumbled, then caught himself, quickly holding up his hand and making a fast sign of the cross, as if to beg for forgiveness.

Klingbile ignored all this, instead doing his able best to keep up with the flow of names, guessing (incorrectly) on the spelling of 'Tumblety' and, in his haste, writing 'James Mason' instead of 'James Maybrick' and 'Freemasons.'

"Then there's Kosminski, the crazed Pole," Barbara continued, searching her brain for the others on the list.

"Not to be confused with Klosowski, the crazed barber," McHugh interjected. He paused for a moment, looking at the scrawl of names on the board across the room. "Um, who have we forgotten in our haste and infirmity? Well, in moving to the second tier, as it were, Lewis Carroll has been mentioned ..."

Barbara looked to him, surprised. "Really? I hadn't heard that one," she said.

McHugh nodded to her. "Yes, apparently he left many a clue down that rabbit hole with poor, addled Alice."

He turned his attention back to the group. "And there are those who lay the blame at the feet of poor Oscar Wilde. Another popular theory at the time was that the killer was actually a homicidal gorilla, escaped from a circus. Not too much stock to be put in that, I think. And, of course, we can't forget my own personal favorite: Unknown Male."

Klingbile had just about filled all the available space on the board. He wrote "homicidal gorilla" in one margin, and then found some space at the bottom of the board to add, "Unknown Male."

"And, of course, we can't forget Miss Thomas' addition to the canon: Robert Louis Stevenson," McHugh added, smiling as the young officer struggled to find remaining space on the board for the unnecessarily long name. "Some think he might even displace the gorilla."

McHugh resumed sipping his tea. Barbara took a breath but decided to let that last remark pass. Harkness, however, wasn't ready to move on.

"Robert Louis Stevenson?" he asked, giving her a hard look. "You mean, the author of *Treasure Island*? That Robert Louis Stevenson?"

Barbara held his gaze. "There is compelling evidence," she said, simply.

"Did he dress up like Long John Silver while committing the murders?"

Barbara looked away and then down at her coffee. "Not that I'm aware of."

"Great." Harkness looked at the names on the board, then at the staff, then at Ben. Finally, he turned back to Barbara and McHugh. "Well, now we know who we're looking for. Thanks for coming in."

The silence that followed said it all. They were no longer needed, if they ever had been. Barbara stood up to leave and McHugh followed her.

* * *

They took the elevator down one flight and then made their way down the long, dim hall, toward the front door.

Barbara felt that she should say something to McHugh, but she wasn't sure what she wanted to say or what needed to be said. She still wasn't certain if his reference to her suspect had been a jibe or just part of the list- making exercise.

McHugh, for his part, was soaking in the ambiance of the police station, the sounds and the smells, and seemed to be in no hurry to leave.

"Mr. McHugh! Miss Thomas!"

They both stopped and turned to see Ben, trotting down the hall toward them.

"I'm glad I caught up with you. Thank you so much for coming in," he said. "I'm sorry that you weren't given a warmer reception."

43

"Think nothing of it, dear boy," McHugh said, placing a reassuring hand on Ben's shoulder. "Back home, every year when the queen comes to open Parliament, the MPs traditionally slam the door of the House of Commons in her face. Well, actually, not literally her face, but the face of her representative. Every organization exerts its independence in a way that is both unique and completely identical to every other."

"Plus, I suspect one doesn't generally look to the NYPD for warm receptions, Detective Black," Barbara added. "I'm just sorry we couldn't be more helpful."

"Oh, you were, you were very helpful," Ben said quickly. "There's just a lot of resistance to outside help in a case like this."

"Particularly from cranks, crackpots and old fools, eh?" McHugh said, then turned to Barbara. "Present company excepted, of course."

"Of course." Barbara smiled. Those Brits could turn on the charm when they wanted to, she thought, and she almost forgot the several swipes he'd taken at her book throughout the day. Almost.

McHugh turned back to Ben. "And you do have bigger problems than we two, don't you Detective? If our killer stays true to form, you've got not one, but two murders fast approaching."

Barbara realized where McHugh was heading. "The Double Event, that's right," she agreed. "Two murders in one night. Catherine Eddowes and Long Liz – Elizabeth Stride."

The three of them stood quietly for a moment as they considered what lay ahead. Their silence was interrupted by an accented voice coming from the far end of the hall.

"Benjamin, did you find the solution to my challenge yet?"

All three looked over to see Isobel, from the Medical Examiner's office, headed toward them. She was a tall, beautiful woman with a dark complexion and a commanding presence. She wore a bright, floral patterned dress, which peeked out from under her white lab coat. Her long, thick hair was pulled back into a businesslike bun, which only served to increase her sexy aura.

"What was it again?" Ben asked. "Gregory Peck to Andre Gregory in two?"

"That's right. And I made it easy for you, because I know your tastes." She gave him a dazzling smile and then turned to the other two.

Ben quickly handled the introductions.

"Isobel, this is Henry McHugh and Barbara Thomas. They're helping us out tonight. Isobel works in the Medical Examiner's office." He considered for a moment, then continued. "I'm going to go with Gregory Peck to Robert Duvall in *To Kill a Mockingbird*."

Isobel nodded. "For you, that's the obvious one."

"And then, let's see." He looked into the distance for a moment, then turned back and smiled. "Oh, then it's easy. Robert Duvall to Al Pacino in *The Godfather*. Pacino then connects with Andre Gregory in *Author, Author*."

"I made it easy for you on that one. Now you make it tough for me."

"Okay, let's make it tough. So you left me with Andre Gregory."

He thought this over for a moment, glancing over at McHugh and Barbara, who were both a bit mystified. "Here's one: Andre Gregory was in *My Dinner with Andre* with Wallace Shawn. Get from Wallace Shawn to Sean Connery. In two."

"In two? I can do that. Next time I see you, I do that." She nodded to the group and then continued on her way, sashaying her way down the hall and around the corner. Ben turned back.

"What was all that about?" Barbara asked?

"Oh, it's a little game we play," Ben said. "It's kind of a six degrees thing, but in our version, you have to get from one actor to another actor who has a similar name, connecting them via people they've worked with. Gregory Peck to Andre Gregory. Bea Arthur to Arthur Kennedy. Bud Cort to Bud Abbott. Then when it's your turn, you have to pick someone that one of them worked with and find an actor with a similar name and somehow connect them. Wallace Shawn to Sean Connery. Which was kind of a cheat, but we don't stick strictly to the rules."

"I see."

"Sometimes it gets a little boring around here and we make up games," Ben explained. "Your tax dollars at work. Although, lately we've sort of had our hands full."

McHugh nodded. "Indeed you have. This is no average killer, as

I'm assuming you've already guessed. This one is on a mission and he's got a very specific – and very deadly – goal. Mercifully, you have a few days breather, one might say, to catch your wind and, with a little good police work and a bit of luck, catch the killer," he said. He looked from one to the other. "Well, if you both will excuse me ..."

McHugh headed toward the front door, still clearly enjoying the look and feel of the police station environment. Barbara watched him go, and then turned back to Ben, trying to generate a reason to lengthen the meeting and coming up empty-handed.

"I should probably go as well," she finally said.

For his part, Ben couldn't think of any other reason to detain her further either, but it was not for lack of trying. She looked great, and he was well aware that accomplishing that feat under fluorescent lighting was no small trick. Only those with natural beauty could pull it off, and she was pulling it off in spades. But he didn't say that, didn't head in that direction, didn't ask her on a date or kiss her hand or propose marriage. He was pleased with the restraint he was showing. So all he said was, "Thanks again."

They stood for a moment longer, and then Ben made the first move, turning away and heading down the hall back toward his office. Barbara watched him go, then, when she was sure he wasn't going to turn back for one more look, she turned toward the front door.

Ben did turn, a moment later, and watched her walk through security and out of the building.

McHugh was just hailing a cab as Barbara exited the building. He looked up and, seeing her, held open the taxi's rear door for her.

"Where are you headed, my dear?" he asked.

"Um ... uptown," she answered.

He made a grand sweeping gesture with his arm toward the open cab door. "Do be my guest."

Barbara stepped into the cab and was surprised when the door shut quickly behind her. She turned to McHugh and spoke through the open rear window. "And where are you going?"

McHugh looked up at the night sky above them and took a deep breath, inhaling the Manhattan air as if it were the lushest of country glades.

"For a stroll," he said. "A well-deserved stroll. This is a grand autumn evening and who knows how many more of these I'll have. I must gather them while I may."

He tipped his tweed hat to her and stepped up on the curb, looking left and right, deciding on a direction and then heading off into the night.

"Where to?"

She jumped at the sound, having forgotten for a moment that she was in a car, a cab no less, and that the driver was waiting for instructions.

"Home. Sixty First and Central Park East," she said.

He engaged the meter and they pulled into traffic, quickly passing McHugh on the sidewalk. He was just turning up his collar to a sudden burst of autumn air before he headed left down Fifth Avenue.

He waved a hand toward the passing cab before he disappeared into the crowd.

CHAPTER SIX

LONDONPRO: BTW, Ripper007, IMHO, your theory doesn't make any sense and you obviously have a very limited understanding of the facts of the case.

RIPPER007: LOL! And how did u pick your suspect? By opening a book & sticking a pin in the first name u saw?

LONDONPRO: I'm not going to waste the digital ether arguing with someone so clueless on the basic facts.

RIPPER007: Clueless, thy name is u.

LONDONPRO: [RESPONSE DELETED DUE TO VIOLATION OF TERMS OF USE]

These were the types of exchanges Ben came across as he spent a little time every day surfing through Ripper websites, trying to learn more about the 1888 case.

He hoped he might pick up some information that might come in handy as they moved forward with their own investigation, which seemed to be going nowhere both quickly and slowly. As he scrolled through the chatrooms on the various websites, he was consistently amazed at the intensity of the on-line dialogs and how quickly an innocent comment could spiral into a full-fledged flame war.

After considerable surfing, he'd come to the conclusion that there were, at best, really only a handful of worthwhile sites on the topic of Jack the Ripper and his crimes. One in particular seemed to provide the most complete combination of hard facts and ongoing dialog from passionate devotees of the case.

Given the popularity of the site, it seemed to Ben that it was possible if not probable that their killer was an occasional visitor. He hoped to find some clues in the often banal, occasionally rabid messages that were posted on the site's various message boards. There were several boards and chatrooms to go through on the site, covering suspects, victims, the police, the press, and many other topics and subtopics of interest to the members.

One exchange in particular caught his attention.

JOHN-NETLEY: This new guy, thiz copycat, hope they nab him quick. Sick stuff.

JACK_RULES: Say what you will about the new killings, this guy has raised murder to an art form.

JOHN-NETLEY: Oh purlease! Just another psycho, needs to be locked up.

JACK_RULES: On the contrary. I think he may become more famous than the original Jack. This one's got style.

Ben considered joining in the debate or sending a private e-mail message to JACK_RULES to test the waters and get a sense of who he was and more importantly, <u>where</u> he was. Visitors to the site appeared to come from all over the United States and Canada, with a few British and Australian posters appearing as well. If JACK_RULES lived somewhere across the country, like Phoenix, Arizona, or across the ocean, there was little need to consider him as a serious suspect. But if he lived in the area, then he would definitely be worth tracking down and speaking to.

But Ben was afraid of inadvertently spooking him and sending him back underground. Instead, he decided it would be more prudent to contact the site's Webmaster and see what information he could get from that source before attempting to contact JACK_RULES directly.

Scrolling through the site he found a "Contact" button and filled in a form with his request: "Police officer seeks information on a subscriber to your site in connection with recent murders. Please reply with best method of contacting you. Detective Ben Black, NYPD."

He filled in his official e-mail address, hit SEND and shifted his attention to some long-delayed paperwork that was further cluttering his already messy desk. He was surprised when an e-mail response popped up just a few moments later.

"Always happy to assist New York's finest," the e-mail said. "E-mail not the best system for this sort of conversation. The walls have ears! :) If you wish to confer, please see me at my office, 111 Worth Street (corner Worth and Lafayette). Signed, Dimitri."

Puzzled, Ben shot off a quick answer. "Thanks for your fast response," he wrote. "Would it be possible for me to call you?"

A few moments later he had his answer: "No phone. Don't own one. Don't trust them. Your options are in person or not at all. I'll be here for a couple more hours. Best, D."

Ben looked at the computer screen for a long moment, then got up and headed out of the squad room, taking the stairs two at a time down to the motor pool.

* * *

Ben found a parking spot on Lafayette and walked to the corner, turning right on Worth. He was looking for 111, but the first doorway he found had the number 115 above it.

He backtracked and crossed Lafayette, only to find that the first door on Worth on that side of Lafayette was listed as 109. He stood on the sidewalk for what felt like a long time, looking up and down Worth Street, scratching his head.

Ben sighed and crossed the street again, walking into the small coffee shop and patiently waiting in line while several customers ahead of him placed their complicated coffee orders. When it was Ben's turn, he stepped forward.

"Welcome to Starbucks, what can I get for you?" The perky clerk gave Ben the impression that in addition to steadily sampling the products, she might also be mainlining caffeine in the back room.

"Nothing to drink," he said. "I'm just trying to find 111 Worth Street and I'm coming up cold. Any idea where it might be?"

The girl shook her head, her ponytail continuing to sway for a few moments after she finished. She yelled to a co-worker who was in the midst of dealing with an overflow of foam on an order. "Hey Howie, where's 111 Worth Street?" she asked.

"What?" Howie shouted over the whir of an espresso machine.

"Where's 111 Worth?" she yelled again over the din.

"111? Um …. That's here. Right here. That's our address." He shook his head as he returned to his foam emergency.

The perky clerk turned back to Ben. "I guess that's the address here," she echoed. "No one's ever asked the address before, so there wasn't really any reason for me to know it. All I know is that we're on the corner."

"No problem."

"Can I get you anything else?" she asked, revving herself back up to her standard level of perkiness.

"No, thanks. I'm good." Ben turned and looked around the coffee shop while the next person in line stepped up and rattled off their order.

Most of the handful of tables were occupied, by individuals and groups of two or three people, sipping coffee, working on their computers, listening to their iPods.

Then he noticed that a lone customer across the room was waving to him. The man was seated by the window and backlit, so it took Ben a moment to recognize him as the black man from the *Star Trek* panel at the Ripper Conference. He was seated alone, wearing headphones connected to the laptop in front of him. He waved Ben over.

Ben navigated around the other tables, finally making his way to the spot by the window. "Dimitri?"

The man took off his headphones and smiled up at Ben. "Detective Black? I figured that was you. What is it about cops that you dudes always look like cops? Damnedest thing, isn't it?"

He laughed and took a sip from his coffee cup, gesturing for Ben to sit across from him. "Now, I know exactly where you're going to go first, so let me beat you to it – you saw the name Dimitri, you figured you were meeting some Russian guy, am I right?"

Ben nodded. "The thought had crossed my mind."

"You're not alone, pal. And you can spare me the Black Russian jokes; I've heard every variation on that sad ass theme."

He set his headphones on the table. Ben could hear some music coming through the tiny speakers. He cocked his head to one side and listened for a moment.

"Roy Acuff?" he asked.

Dimitri smiled. "You've got a good ear, Detective. It is indeed. *Back in the Country*, off his Greatest Hits, Volume One."

He pushed a key on the keyboard and the tinny sound stopped. "Interesting dude, Roy Acuff. Did you know when he started out, before he formed The Crazy Tennesseans, that he used to perform in blackface?"

"Really?"

"It's the stone-cold truth. You don't see much of that these days, do you? Blackface performers, I mean."

Ben shook his head. "Not so much, no."

Dimitri laughed and leaned back in his chair, stretching his legs and putting his hands on the back of his head, interlacing his long fingers. He looked up at the ceiling fan overhead, which revolved lazily with just the hint of an occasional wobble.

Just as the first time Ben had seen him, he was dressed sharply, in a tailored blue suit, bright white shirt and a patterned red tie.

"Here's another interesting truth about Roy Acuff," Dimitri continued, still looking at the ceiling. "Did you know he was a Mason? A 33rd Degree Mason, no less."

"A Mason? Acuff?"

"That's what I'm saying." Dimitri leaned forward, looking Ben in the eye. "That's what's so weird about it. You think Roy Acuff, you don't immediately go there, do you? You think Roy Acuff, you think Grand Old Opry, you think 'King of the Hillbillies,' you think, 'Oh, yeah, he's the cracker that was one of the first to record *House of the Rising Sun*.' You think all that, but sure as I'm sitting here, you don't immediately think, 'Oh, right, Roy Acuff … the Mason.'"

Dimitri laughed again as he once more leaned back in his chair.

"Do you know a lot about the Masons?" Ben asked, trying not to attach any significance to the question.

"You'll find that I know a little about a lot of different things," Dimitri said. "Anyway, Detective Black, welcome to my office." He gestured with one hand to the rest of the coffee shop.

Ben looked around quizzically. "Starbucks is your office?"

"Why not?" he asked, giving Ben a serious look. "I'm starting to get the sense you're not a Starbucks guy."

"No, probably not. I mean, I like coffee and all, just not at these prices. Back at the Precinct, we call it Fivebucks. None of us are really into paying that much for just a cup of coffee ..."

"That's 'cause you're not the target market. But, trust me, lots of people are. Lots and lots. They're not paying for a cup of coffee. They're paying for the experience, the music, the smell, the CDs at the counter, all that folderol. These Starbucks folks, they've got it going. You know, the whole enterprise is based on the premise of being the Third Place ..."

"The Third Place?"

"Yeah, the Third Place. Check it out: The First Place is home, second is work. For my money, I would have thought Church might have ranked up as high as third, but I guess that's the world I want and not the world that is. So Starbucks is the Third Place and I come here and I work on the Fourth Place." He tapped his computer with one hand.

"The Fourth Place?"

"You got that right. The Internet. Nowadays, people – when they're at home, at work, even at Starbucks – they also exist in the Fourth Place. And that's where I make my living."

"On the Internet? With the Jack the Ripper site?"

Dimitri smiled proudly and nodded. "On the Internet," he said, "but not just with that one site. I've got a lot of sites that appeal to a number of broad and varied constituencies."

He saw a look pass across Ben's face and immediately added, "No and it's not porn, like you're thinking. Sure, you can make money with porn on the Net, bushels full, but really, is that a business for serious men? I don't think so. At least, it's not for me. Got no stomach for that."

Ben nodded and eased back into his chair. "So, how did you get started on this Jack the Ripper site?"

"Well, now, that's a good question." Dimitri shut the laptop and leaned forward, resting his hands on the computer. "You see, one night I'm flipping channels on TV and I come across this movie with

David Hasselhoff – you know the dude?"

Ben nodded. "*Knight Rider* and that lifeguard show with Pamela Anderson, right?"

"Exactly, that's the guy. Anyway, it's this terrible movie about how they moved the London Bridge to Arizona or someplace like that, and then the Jack the Ripper murders start up all over again."

Ben shrugged. "Never heard of it."

"Well, don't bother rushing home to add it to your Netflix queue, trust me on that. But later I was surfing around and just for fun I typed 'Jack the Ripper" into Google and you know what popped up?"

Ben shook his head.

"I'll tell you what popped up: over three million hits, that's what popped up. And I got to thinking, there's a lot of interest out there for this dude, lots of movies, lots of books – fiction, non-fiction, you name it."

Dimitri leaned back in his chair and took another sip from his coffee cup. "And I figured if the general population is that interested in Jack the Ripper, then a certain percentage of that population is going to show up if you create a central repository of information on the case. Some place where they can read about the suspects, the victims, look at maps, read old newspaper accounts, and of course carry on endless conversations with other like-minded individuals. And you want to know the beauty part?"

"What?"

"The site pretty much built itself. I'm being straight with you. It built itself."

"How'd you manage that?"

"Simpler than you might think. You know that writer, Douglas Hofstadter?"

Ben thought it over for a moment. "Yeah, he wrote a book. Something about Bach and some other guys, right?"

Dimitri laughed. "Well, yeah, some other guys. '*Gödel, Escher, Bach: An Eternal Golden Braid,*' but that's not where I'm headed.

"You see, Hofstadter had an idea for a book, which he was going to call '*Reviews of This Book.*' His idea was that he'd start with a blank sheet of paper and send it to a reviewer, and that reviewer would write a review about the blank sheet. Not much you can say about a blank sheet of paper, but, trust me, there are writers out there who can gen up 500 words on the subject. Then Hofstadter would take that review and send it to another reviewer, who would write a review of the review of the blank sheet of paper, and then it goes to another reviewer and then another. And before you know it, you'd have a book of reviews."

He picked up his cup and finished his coffee, then gestured toward the counter. "Can I get you something? They like me here, might not charge the full five bucks."

Ben shook his head. "No thanks. Getting back to this book that writes itself ..."

"Oh, yeah. Well, the website is pretty much the same idea. You put up a website that claims to be the do-all and end-all on Jack the Ripper, pretty soon you're getting e-mails from all these Jack the Ripper experts sending you stuff, asking if they can write the section on this victim or that victim, wanting to give you bios on each of the suspects, send you photos of the crime scenes or newspaper accounts that they've scanned. People send you their research, their dissertations. And before you know it, with very little effort, you've got a website with all the information on Jack the Ripper."

"Just like that?"

"Just like that. The best site out there, and that's not just me saying it. That's the word on the street. And the beauty part, once it's up and running, the sucker pretty much takes care of itself."

Ben nodded appreciatively. "And you can make a living doing that?"

Dimitri laughed. "Yeah, a living, but nothing exceptional. I mean, I got ads on the site and every time someone clicks on one, I make some coin. Or they click on a book or a movie, they're whisked away to Amazon and I get a cut of that action. Like anything else, it's all about margins and volume. Which is why I started the other sites."

"Other sites? Oh, that's right, your other broad and varied constituencies." Ben smiled. "Which means what, exactly?

"Other serial killers, of course." Dimitri opened his laptop and quickly typed a few keystrokes.

He spun the computer around so that Ben could see the screen. "This is my Jeffrey Dahmer site. Averages two thousand hits a day. Less than six months old, and it's the definitive site on that crazy-ass dude."

Ben looked at the screen, which resembled the layout of the Jack the Ripper site, with links for Victims, Photos, Maps, Timelines, and of course, Message Boards. Ben moved the cursor around and then looked at Dimitri, who gave a quick nod of approval. Ben clicked on the Message Boards and scanned through the topic list that popped up.

"It's a cottage industry at its best," Dimitri said, watching while Ben looked through the Message Boards. "I've got sites on Ted Bundy, the Boston Strangler, Son of Sam, Ed Gein, Charlie Manson, John Wayne Gacy, the Zodiac Killer. You name a serial killer, I've got a site about him. And those sites have lots and lots and lots of visitors, all clicking away like crazy on the ads and the books and the movies.

"If I've learned anything, it's that you should never underestimate the public's interest in multiple murders and the lunatics who commit them."

Ben looked up from the computer. "I see that exchanges can get pretty heated on this site as well."

"Oh, man, they get heated on every damn site. It's just human nature. You put people in a room – cyber or otherwise – and get them talking about something they're passionate about, some sparks are going to fly, some cross words are going to get typed and before you know it, you've had to ban some stupid schmuck from the site for violation of the terms of use."

"So, who exactly does the banning? Is that you?"

Dimitri shook his head. "No, I'm a firm believer in delegation. Here's how you do it: You get some of the better-behaved ones on each site and you make them the monitors, give them a bit of power and they do all the policing. Give them a special title, like Chief Inspector. People eat that shit up. They do all the watching, they handle the conflicts, they weed out the troublemakers. Like I said before, these sites pretty much run themselves."

"So," Ben said, turning the computer back around to Dimitri, "if I were trying to track down someone possibly connected to the recent copycat murders who's been leaving messages on the boards on your Jack the Ripper site –"

Dimitri held up his hand. "Well, first I'm sure you'd have a court order of some kind. I mean, that would be your first step, right? That is to say, you would have talked to a judge and he would have completed the paperwork, right? Or we wouldn't be having this conversation, am I right?"

They looked at each other for a long quiet moment.

"Sure," Ben said finally. "I'd have a court order, and I'd most likely have it right here." He patted his breast pocket.

"Doesn't look like a very big court order," Dimitri said wryly.

"Be that as it may," Ben continued, "before I go to the trouble of taking it out and presenting it to you officially, what do you think I'll find with this court order? Hypothetically, I mean."

"Well," Dimitri said, taking his time, "Odds are pretty good you won't find jack shit."

"Really? How do you figure?"

"Well, let's break down what you're looking for: you want to track down a dude who's leaving messages on the Jack the Ripper site. That means, he's filled out a profile and given me his e-mail address. Now, we both know if this is your killer, he lied on every question in the profile and he used an e-mail address that you can't possibly trace back to him. Which is a pretty easy thing to do."

"Which means?"

"Which means, you serve me with the court order, I take it to my attorney, he charges me several hundred bucks an hour to fight the order on First Amendment grounds, we lose due to the pressing nature of the case, I give you all the information I've got on the dude – his fake profile – and you're no further along than you were before.

"And I'm out attorney's fees and to be honest, I'm pissed about it. Which, I have to tell you, would have a detrimental impact on our relationship." He smiled at Ben. "That's option one."

"What's the other option?"

"The way I see it, you've got nothing but options, Detective Black." He looked into his empty coffee cup and then set it aside.

"But I suspect the most fruitful avenue you could pursue would be to keep your imaginary court order in your nice, neat off-the-rack

Men's Warehouse suit coat. Keep it there. And instead, ask me in a nice way to keep an eye on the messages coming in and out of my sites – Jack the Ripper and all the others – and to let you know if I see anything that one might deem suspicious.

"And if I do, ask me to use my considerable resources to glean whatever information I can about said suspicious character, through channels as it were. I think that would be your best option."

Ben sat silently for a few moments, considering what to do next. "Are you planning on creating a website about this new killer?" he asked finally. "This Jack the Ripper copycat?"

Dimitri considered this briefly and then shook his head. "Nah, not this one."

"How come?"

He continued to shake his head. "I don't want to be that guy. I don't need the business that bad. Let somebody else be that guy."

Ben stood up and pulled a card out of his pocket. "Here's my phone number. Any point in giving it to you?"

"Sure, if it makes you feel better. But if I need to get in touch, I'll send an e-mail. Plus, you can just about always find me here."

"In your office? Dressed in a suit, drinking a double mocha?"

"Actually, it was a cinnamon spice mocha with soy milk. But yeah, well, it's better than sitting in my underwear in my apartment drinking Red Bull."

He put Ben's card in his breast pocket without looking at it. "The way I see it, Detective, if you're going to go into business, then treat it like a business. Otherwise, no one else will."

He slipped on his headphones and touched a key on the computer keyboard.

A moment later, Ben could hear the tinny voice of Roy Acuff, singing in his twangy voice about the many benefits of being back in the country again.

CHAPTER SEVEN

"Please, please, please tell me you're joking."

Val Howard leaned across her massively messy desk which sat in the center of her equally cluttered office, her hands clasped together in mock prayer. As always, she wore a skirt that was too short for a woman her age, a blouse that was too tight with a neckline that plunged further than it should have.

Adding to her overall look was a dazzling assortment of bracelets, necklaces and over-sized earrings that made her small head appear even smaller. Her salt-and-pepper hair had recently been permed, giving her the look of the world's first fifty-something cheerleader.

"This is a publisher's wet dream," she continued. "Now is the time to pounce."

Barbara, seated in front of the desk on a terribly chic and terribly uncomfortable chair, shook her head. Again. For the third time. This time, with what she hoped appeared to be even more resolve.

"I just don't think 'pouncing' is the appropriate response," she said.

Val rocketed out of her chair as if it were an ejector seat.

"Hello! You've written a new, hit book about Jack the Ripper. Someone's reproducing the crimes in all their glorious, gory detail. The police have asked you to be a special consultant on the case. It's like the perfect publicity storm – I wish to God I'd thought of it myself.

And you won't allow as much as a press release? I could have you on all the morning shows first thing tomorrow – ABC, NBC, CBS, FOX, boom, boom, boom."

Val sat back down, now perching on the edge of the desk, her voice becoming quieter and more pleading. "And who does it hurt? No one," she said. "And what does it do? Sell books. You're still in that business, aren't you?"

"Val, I just don't feel comfortable in that position. Plus, I'm not really an expert on Jack the Ripper."

"The hell you're not," Val said, heading back to her chair. "Have you read your dust jacket?"

"Yes, well, but didn't you once warn me never to believe what you read on a dust jacket?" Barbara asked.

Val waved the question away with her hand. "I was joking," she said. "Or lying. Or both." She plopped back into her chair like a disappointed toddler.

"What I meant to say," Barbara continued, "is that there are people out there who know a lot more about Jack the Ripper than I do."

She didn't mention specific names, but she was thinking about the man at the conference who had so kindly annotated her book with Post-It notes, and about McHugh, still feeling a bit stung about his correct prediction of the objects that would be found around Annie Chapman's body. That was an easy one, she thought. She shouldn't have missed that.

Val leaned forward and glanced at her computer screen, quickly typing a response to an e-mail. "Yeah," she said as she typed, "and not one of those so-called 'experts' is going to mention your book on national television. Not one. I can guarantee that."

"I think I can live with that," Barbara said as she got up and walked to the window.

It was a beautiful morning and the view from Val's office window was always stunning, with the Empire State Building two blocks away on the left and the East River in the distance. She looked at the view for a few moments, then turned back to look at Val. "Didn't you have something you wanted to show me?"

"I did?" Val was lost in her e-mail for a moment. "Give me a second." She reviewed what she had typed, then hit the send button.

"That's the last time that little dick gets any ARCs from me." She turned toward the window. "Where were we?"

Barbara smiled. "The reason you wanted me to come in?"

"Oh, yeah," she said. She turned and reached over to a stack of mock-ups on the table behind her desk. "We've got a cover design for the new paperback."

She dug through the pile, finally pulling out a board with the proposed image: A busty woman in peril, with an ominous grandfather clock looming behind her. Small drops of blood dripped from the hands of the clock. The title, *Hickory Dickory Homicide*, filled the top quarter of the cover, while Barbara's name took up the bottom quarter. The woman's cleavage took up the rest of the space on the cover.

Barbara took the board from Val and studied the artwork. She was always impressed at how each of the covers for her books looked exactly the same as the last book ... but also somehow different. Each was a little sexy, a little scary, and to a degree, a little tongue-in-cheek.

"This looks sufficiently lurid," she said.

"That's what we're aiming for," Val said. "The art department always has fun with your stuff."

Barbara had to agree. The art department – in fact, the whole publishing house – loved her stuff because it sold and it sold and it sold. From the very first title in the series, *The Mother Goose Murders*, Barbara had leapt from being a barely-successful author of romances to a (seemingly overnight, although she knew it was a longer process) wildly successful author of nursery rhyme-themed murder mysteries.

The second book in the series (*Humpty Dumpty: A Scrambled Suicide*) had outsold the first, and the one after that (*Murder In St. Ives*) did as much as the first two combined.

The first book had been something of a fluke. She had written the story quickly and was surprised (flabbergasted, actually) when the book became a hit and the publisher wanted a second one.

She struggled with it at first, but then she figured out the formula: Someone is killed in a manner that in some way evokes a well- known nursery rhyme, and then her detective, Hilary Webster, is called in to solve the case.

Once Barbara had landed on that pattern, it was then just a matter of going through the best-known rhymes and devising grisly but fun deaths for her homicidally luckless characters.

If pressed, Barbara would doubtless admit that some of the books in the series (like *Georgy Porgy: Pudding and Die* or *Simple Simon: A Taste For Murder*) were some of her best work, while others (like *One, Two, Buckle My Shoe [Three, Four, Kill Some More]* or *Blind Fury: Revenge of the Three Blind Mice*) never really congealed, despite her best efforts.

However, Val would tell her that she was nitpicking. They all sold and they sold remarkably well. And they kept selling, in ebook, paperback, hardcover and audiobooks, in English and now in at least 23 other languages.

It was due to the mind-boggling success of this series that she was able to get Val to back her foray into non-fiction, with her Jack the Ripper book. Of course, Val had insisted that she follow it up immediately with another book in the series (*Jack Sprat: DOA*), so the publishing house had covered their bets pretty cleanly and it was, as Val put it, "a win-win-win situation for everybody and his freakin' brother."

So, why Jack the Ripper? That was invariably the first question interviewers had been asking about this book, and although it had taken her a while to come up with it, by now she had a pretty good soundbite prepared. They called it your "elevator speech" – what you'd say about your book to someone important if you only had the length of an elevator ride to say it. Barbara would say that as a mystery writer, all mysteries were of interest to her.

Then she'd go on with something along the lines of, "How many mysteries that are over a hundred and fifty years old still inspire the same feelings of fear and dread as the Jack the Ripper killings? Very few. And why is that? Why do the murders of five women in 1888 still intrigue us? Because, on a primal level, we wonder which of us would be capable of such horror? This book explores, for the first time, the psychological underpinnings of that murderer and reveals not only who he was, but also why he did what he did."

Of course, deep down she knew why she had picked this book to write: she wanted to sit at the grown-up table, with the non-fiction writers, and get away from the mystery ghetto, if only for one book.

And unlike others in the field, she had the money to take a year off, the money to travel to do the research, and the money to pay for some new investigation techniques that (as luck would have it) helped support her case that Jack the Ripper was none other than Robert Louis Stevenson.

It had been a fun project and she recognized that it gave her self-esteem a bit of a boost to see her name on the non-fiction best-seller list at the same time as she had a book on the fiction list (and two books on the paperback best-seller list, if anyone was keeping count, which to be honest she was).

Although she would never admit it publicly, or even say it out loud, secretly Barbara was glad that the Ripper book was behind her and that she was back in the world of fiction. While she had enjoyed the year she spent researching and writing the Jack the Ripper book, there was something warm and almost comforting about getting back into fiction.

Oddly enough, she had found that the non-fiction world could be a brutal place. While Val had gathered a number of glowing blurbs for the back of the Jack the Ripper book, there were just as many (probably more) vicious pans of her work. Barbara had crossed a line when she moved from fiction to non-fiction and a lot of reviewers made it clear which side of the line they felt she belonged on.

And that didn't even take into account the reactions of the so-called experts in the study of Jack the Ripper (they liked to be called "Ripper-ologists," she had learned) who immediately attacked her theory and her methods, even those who promoted theories that were more ludicrous and far-fetched than her own.

"Please, please, please..."

Barbara looked up from her reverie to see Val, leaning across her desk, doing her best impression of a whining child.

"Can't I just plant one little item in *The Times*?" Val pleaded. "A teeny, weenie little blurb? An unsubstantiated rumor? A deep background quote from an unattributed, unnamed source?"

Barbara placed the mock-up board back into Val's outstretched hands. "No," she said. "I've had my fill of Jack the Ripper this week. This month. This year. It's time to move on. Come on," she said, crossing the room and picking up her purse from the floor next to that terribly uncomfortable chair. "Let's get lunch."

Val could tell she was beaten, at least for now, so she dropped the pleading posture at the same time that she dropped the cover mock-up on the table behind her desk.

"Lunch it is," she said. "My treat." She grabbed her own purse off the back of her chair and headed toward the door, with Barbara right behind her.

"Your treat? That's very nice of you," Barbara said.

Val held the door open for her. "Yeah, I'm a freakin' saint. Of course, you know," she continued, "that we just apply the cost of the lunch against your future royalties. So, when it's all said and done, you end up paying for it anyway. And for all I know, we mark it up."

Barbara laughed. "That's what I love about publishing. You've even found a way to make money on lunch."

* * *

As was often the case when she went out with Val, lunch turned into a short shopping spree, which then turned into drinks with some of Val's co-workers, which then turned into a happy hour meeting with a couple of her new authors.

As a result, it was nearly dusk and Barbara's side of Central Park was already heavily in shadow when the cab pulled up in front of her apartment building. Barbara struggled with her shopping bags as she paid the cabbie, then struggled again, this time with the lobby door, before Hector the doorman, finally noticed her and came to her rescue.

"Sorry about that, Miss Thomas," he said, opening the door with one hand and taking a couple of the bags with the other. "I didn't see you drive up."

Hector was often conveniently late in this manner, Barbara had noticed, but his tardiness tended to diminish as the holiday season drew near. If this had been late December instead of early September, she mused, he would have been standing and waiting at the curb as her cab pulled up.

Barbara assured Hector that she could get upstairs without further aid, and after grabbing her mail from her mailbox, she took the elevator up sixteen floors and let herself into her apartment. Still struggling with the bags, she closed the heavy door with her foot, then realized that the lock hadn't quite latched (a problem the Super had promised to repair weeks ago).

Her hands were still full of shopping bags, so she followed the path of least effort and simply backed into the door with her butt until she heard the reassuring snick of the lock. She dropped her purse and the shopping bags on the couch, tossed the mail on the table by the door, and kicked off her shoes. It was good to be home.

She headed toward the second bedroom that she used as an office to boot up her computer. A few minutes later, as she was boiling water for tea in the kitchen, she heard the familiar incoming mail chime from down the short hall.

By the time she settled down in front of the computer screen, her tea was sufficiently steeped and ready to be sipped.

She scrolled through what seemed to be an ever-increasing number of spam e-mails, many offering to increase her manhood ("Who answers these things?" she wondered and then decided she didn't want to know), and a couple that alerted her to a unique money-making venture that involved her bank account and the recently-deceased Prime Minister of Nigeria.

She kept scrolling and deleting, scrolling and deleting, until one e-mail caught her attention. She didn't recognize the return email on the screen, but she immediately recognized the two words that made up the subject line.

It read, simply, "Dear Boss."

Barbara opened the e-mail and as soon as she had read the first two sentences of the message, she set down her tea and picked up the phone.

CHAPTER EIGHT

When the elevator door opened, McHugh stepped out, then stopped, not sure that this was, in fact, the sixteenth floor. He stepped back into the elevator, checked the lit numbers above the door (Yes, the sixteenth floor) and then moved back out into the hall and turned right.

He should have turned left, he realized almost immediately, because the apartment numbers were going in the wrong direction, up instead of down. When he turned to retrace his steps and find the right number, he saw a uniformed patrolman standing outside an apartment door further down the hall. Uttering a muttered self- derogatory comment, McHugh shook his head at his own directional impairment and headed toward the patrolman.

Just as he reached the door, two other patrolmen came out of the apartment, with that young detective, Ben Black, right on their heels. Ben was about to give some instructions to the patrolman at the door when he noticed McHugh.

"Mr. McHugh," he said, taking and shaking McHugh's hand and guiding him into the apartment. "Thanks so much for coming on such short notice."

"My pleasure, my boy," McHugh said, glancing around the large, airy – and probably, he thought, very expensive – apartment, surprised to see several more police officials in the room, including that most unpleasant Lieutenant Harkness. "To what may we attribute the urgency, if I may ask?"

Ben glanced over at Barbara, who was coming through the living room toward them. "Miss Thomas received a disturbing e-mail today," he said. "And I wanted to get your opinion on it."

"Actually," Barbara said as she reached the two of them, "it was my idea to call you."

McHugh nodded a greeting at her while Ben pulled a hardcopy of the e-mail out of the folder he was holding. "We were hoping to get your thoughts and insights on this," Ben said.

"Certainly," McHugh said. "By all means."

McHugh rifled through his coat pockets, first the outer pockets and then the inner pockets, finally finding the object of his search: his reading glasses. He took the printout from Ben and scanned the contents of the paper, holding the glasses in front of his eyes without taking the time to actually put them on. He read the subject line aloud.

"'Dear Boss.'" McHugh lowered the sheet of paper and looked from Barbara to Ben and then back to the paper. "Oh, dear."

* * *

"The 'Dear Boss' letter is a significant artifact of Ripper correspondence and miscellanea for several reasons," McHugh said. He looked up at Barbara. "As I'm sure you're aware."

He was seated at the large, oak table in the apartment's dining room, which adjoined the living room on one side and a pass-through kitchen counter on the other. Barbara was just setting a cup of tea in front of him.

Ben, unwilling to sit, stood near the table, listening intently. Harkness, who was across the living room talking loudly on his cell phone, was also listening, although he pretended to be ignoring their conversation.

Barbara stopped as she set the tea down, realizing that they were all waiting for her response.

"Absolutely," Barbara said, feeling very much like an unprepared student in the midst of a surprise final exam. She took a breath and plowed forward, racking her brain for facts as she spoke.

"It was very significant. First and foremost, the 'Dear Boss' letter was the first time anyone used the name 'Jack the Ripper.' It's also one of the few letters, of the hundreds that the police received, that many experts agree is authentic."

McHugh clucked his tongue at this. "Many," he said, "but not all."

Ben pointed to the copy of the e-mail in McHugh's hand. "So," he said, "is that the text of the 'Dear Boss' letter?"

"At first blush, I'd have to say yes. Of course, I'd need some time to do a word-to-word comparison," McHugh said. "The font looks to be one of the 'Ripper' fonts that one might purchase on the internet, but our author does not appear to have done any significant re-writing from the original."

McHugh put his glasses on again and read a portion of the printed e-mail aloud. "'I am down on whores and I shan't quit ripping them till I do get bucked.' Blah, blah, blah. 'My knife is nice and sharp. I want to get to work right away if I get a chance. Good luck. Jack the Ripper.'"

He set the sheet back on the table with a sigh. "It appears to be identical to the original, in the text at least."

"But you don't think the original letter was authentic?" Ben asked.

McHugh looked up at him. "I stand in the minority, but no, I do not. To my ear it's always read like an educated person trying desperately to sound semi-literate." He pointed to a line in the e-mail. "'I saved some of the proper red stuff in a ginger beer bottle over the last job to write with, but it went thick like glue and I can't use it. Red ink is fit enough I hope ha ha.'"

McHugh tossed the paper aside again. "Rubbish," he said, taking a sip of his tea. His face registered surprise at how much he liked it. He nodded at Barbara appreciatively.

"Yorkshire Gold?" he asked. "If I'm not mistaken?"

"Yes, isn't it the best tea?" she said. "I started drinking it last year in London. When I was there doing my research."

"An unintended consequence, but a deeply appreciated one," McHugh said, taking another sip. "The next time you're back in London, there's a shop in Covent Garden just down from Neal's Yard that I can recommend to you without hesitation. They offer a stunning selection of teas, and not just from India and the West Indies and China, but from locales where you'd never expect to find tea at all, let alone outstanding tea, but believe me –"

Ben, who didn't want to spend the remainder of the evening talking about tea, quickly interrupted.

"So, if the original was a fake," he said, "why did our killer bother sending it? And why send it now?"

McHugh sat back in his chair. "Perhaps you are examining this from the wrong direction. You need to reframe the question. It's like that classic logic puzzle, you know the one, how does it go again?" McHugh sipped his tea for a moment. "Oh yes. A man buys some rare tea for five dollars a pound and sells the tea for three dollars a pound and becomes a millionaire. How did he do it?"

He sat back and watched while Ben and Barbara exchanged a look, each hoping the other had the answer on the tip of their tongue. They each turned back to McHugh as they jointly shook their heads in defeat.

McHugh smiled at them. "The answer is, he started out as a billionaire. And then became a millionaire. You have to reframe the question." McHugh smiled and leaned forward, picking up the printout of the e-mail. "You see, to my mind, what's most interesting about the original 'Dear Boss' letter," he said, "is not what it says, which is nonsense, but to whom it was sent."

"Who was it sent to?"

Barbara knew this one, so she answered before McHugh could. "The London newspapers of the day," she said, glad to finally be able to contribute something to the conversation. Her elation was short-lived.

"Not quite," McHugh said gently, shaking his head. "The author of the 'Dear Boss' letter sent his handiwork to the Central News Agency, which was sort of the Associated Press of its day. They gathered and wrote news stories, and then sold them to all the papers. Our original 'Dear Boss' author understood that sending the letter to the Central News Agency, instead of to a particular newspaper, meant his work wouldn't appear in just one newspaper ..."

Barbara finished his thought. "It would appear in all of them."

"Exactly," McHugh agreed. "Which is the reason why, parenthetically, I believe the original author was a reporter and not the killer we've come to know as Jack the Ripper." McHugh leaned forward and picked up the printout again. "So ... just as with the original, we have to ask, why send *this* letter to *this* person?"

He gestured toward Barbara, then set down the paper and picked up his tea.

"The answer to that question," he said, "will, I suspect, also satisfy many other questions."

He finished sipping his tea and handed the cup to Barbara, his body language making it very clear that another cup would be appreciated, thank you very much.

* * *

"I'm not convinced that this has anything to do with our thing." Dale Harkness was standing in the doorway to Barbara's apartment, not making much of an effort to lower his voice and keep the conversation between just Ben and himself.

"Which means what?" Ben asked quietly, hoping that Harkness would match his hushed tone.

"Which means the lady just wrote a book about Jack the Ripper," Harkness growled, "and wouldn't it be nice to get a big fat bunch of publicity by receiving e-mails from our killer?"

Ben shook his head. "She didn't fake this."

Harkness shrugged. "Maybe she did, maybe she didn't. All I'm saying is, I don't want this to go any further than this room." He turned and gestured to the two remaining patrolmen, who were waiting in the hallway just outside the door. "Let's go."

Ben watched them head toward the elevator, then turned and walked back into Barbara's apartment, shutting the door behind himself, giving it an extra push until he heard the satisfying 'click' of the lock sliding into place. Barbara was in the small kitchen, cleaning up the tea things.

"So, what's the verdict?" she asked as she opened the compact dishwasher and placed the cups and saucers into it.

"No verdict, really," Ben said, as he leaned against the doorframe.

"Our semi-official position is that we'd appreciate it if you didn't talk to anyone about the e-mail, or anything having to do with the ongoing case. For a while at least."

"Sure. No problem." Barbara straightened up and leaned against the sink, turning to meet Ben's gaze. "He doesn't like me much, does he?"

"Who, Harkness? Oh, don't let that bother you. Dale Harkness doesn't like anyone much," Ben said. "So, I wouldn't take it personally. I thought for the first few years that he didn't like me, then figured out I was right. I suspect even his mother has a hard time summoning up warm feelings for our friend Dale."

Barbara smiled as she thought about this for a moment. "Is it just me or does he seem sort of young to be in charge of ... well, anything, I guess," she said.

Ben nodded. "Yeah, well. You know how it is: some people have careers that move like rockets, other people ... well, you know." He didn't finish his thought and Barbara didn't push it.

"So," she said, after a long, quiet moment. "What should we do now?"

Ben hesitated and then, gathering his courage, said, "Well, at the risk of sounding forward, what would you say to going out to dinner?"

The answer to his question came from the hall outside the kitchen, as McHugh made his way out of the bathroom toward them.

"Splendid idea," McHugh said, still wiping his hands with one of Barbara's guest towels. "And I know just the spot!"

He handed the soggy towel to Ben as he headed to the couch to retrieve his hat.

* * *

"I know I shall be marked a traitor to my Queen and country," McHugh said in full raconteur mode, finishing off the last of his medium-rare steak and taking a healthy sip of the restaurant's best red wine, "but one of the most sublime joys of leaving Britain is escaping our terrible food. I've said it before and I'll say it until the day I die: If

71

it weren't for our Indian restaurants, I'd never get a decent meal when I'm at home."

He sat back, fully sated. "During the war, we could blame rationing," he continued. "But we lost that excuse years ago. The awkward, painful truth is that our English cuisine is a disaster!"

"I've never been to England," Ben said, "so I'll have to take your word for it."

"I'm going to have to disagree. I've had some very fine meals in London over the years," Barbara said, pouring a bit more wine for herself, and then gesturing to the others with the bottle. Ben, who hadn't had any wine with dinner (maybe it's because he's on duty, she thought) shook his head, while McHugh polished off the remainder in his glass and held the empty vessel forth for more.

"If you had a good meal in London," McHugh said, "then I'd be willing to wager that you must have been in love at the time."

Barbara laughed. "As a matter of fact, I was."

McHugh grunted an assent. "I've often thought a great research study could be done on the effects of love on the taste buds," he said. "From the anecdotal accounts I've assembled, love is not only blind but it also wreaks havoc on one's critical faculties in relation to the quality of the local cuisine."

His further thoughts on that topic were interrupted by the waiter, who expertly cleared away plates and the empty wine bottle.

"Can I tempt anyone with dessert tonight?" he asked as he worked.

"I can't speak for the younger members of my party," McHugh said, placing his napkin over the remains of his steak, "but before temptation overcomes me, I must bid adieu and take my leave." He stood to go. "But don't let my exit put an end to this delightful and diverting evening," he said to Barbara and Ben. "I'm sure you two have much to discuss."

Barbara noticed that the waiter was quietly waiting for a reply. "I'll have a cognac," she said.

The waiter looked to Ben, who shook his head.

"Nothing for me, thanks."

As the waiter headed off to turn in the order, McHugh pushed his empty chair back in to the table. "I thank you both for this charming respite," he said. Then he turned to Ben. "And, Detective Black, I leave you with one thought before I go."

Both Ben and Barbara looked up, expecting another joke. But McHugh's tone had become solemn, almost sad.

"There are three women out there tonight who are desperately in need of your help," he said quietly, his voice little more than a whisper. "Their safety and well-being will require every iota of energy, tenacity and wisdom you can muster. Elizabeth Stride. Catharine Eddowes. And Mary Kelly. They're depending on you. It's true, for the moment you've got the gift of time, but it's a stingy gift indeed. They will be expecting your very best. And they deserve nothing less."

He picked his hat up and bowed to both of them. "Good evening," he said. And then he was gone.

They were quiet for a moment. Barbara spoke first. "You realize what he's done, don't you?" she said.

Ben nodded, slowly. "Yes. I do. I guess he's issued a kind of challenge," he said. "And he's expecting me to rise to the occasion."

He looked at Barbara and was surprised to see that she was smiling. No, not just smiling. She was trying not to laugh.

"Well, yes, I suppose he did that," she said. "But he's also gone and stuck us with the check."

Ben smiled back at her. "Yes, he did that, too. That was going to be my second guess."

They both laughed and Barbara shook her head, gesturing in the direction where McHugh had gone. "Well, after what he's been through, I don't mind buying the man a meal or two."

"What's he been through?" Ben asked, wiping the corners of his mouth with his napkin.

Barbara was about to begin her narrative just as the waiter arrived with her brandy. Once he was out of earshot, she settled in to tell the story.

"Well, the way I've heard the story, McHugh was with the London police force for years. About the time he was getting close to retirement, he published his Ripper book, which is considered to be the definitive text on the subject."

Ben raised an eyebrow at this. Barbara laughed. "It's true. Everybody tells me that when they're buying my book. They say things like,

'Well, yours is okay, but McHugh's is the definitive book.' Believe me, I'm used to it.

"So, one night," she continued, "he's out with his wife, they've just had a nice dinner like this, they're on their way home, and they get mugged. A guy with a gun pushes them into an alley, says he wants their money. Now, McHugh's a cop, but British cops don't carry guns, on duty or off, so he does the smart thing. He gives the mugger all his money, his watch, his wife's jewelry.

"The mugger sticks the stuff into his pockets, turns to leave, and then – for no reason at all, apparently – he turns back and shoots McHugh and his wife. Point blank. Right there in the alley. They're rushed to the hospital. Long story short: she dies, he lives. Just like that. His life changed, shattered, in the course of about 30 seconds."

Ben sat back in his chair and looked around the restaurant, then back at Barbara. "Well," he said, "under the circumstances, I don't mind buying the guy dinner." He played with his spoon for a moment, then set it back on the table. "Of course, I'm not going to make a habit out of it."

They both laughed. Ben took a sip from his water glass while Barbara took a sip of her cognac, watching him all the while.

"Hey," he said, suddenly remembering. "I forgot to tell you. I read one of your books this week."

"You didn't."

"Swear to God. *Murder in St. Ives.*"

"So, how'd you like it?" she asked, surprised at how nervous she was about what his response might be.

"It's not a bad read," he said. "I'd give it … let's say, four out of five stars."

"Not five stars?"

"No offense, nothing gets five stars. Well, maybe *To Kill a Mocking-bird*," he said. "But I've got to tell you, you did that thing all you mystery writers do, and I gotta be honest, it bugs the hell out of me."

"What was it," she asked, leaning forward. "Tell me, and I'll tell the others."

"Right before the last chapter, your detective–"

"Hilary Webster."

"Right, Hilary," he said, snapping his fingers. "So, anyway, in the second-to-the-last chapter, Hilary says something like, 'I went down-town and spent the afternoon at the public library, following up on some hunches. By the time I got back to my office, I had all the pieces put together.' And I'm thinking, 'Of course you have all the pieces put together, and I would too if you told me what you found at the darned library!'"

"Well, that's one of our dirty little secrets, we mystery writers," Barbara said, sitting back and taking another sip of cognac. "We don't play fair. It's that simple. If we told you what Hilary found in the second-to-the-last chapter, you wouldn't need to read the last chapter."

"Damn straight," Ben said. "So, what are the others?"

"Other what?"

"The other dirty little secrets of mystery writers?"

Barbara considered this. "Let me see." After a moment, a thought occurred to her. "Well," she said, "this is true of all writers, not just mystery writers. We face our books."

"You do what?"

Barbara smiled, lowering her voice to a more conspiratorial tone. "We face our books. When we're in a bookstore, and we're checking out the section where our book should be – and we ALL do that – we face the book."

Ben shook his head. "Sorry," he said, "I'm not tracking with you."

Barbara sat back and started to use her hands to describe what she meant. "You know how when you go into a bookstore, all the books are turned so you can read the names on the spines, but then every once in a while, right in the middle of the shelf, one of the books will be displayed with its cover facing out?"

"Yes, I've seen that. It takes up more space, but that way you can see the cover. They probably do it with the more popular books."

"That they do, but like you said, it takes up more space, so there's a lot of jockeying for that position. So the bookstores only do it – it's called 'facing' – they only face a few books and usually, if you're a writer checking out the store, it isn't yours.

"So, if you're a writer and you're in a bookstore, here's what you do: You take your book and pull it out, move some of the other books on that same shelf aside, and put yours back with the cover facing out, so people will be more likely to buy it. At least, that's the theory behind it."

"And you all do it?"

"Never met a writer who didn't."

"Well, your secret is safe with me." Ben noticed the waiter passing by and flagged him down. "Can we get our check, please?"

"The check?" The waiter took a moment to remember the status of their check. "Oh, yes," he remembered. "The gentleman, the older gentleman, he took care of it on his way out. He's quite a character, isn't he?"

Ben nodded. "Yes, you could say that."

"Anyway," the waiter continued. "You're all set. Have a great evening."

The waiter headed across the dining room while Ben and Barbara exchanged a bemused look. "I guess we're all set," Ben said.

"I guess we are."

* * *

"So, tell me, how does someone become a world-famous writer?"

It was a question Barbara got a lot, in various forms, but usually not so directly.

She and Ben were walking the last block or so to her apartment. Although it wasn't late yet, it was closer to late than she'd experienced in a while. She was enjoying the sensations of being out and on something that seemed, in many ways, very much like a date.

"Do you really want to know? Or are you just making conversation?"

Ben laughed. "Making conversation is not one of my skills, as you will discover. And, yes, I am interested."

"Well, the short version of the story is that I got lucky."

Ben shook his head and looked ahead up the street. "That's great, but we've got at least a block until we get to your apartment. So I'm guessing we have time for, if not the long version, at least a version that isn't quite so abbreviated."

Barbara flushed a bit. "Okay." She wasn't good at talking about herself, which can be a minor liability when you're on a book tour and

76

is just plain awkward when you're on a first date. If this was, in fact, a date.

"I wrote a romance novel," she said, starting at what felt like the beginning.

"What's that?"

Barbara gave him an annoyed look, but he held up a hand in mock defense. "I'm a cop, not a book critic."

"Maybe, but you don't look like much of a cop carrying that tinfoil swan."

She had a point. Ben looked at the tinfoil swan the restaurant had so thoughtfully provided him when his entrée proved to be too large to eat in one sitting. He continued walking, casually holding his hands behind his back to hide the swan and the shame.

"Seriously," he said, "what's a romance novel?"

"Well, nowadays they might classify them differently, but they're basically novels that women read that are filled with a lot of romance and a little sex."

"So it's like soft core porn, but for women."

"Sort of, but the books are also about relationships and feelings and shopping and all the men are hunky, and the women are either bitchy or saints. There's a real formula to it."

"You can make a living doing that?"

Barbara laughed. "Well, some people can, but I couldn't. So I did temp work. But I did sell a couple of short stories, and then a romance novel and I was just starting to think it might become an actual career."

"And then ...?"

Barbara sighed. "Then I got lucky. I was reading nursery rhymes to my four-year old niece (who is now fourteen, oh my God), and the idea for a book came into my head, full-blown. Which never happens, I mean not ever.

"So I went home and wrote down the idea and then I wrote the first couple of chapters and showed them to my publisher. He wasn't interested but he knew someone who had just moved to another publishing house and was looking for that sort of thing and suddenly I sold the book.

"That first one, *The Mother Goose Murders*, was a modest hit, and then they wanted another one, and they wanted it to have a similar, nursery rhyme title, and before I knew it, I was trapped with a semi-successful series of books with increasingly odd titles."

"Gee, that's tough," he said, stopping and looking up at her building. "I mean, having to live on Central Park East and all."

Barbara smiled. "Yes, it's been a horrible inconvenience. One that I'm learning to live with on a day-to-day basis."

"One day at a time," he said in agreement.

Here's that awkward moment, Barbara thought, as they stood by the building's front door. Is it a date or just a dinner or what? They both stood there for a moment. A long moment.

Barbara finally was the one to give in and break the silence. "Well, I'd invite you in," she said, "But –"

"But we wouldn't want to wake your doorman," Ben said, finishing her sentence for her.

He gestured through the glass door. Barbara turned and wasn't at all surprised to see Hector, in his full doorman uniform, including the cap, sleeping soundly in one of the high-backed lobby chairs. Hector nodded a little, righted himself, and then slipped immediately back into sleep.

Barbara turned back to Ben and smiled. "Yes, I suppose you're right. They're so adorable when they're sleeping, aren't they?"

"I can't say. We've got a guy who stands outside my apartment building, but he thinks he's General MacArthur and that our building is The Philippines. He doesn't sleep much. On the upside, though, I don't have to tip him at Christmas."

Ben pushed the door open for her and she stepped into the lobby. She turned back to him and he held up the tinfoil swan, extending it toward her.

"Here, you can have this," he said. "You took enough of it off my plate during dinner, so by the right of eminent domain it's technically yours."

Barbara took the foil bird, which was still warm to the touch. "Are you sure you don't want it?"

"Yes, I do want it," he admitted. "I just don't want to be seen carrying a tinfoil swan in my neighborhood. A guy can get beat up for less." He turned to go, and then turned back, starting to say something, then stopped. "So, earlier, when you said you'd been in love in London ..." He hesitated again before finishing his thought. "That guy. Is he still around?"

"Actually, in the interest of full disclosure, it was two guys," Barbara said, adding quickly, "But not at the same time. And I lost both of them while in London."

Ben did his best not to look pleased. "Oh," was all he said, as he started to walk away. After taking a few steps, he turned back.

"Well, you know what they say," he said. "To lose one boyfriend in London may be regarded as misfortune ... to lose both seems like care-lessness."

Barbara laughed. "Thank you, Oscar Wilde. And good night."

She walked into the lobby, still holding the tinfoil bird. Ben watched as she pushed the button for the elevator. When it arrived,

she stepped in and a moment later the doors shut. Hector remained in his chair, still sleeping comfortably.

Ben waited a few more moments, letting the feeling of the evening sink in a bit, enjoying how he felt for the first time in a long time. Then he walked to the curb and hailed a cab.

CHAPTER NINE

The message light on Ben's desk phone was blinking when he sat down at his desk the next morning. He turned on his computer and while waiting for it to boot up he scraped some ancient non- dairy creamer into his coffee cup, which helped to dull the sting of the precinct's legendarily bad coffee.

He was about to pick up the phone and retrieve the message when his cell phone, which was sitting in its charger on the far corner of his desk, began to chirp loudly. He replaced the receiver on the desk phone and reached for the cell phone, narrowly avoiding spilling his coffee in the process.

"Ben Black here."

"Where are you?" demanded a husky voice with a rich Jamaican accent.

"Good morning to you, too, Isobel." He began logging into this computer with his free hand. "If you must know, I'm sitting at my desk, multi-tasking."

"Ah, I don't think that is entirely true. I just called your desk. You did not answer your telephone."

"You really can't get anything past you Medical Examiners can you? As it turns out, I just sat down."

"I called your cell phone first, but you didn't answer that either."

"Not that this is really any of your concern, but that's because my cell phone was in its charger at my desk."

He heard a deep, disapproving sigh through the phone. "And what earthly good is it to have a cell phone at your desk and not on your person, please tell me?" she asked.

Ben decided to treat the question as rhetorical and changed the topic. "Isobel, what can I do for you this fine morning?"

"If you must know, I'm at a crime scene and think it may be connected to the case you're working on."

Ben sat up in his chair. "A murder?"

"Yes, it appears to be very much so."

"What's the victim's name?" He flipped open the notebook on his desk and began to thumb through the pages. "Is it Elizabeth Stride? If it is, it's way too early for Elizabeth Stride."

"No. This is not a female. What we have here is a male victim."

Ben stopped paging through his notes. "A guy? Then what makes you think it's connected to my case?"

"You come. You look. I think very quickly you agree with me."

"Sure, okay. Where are you?"

He jotted down the address as she rattled it off. He hung up the phone and was just standing to leave when he noticed that the e-mail indicator had popped up on his computer screen. He clicked on the indicator and a brief e-mail opened on the screen.

"Something of interest has come to my attention. Stop by the office today. I'll be here until noon. Dimitri."

"I guess it's going to be a busy day," Ben said to no one in particular as he pulled on his suit coat, took one more gulp of painfully-bad coffee and headed out of the office and down to the motor pool.

A moment later, he returned to his desk and picked up his cell phone, pocketing it as he headed back toward the door.

* * *

The address Isobel had provided took Ben to an apartment building several blocks north of Little Italy. The building was one of three identical-looking structures, all clustered across the street from Roosevelt Park. The post-war buildings appeared to be popular with young singles and couples with small children, as evidenced by the bicycles, tricycles and strollers stored on nearly every terrace that jutted out on every floor.

A patrolman manning the front steps recognized Ben and opened the door for him.

"It's up on five," he said.

Ben moved through the worn but spotlessly clean foyer and pressed the button for the elevator. When it came, he stepped in, joining a severe-looking middle-aged woman holding a large laundry basket filled with neatly folded clothing. He pressed the button for five, noting that the light was already lit for the top floor, which was six.

The woman gave him a sidelong look, and then looked away when he glanced at her. She was wearing flip-flops, her hair was wrapped in a light blue scarf, and she was wearing what his mother used to call a 'housecoat,' which he always considered to be a fancy name for a bathrobe. Two well-thumbed copies of *People* sat atop her pile of laundry. She shook her head and mumbled.

"Excuse me?" Ben said.

"I said, it's a shame," she answered in a surprisingly deep and gravelly voice for such a tiny, thin person. "The damn place will never be this clean again."

"How do you mean?" Ben asked.

"Our building. Big Billy. He was the Building Caretaker; he kept the place clean, the walk swept, garbage out of the halls. He was good at it. And now he's gone, poor soul, and the place will go to hell, you can mark my words."

"Big Billy?"

"Yeah, up on five. You're a cop, right? You're here about Big Billy, right? The cops have been here all morning. Ever since they found him. Poor soul."

The elevator arrived on five and the doors opened. Ben stepped out into the hall and turned back to the woman. "It's down there at the end," she said, gesturing with a sharp tilt of her head.

"Thanks."

She clucked her tongue as the elevator door slid shut. "Never be this clean again," she muttered.

She had a point, Ben had to agree. The hallway was clean, the fixtures shiny, and the carpet, although old, had clearly been vacuumed and shampooed on a regular basis.

He headed down the hall in the direction she had indicated and had little trouble finding the apartment. The front door was open and several people Ben recognized were moving through the neat one-bedroom apartment, each actively engaged in their respective duties. One was dusting for fingerprints, another taking photos, and a third was seated at a small desk, typing on a keyboard and looking through the contents of the victim's computer.

Only one person wasn't moving, Ben noticed, and that was a body on the floor in the center of the living room, covered by a sheet.

Ben was surprised at how small the lump under the sheet appeared to be and for a moment he was afraid that the victim was a child. The purplish pallor of a pudgy, obviously adult hand, poking out from under the sheet, put his mind at ease. It was clear that there was an exceptionally short adult corpse on the floor.

Ben glanced around the rest of the apartment and was instantly struck at how incredibly neat and clean the small place was. The kitchen floor shone, the walls looked freshly painted, the couch and two chairs were covered with crisp plastic covers. Books, DVDs and CDs in the bookcase were arranged with painful precision.

A wooden library ladder leaned against one wall, looking a little out of place, as the tallest bookcase was well short of eight feet. The only thing that broke the spell of tidiness was the lumpy shape under the sheet in the middle of the room.

Isobel stepped out of the bedroom, saw Ben and made her way across the room toward him. She gestured toward the sheet-covered figure as she walked.

"William Burke, age forty-three."

Ben nodded. "Big Billy."

Isobel looked up from her ubiquitous note pad, her eyebrows arching. "You know him?"

Ben shook his head. "No, no," he said. "I ran into another tenant in the elevator. Apparently, Big Billy was something of a clean freak and the people of this building are going to miss him."

"Clean freak, that's what they say? Well, they be right about that. But he's a bit of a mess now, sad to say."

She crouched down and pulled back the top of the sheet, revealing Big Billy's face. His eyes were closed, but he didn't look particularly peaceful. His face was frozen in a painful grimace and the white of his skin had begun to take on a purple hue.

Wrapped around his neck was a black cord, barely visible under the layers of skin that comprised his double and triple chins. Where the cord was visible, Ben could see that it had cut deeply into Big Billy's neck.

"Strangled?" Ben asked. "With that cord?"

Isobel nodded. "That's probably right."

"When did it happen?"

"Late last night. Early this morning. Ten, twelve hours ago."

Ben looked down at Billy and then up at Isobel. "So, how are you coming with my challenge? Wallace Shawn to Sean Connery?"

She smiled at him, shaking her head. "Games, games. You and your games. I am making progress, don't you worry."

Ben nodded and looked around the apartment. "So, what do you think? Robbery?"

Isobel shrugged. "How do I know, I'm a medical examiner? You have questions about the bodies, the dead ones, I'm the one you see. Don't look to me for information about robberies. But there is something here that is interesting. Most interesting."

She stood and walked over to the desk where one of the techs was seated, working on the computer. Ben followed.

"Tell him what you found on the computer," Isobel said to the tech. He looked up from his work, first at her, then at Ben.

"Nothing," he said.

Ben waited a moment, thinking there must be more to it. "Nothing suspicious?" he asked.

The tech shook his head. "No, nothing. Absolutely nothing. The computer was wiped clean. All the files, all the programs, everything." He gestured to the blank screen on the monitor. "It's like it just came from the factory, except even a factory computer comes with an operating system and a handful of programs. This sucker was cleaned right down to the mother board."

84

Ben looked at the monitor and at the computer tower on the floor by the desk. "But this is not a new computer."

"You've got that right," the tech agreed. "It's about two years old. And it's completely blank. But I suspect that, until recently, all those programs were on this computer."

He pointed to several software boxes, lined up neatly on a shelf behind the desk. Ben stepped forward and looked at the product names: Photoshop, Illustrator, PaintShop Pro, and Lightroom. Next to the programs were several photography textbooks.

"This guy was a photographer?"

The tech looked up at Isobel, who shrugged. "Maybe. Maybe not. But not so much anymore."

Ben looked at her and then over at the body on the floor. "So I don't get it. How is this case connected to my case?"

Isobel moved back to the body and, crouching down, took the loose end of the black cord in her fingers. She pulled the sheet back further, revealing that the cord around Big Billy's neck continued down his chest. At the end of the cord was a white square encased in a plastic cover. Isobel pointed to the square and Ben moved closer to inspect it.

It was then that Ben realized that the cord around Big Billy's neck was a black lanyard, and at the end of the lanyard was a nametag. Handwritten on the nametag were the words "Big Billy, Official Photographer."

Beneath his name, printed on the card, was the logo for the 15th Annual Jack the Ripper Conference.

* * *

"Oh, poor Billy. Poor, poor Billy."

Grace Marquardt wrung her hands together and then reached for a tissue, gently dabbing at the corners of her eyes. She quickly ran the tissue under her nose and then delicately crumpled it, hiding it in her sleeve and making it disappear, like a magic trick performed by an aged but still skillful magician.

Ben sat across from Grace in her apartment in Brooklyn's Red Hook neighborhood. The apartment was much like its resident: overstuffed, a bit garish and long overdue for a makeover. He sat on a lumpy couch, upholstered in a busy, red chintz pattern. Grace sat across from him in a padded rocking chair, gently rocking back and forth. For a few moments the creaking of her chair and Grace's gentle sniffling were the only sounds in the apartment.

"Did you know Billy well?" Ben asked, breaking the silence.

Grace nodded and sniffled again, effortlessly producing the tissue from her sleeve, wiping her nose and just as skillfully making it disappear a moment later.

"I suppose," she said. "As well as you know anyone you see once a year. He came to all the conferences, perhaps even from the beginning. Certainly, for the last dozen years or so."

"And he was the official photographer for the Conference?"

Grace smiled. "No, not really," she said, shaking her head at the memory. "We gave him that title because, well, because he was always taking pictures. Every year, at every Conference, you could count on seeing Big Billy with his camera, just snapping away."

Ben nodded and made a note on his pad. "So, Billy had a long- time interest in Jack the Ripper?"

Grace stopped rocking and leaned back in her chair. She was a large woman and Ben was amazed at how she had not only squeezed effortlessly into the tight confines of the chair, but even appeared to be completely comfortable.

"No, I wouldn't say that about Billy," she finally said, resuming the rocking motion. "We get all levels of interest at the Conference, from the neophytes to the truly scholarly. For Billy, his interest in Jack the Ripper was, I think, purely social. And perhaps economic."

Ben looked up from his notes. "How do you mean?"

"I mean, Billy was an outsider his whole life and I think, in some small way, coming to the Conferences made him feel like he was a part of something. He was accepted. He belonged. And, given his ... handicap ... I don't think that Billy experienced that often in his life."

"So he didn't make his living as a photographer?"

Grace shook her head, stifling a laugh. "Goodness no. To be honest, he wasn't a very good photographer, really. And I don't think he ever made much of a living. I think he received a Social Security check each month, and his parents might have left him a bit of money. But, no, he didn't make his living as a photographer or anything else, really."

"So, what did he do?"

Grace shrugged. "Like I say, I really only saw him at the Conference each year. Occasionally he'd show up at a committee meeting, but he wasn't what you'd call a regular. And, of course, I often received e-mails from him," she added, gesturing to a MacBook which sat anachronistically atop an antique desk across the room.

"He spent a lot of time on-line, in the Ripper chatrooms. And he bought and sold Ripper items on eBay, I believe. I don't think he ever made much money at it, but he was always looking for that one rare item that would make his fortune."

Ben shifted his position on the couch, trying to find a spot that was, if not more comfortable, than at least less painful. "What sort of thing would that be?"

Grace laughed and used her magical disappearing tissue to wipe away one final tear. "Oh, who knows? A rare book, an original photograph, a letter, a manuscript, some curio or miscellanea. He wasn't the only one. Some people are attracted to subjects like the Ripper simply because it provides the hope of making their fortune. Of course, hardly anyone ever does. Fortunes are hard to come by in the Ripper world. That's true in the real world as well."

Ben nodded in agreement. "Tell me about it," he said rhetorically, closing his notebook.

Unfortunately, rhetorical statements were wasted on her, and so for the next hour and forty minutes, Grace Marquardt did just that.

* * *

Ben was halfway through the Brooklyn-Battery tunnel on his way back to Manhattan when he remembered the e-mail he'd received earlier that morning from Dimitri. He quickly checked his watch and realized that – if traffic was with him and road construction was at a minimum – he could just make it to the Starbucks at the corner of Worth and Lafayette before noon.

The coffee shop was crowded but Ben had little trouble spotting Dimitri, in what appeared to be his regular spot by the window. He wore headphones and tapped at the keyboard on his laptop, stopping only when he realized that Ben was standing over him. He looked up at Ben and then pulled off his headphones as he glanced at his watch.

"Cutting it close, Detective. Cutting it very close. I was about to be gone."

Ben listened for a long moment to the mournful sound coming out of the headphones on the table. "Harry Nilsson?" he asked, tentatively. "But maybe Randy Newman," he added, covering his bet.

"Your confusion is completely justified," Dimitri said with a quick smile. "It is in fact Mr. Harry Nilsson, but in this instance the cat is singing one of Mr. Randy Newman's classic tunes, *Dayton, Ohio 1903*. I'm going to give you that one, so you are officially two for two. Don't kid yourself, you're good at this."

"And you have eclectic musical tastes," Ben replied, pulling over a chair from a nearby table.

"What did I tell you last time? I know a little bit about a lot of things, and that applies to my taste in music as well." He tapped a key on the keyboard and the sad, tinny music was silenced. "Can I get you a wildly over-priced hot or cold beverage of your choice?"

Ben shook his head.

"Oh, that's right," Dimitri said, smiling. "You don't partake of the pleasures of the Third Place."

Ben nodded. "I'm still recovering from a cup of precinct coffee I had earlier this morning."

"That cop coffee will kill you, man."

"That's what they tell me." Ben settled back in his chair and stole a glance at his watch. "So I got your e-mail. Am I keeping you from anything if this goes past noon?"

"I've got a date with an elliptical trainer, but that's flexible," Dimitri said. "Fact is, I might just blow off today's exercise regimen and take in a movie, depending on what's showing at the Regal in Union Square. There's a new zombie movie I want to catch while it's still in the theaters."

Ben smiled. "You like zombie movies?"

"Hands down, my favorite genre. And, man, you ain't seen a zombie movie 'til you've seen it with a true-blue New York audience. That can be a life-changing interactive experience. Of course, none of the current crop of zombie flicks lives up to the original, *Night of the*

Living Dead, but that's just another indication of the sad state of the American cinema."

"*Night of the Living Dead*? That's the black and white one, right?"

"You got it, Detective. Significant for me because it was the first horror film that I ever saw as a kid that had a black man in the lead. Revolutionary, I tell you, revolutionary. Mr. George Romero, if you'll pardon the expression, is the shit."

Ben leaned forward. "Yes, but doesn't the black guy get shot in the head at the end of that movie?"

Dimitri nodded, frowning. "Yeah, the dude got shot, but for one of the first times in the cinema of my experience, it wasn't simply because he was a black man. Consider that." He took a long sip of coffee and then started moving his fingers quickly across the keyboard. "But you didn't come here for a symposium on black cinema, did you?"

Ben shrugged. "I'm not entirely certain why I'm here, but I'm always up for a conversation about movies and I'll happily debate the relative merits of Fred Williamson against the significant contributions of Pam Grier."

"A well-rounded cop. Will wonders never cease." Dimitri gave a short laugh, then returned to his typing. "So, here's what's up. We had a little incident early yesterday on the Ripper website. At first, I didn't think much of it, but then I started digging a little deeper and I realized that what we had might be of interest to you. Take a look at this."

He spun the laptop around on the table and Ben leaned in to look at the screen, tilting it back a bit to eliminate the glare from the overhead light. On the screen he recognized a thread from one of the Ripper message boards.

The particular forum was titled "General Discussions," and the thread that was open was called "Conference Photo$." Ben read the only message under that heading: "Here'$ just one of the great photo$ I snapped at our recent Ripper Conference. Lot$ of other$ are available, including $ome revealing $hots that could CHANGE your life."

He realized immediately what was so odd about the posting. All the Ss in the ad had been replaced with dollar signs.

Ben scrolled down further, revealing a photo that filled the bottom half of the message space. Although he'd never seen the photo before, Ben immediately recognized the location and subject matter.

89

The image was of a hallway at the Ripper Conference, right outside the book room. The people moving past in the shot were hazy blurs, but one part of the photo was in sharp focus: Near the center of the frame Ben could see the white-clad and white-faced figure of the newsboy statue, holding his newspaper with the headline, "Jack the Ripper Strikes! Claims First Victim!"

Ben looked up at Dimitri. "Okay, it's from the Conference, that's clear." he said. "But I'm not sure I understand the significance."

"I didn't either, at first. I get people trying to sell things all the time. You see, one of the rules of the board is that you can't use it to buy or sell items. My policy has always been, if you want to do that, get your ass over to eBay."

Ben tilted his head to the side. "I would have thought that on- line auctions would be a great profit center for you."

Dimitri nodded. "Yeah, you'd think so, but once you start over-seeing the buying and selling of goods, you expose yourself to all kinds of bothersome liabilities. And that's not for me. Plus," he added, gesturing to the coffee shop around him, "I'm a firm believer in sticking to your core and outsourcing the rest of that nonsense."

Dimitri leaned forward and pointed to the text on the screen. "The dollar signs he used were his lame attempt to get around our no-selling policy. The thing is, he's not all that clever, because a dollar sign in a message sends an alert to the moderator, who then looks at the message and pulls it if he thinks it's a violation of the terms of service. Which is what happened in this case: the moderator got the alert, looked at the message, determined that this cat was trying to sell some-thing and pulled the message.

"And, because this particular member has been reprimanded in the past for trying to sell items on the site, the moderator passed all this up to me."

Ben nodded. "So, this message is no longer on the board?"

"That's right. I kept a copy, but we pulled it from the live board a couple hours after it went up."

"And you contacted the member?"

Dimitri leaned forward. "Well, you see, that's where it starts to get interesting. I e-mailed the dude and it bounced back, which is weird, because a few hours before the guy had posted this message using that same e-mail address, and all of a sudden, the system was saying that this e-mail address didn't exist. That doesn't make much sense, particularly if you're using your e-mail address to try to sell something."

Ben nodded. "I see your point."

"On top of that, I recognized the e-mail address, because this guy has a history of trying to buy and sell shit on my boards. So, I was confident that it was the right address. This got my curiosity up, so I went into his profile on the site and saw that among all the other trivial things that people put in their profiles, he'd listed his phone number. So, I tried to call him."

Ben looked surprised. "You used the phone? You actually placed a call on a telephone?"

Dimitri smiled patiently. "Yeah, I broke down and used the phone. 'Course, you can't find a payphone in this town any more for love or money, so I borrowed a phone from one of the kids behind the counter."

"And you talked to the guy?"

Dimitri shook his head. "Nope, I talked to a cop, because that's who answered the damned phone when I called. I asked for Big Billy, the guy identified himself as a cop and asked me my business, and I said that I'd call back later and hung up. I didn't want to get caught up talking to a cop. Present company excluded, of course."

Ben sat forward suddenly. "Big Billy? You were calling Big Billy?"

"Isn't that what I just said?" Dimitri gave Ben a long look. "So, what are you saying, you guys are familiar with Big Billy?"

"Well, we are now. He was found murdered this morning."

Dimitri gave a low whistle and sat back heavily in his chair. "No shit?"

Ben nodded. "Looks like he was strangled sometime last night. And whoever did it, it also looks like they wiped his computer clean."

"Must have wiped out his e-mail account as well," Dimitri said. "Because there's no trace of it now."

"Do you think it had something to do with this photo?" Ben asked, gesturing toward the image on the computer screen.

Dimitri bit his lower lip for a moment. "Probably," he said finally. "Or, this photo was just the bait and Big Billy had other photos that were, in some way, more damning. He said in his message on the board that he had some revealing shots that could change your life."

"Well, they certainly changed his life."

"You got that right. But for my money, I'd say the answer is tied up with that crazy-ass mime. I mean, nobody in their right mind would show up at a Ripper Conference hawking a mistake like that one, unless they meant to stir things up."

Ben leaned in and examined the photo more closely. "What mistake?" he finally asked.

Dimitri shook his head sadly. "Man, you are a pitiful excuse for a detective, aren't you? Look at the headline. What does it say?"

Ben read the headline on the mime's newspaper. "Jack the Ripper Strikes! Claims First Victim!" He looked at it for a long moment, then looked over at Dimitri. "I'm stumped. Where's the typo?"

Dimitri pulled the laptop back toward himself. "It's not a typo. It's a simple factual error, and if you spent any amount of time at all on my Ripper website, you'd have understood it in an instant. You are a newbie, man, a total newbie."

Dimitri used one of his long fingers to point out the words on the headline in the photo. "Jack the Ripper Strikes. Claims First Victim! You see, the thing is, nobody called the dude Jack the Ripper or even Jack until after the second murder. So, you never would have seen that headline in real life. Unless …"

Ben looked up from the photo. "Unless what?"

Dimitri looked around the room and lowered his voice. "This photo was taken at the Ripper Conference, which took place after the first victim was murdered. What if this dude is using this get-up–this mime statue shit–as his own, sick and twisted way of announcing that he's claimed his first victim?"

He pointed at the headline and then at the white-faced statue. "Jack the Ripper Strikes. Claims First Victim."

"So," Ben said, drawing out the word to three syllables, "you're saying that this might be our murderer?"

"Could be. And what if he changed into that get-up somewhere around the hotel and Big Billy happened to snap a shot or two of him in his 'before' stage?"

Ben nodded along. "And then Billy saw the headline, recognized what it really meant and put two and two together."

"And thought he could make a bit of money with the information." Dimitri sat back and finished his coffee. "He posts the message. The mime reads it, gets in touch with him, goes to his apartment under the pretense of wanting to pay him for the photos…"

"And strangles him. Using Billy's nametag lanyard from the Conference as the murder weapon."

Dimitri winced. "Oh, that's tight. Very tight."

Ben pointed toward the image on the screen. "With the costume and the make-up and the lack of clarity, this could be anyone. You can't tell for sure if it's a man or a woman, white or …" Ben stopped short, not finishing his sentence.

Dimitri laughed. "Man, another liberal, lord help us. Just say the word. The word is black. You can't tell if he's white or black."

Ben plowed ahead. "Or Hispanic or Asian for that matter. The clothing could be padded, so you can't get a decent guess on the weight. Plus, it doesn't help that Billy shot it from a low angle, so you can't really get a handle on the height of the subject."

Dimitri folded his arms. "Yeah, well, my understanding is that Big Billy shot everything from a low angle. He was, as they say nowadays, vertically challenged."

Ben chuckled grimly. "Yeah, I guess he was." Ben sat back in his chair. "Well, I guess this helps us, but I'm not entirely certain how. But thanks."

Dimitri stood up and pulled on his suit coat. "No problem. Just don't be dragging any of this back onto my doorstep," he said as he shut the computer and began to pack it into its carrying case. "Now, if you'll excuse me, I've got a date with a zombie. You're free to join me, if you like."

Ben thought over the offer. "That's very tempting," he said. "It's been a long while since I saw a good zombie film."

Dimitri shook his head. "Man, don't be thinking like that, it will just lead to heartbreak. Trust me, there ain't no such thing as a good zombie film. They don't exist on that critical plane. You just have to take them for what they are."

"Really? And what are they?"

"Well, in the hands of a master like Mr. Romero, they tend to be insightful critiques of the human condition."

"With buckets of blood."

"Well, yes, but understand that blood and viscera are just necessary elements of the convention. You're in homicide. That's shouldn't be a surprise to you."

Ben thought about it for a moment longer and then stood up.

"I'm in," he said, and a few moments later he and Dimitri were headed toward the door.

CHAPTER TEN

The blade was sharp. Very sharp. Far sharper than it needed to be. The word 'overkill' came to Jack's mind, and when it did it made him smile.

Still he ran the blade through the sharpener, to make sure it was as sharp as possible, and as he did, he immediately thought of Proverbs 27: "Iron sharpens iron."

He'd had the blade for a long time now and he kept it at the very peak of sharpness. It had proven to be a very versatile tool, and although he had acquired two other blades in his travels, this was the hero blade, the one he returned to again and again.

As he examined the knife, he was glad again that he had not used it on the midget photographer. For that little annoyance, he had used other means; in his heart he knew the knives were sacred and not for such trivial adventures.

The knives, and this knife in particular, were special.

Working slowly, deliberately, he used the blade to cut through the thick, white paper. Jack was using a straight edge to guide the blade, but he almost didn't need it; the blade was wicked sharp, and it just sailed through the paper fibers without a hitch or a snag. When he'd gone to the office supply store to buy the roll of paper (using cash, of course, he was no dummy), the clerk had called it "butcher

95

paper."

And he'd thought, *Lady, you don't know how right you are.*

He finished cutting a large enough section of the paper for his purposes and set the rest of the roll aside. There was a lot of paper left over, which seemed a shame. Perhaps he would donate the rest of the roll somewhere. Maybe an art school for poor kids.

He'd have to look into that, he thought as he spread the cut paper across the top of the table. The paper started to roll up a bit at the corners, but that was okay. He could handle that. Not a problem.

Jack opened the refrigerator. The light didn't come on, but that was okay, too. There wasn't much to see in there, except for an orange, a pint of milk, two sticks of beef jerky and a small white cardboard box. It looked like one of those boxes you got when you took home Chinese food – not the big ones, but the little ones that they put the rice in, cheap bastards. Like it would kill them to fork over a little more rice.

He didn't like Chinese food, but that was okay because there wasn't any Chinese food in the little white box. Nor any rice, for that matter.

He put the small white box on the white paper, and he picked up the packing tape, which was clear and profoundly sticky. Then he started folding and taping and folding and taping. Like that lady did once at that store he'd gone to before Christmas years ago, when she'd offered to wrap the present he'd bought. She was a pro, that lady, making every fold perfect and taping it in such a way that it almost hid the folds. She'd done a very good job.

He'd appreciated what she'd done and told her she'd done a good job and she said that was because she was "a professional wrapper," and then she'd laughed, and then the other lady who worked with her–the really heavy one with the mole on her round, fat face–she started laughing, too.

They'd laughed and laughed, two happy, heavy wrapping ladies. He still wasn't sure why it was so funny.

Of course, he did a good job, too. Not as good as she had done, but he was not a professional wrapper. But when Jack was finished taping, the box was all wrapped and sealed and ready to be delivered.

And best of all, it wasn't leaking.

Not a drop. At least not yet.

CHAPTER ELEVEN

Ben was seated at his desk, scanning through a particularly intense flame war on Dimitri's Ripper message board, when a newspaper landed with a stinging smack on top of his hands. The immediate consequence was that he involuntarily scrolled past several messages on the site.

Ben looked up to see Dale Harkness glaring down at him; then he looked down to see the headline on *The New York Post* which lay across his keyboard: 'Desperate Cops Turn To Author For Help Finding New Jack The Ripper.' The sub-head read, 'Police Otherwise Clueless In Recent Murder Spate.' There was a photo of Barbara next to the headline and a recent crime scene photo right beneath it.

"This is her idea of keeping a lid on it?" Harkness asked, spitting out his words.

Ben picked up the paper and scanned the first couple of paragraphs. As he read the story, he could feel Harkness seething next to him. He didn't let that bother him. In fact, the longer he read, and the more Harkness seethed, the better Ben felt about himself. So he took his time.

After a few moments, Ben finally put the paper down. He looked up at Harkness, who was glowering down at him.

"Well," Ben said, "I'm guessing you'll want to talk to her."

"Good guess, Sherlock. And her publisher – the one who's quoted in there about a gazillion times – get her ass in here as well."

Ben glanced back at the paper. "Valerie Howard. Sure thing. How soon?"

But by that point Harkness had already stormed away. Ben could hear an office door slam further down the hall.

"I'm guessing pretty soon," he said to no one in particular. He picked up his cell phone, which was sitting in a charger on the desk, and then realized as he started to dial the cell phone that he had a desk phone at his disposal.

So he set the cell back in the charger and picked up the desk phone, then started flipping through his notes to find Barbara's phone number.

* * *

Barbara and Val were seated, none too comfortably, in the small, drab interrogation room on the third floor of the precinct station. Val was, as always, in a too-short skirt and too-low-cut blouse, both wrists over-loaded with bracelets. Barbara, the picture of decorum next to her, was in slacks and a cashmere sweater. Harkness paced in front of them, holding–no, clutching–a piece of paper.

"So, what you're telling me is," he said to Val, brandishing the sheet of paper, "that you didn't write this press release, you didn't authorize this press release, you didn't e-mail this press release ... but when reporters called you in reference to this press release, you saw no reason not to talk to them about the press release. In grand and glorious detail."

Val nodded. "That's what I'm saying."

"Is that standard practice?"

"Honey, I'm in the publishing business. In our world there's no such thing as standard practice."

Harkness gave her a long look, which didn't seem to faze her one bit. "But you didn't write it and you didn't send it."

"Yes, Lieutenant Harkness, for what I swear to God must be the one millionth time, that's right."

Harkness continued to pace, now with his back to them, facing the large mirror that took up much of one wall. Barbara looked up at the mirror and guessed that Ben, among others, was watching from behind the glass. Val looked at Barbara and then followed her gaze over to the mirror. Val got up, deciding this would be as good a time as any to refresh her lipstick.

Harkness, hearing her get up, turned and watched with astonishment as she walked past him to the mirror, took a bright shade of red lipstick out of her clutch purse and diligently began applying it to her lips.

"You expect me to believe you had nothing to do with this, even though the press release is on your company's letterhead and appears to have been e-mailed from your computer?" Harkness directed his stare at Val's reflection in the mirror.

She finished her lipstick, recapped the tube, replaced it carefully in her purse, then turned to him and held his gaze, expertly. "Weird, isn't it?"

"It's not just weird, Miss Howard," he said. "It's also very likely prosecutable."

Val shrugged. "I doubt very much that's even a word and I edit books for a living," was all she said as she headed back to her straight-backed chair.

She sat with a defiant sigh, crossing her legs and making a point not to look in Harkness' direction. Next to her, Barbara was becoming frustrated at the circular nature of the argument.

"Look, Lieutenant," Barbara said, "if Val said she didn't send it, then she didn't send it."

Harkness moved his gaze from Val to Barbara without turning down the intensity one degree. "I'm not so sure I want to take her word for it. Or, yours for that matter."

"Right now, it looks like that's all you've got," Barbara said.

Harkness continued staring at her. He was clearly disgusted with her, with Val, with this situation, and the world in general. If there were a puppy in the room at that moment, Barbara thought, he probably would have hated it, too.

"I'm painfully aware of my options, Miss Thomas," he said as he walked out of the room, slamming the door behind him. This was no small trick, Barbara noted, because the door had an automated door closer on it, which allowed it to close slowly and smoothly.

But Dale Harkness' anger somehow defeated the mechanism and the door closed with a resounding slam.

* * *

"Here I'm thinking we're going to meet the real-life equivalent of Benjamin Bratt or Jimmy Smits or even William Peterson, and we get stuck with a constipated Doogie Howser," Val complained as she and Barbara made their way out of the interrogation room once they'd been released. "I gotta tell you, I feel cheated."

"Doogie Howser was a doctor, not a cop," Barbara reminded her.

"Whatever."

At that moment, Ben came out of the viewing room next to the interrogation room and joined them in the corridor.

"I think that went well," he said, keeping pace with them as they made their way down the hall.

"You do?" Barbara was surprised at his assessment.

Ben shrugged. "Relatively well."

"Relative to what?"

Ben didn't answer her, but instead turned to Val. "Call us immediately if you hear from anyone who says you sent them an e-mail that you didn't send. Or if anything else out of the ordinary happens."

"Sure thing," Val said. "Who do I call, you or your charm- impaired boss?"

They had reached the elevator. Ben produced a card from his coat pocket. "Call me. Generally, I'm more user-friendly than Lieutenant Harkness."

"Thanks, but the bar's not set all that high around here."

Ben smiled as he pressed the "Down" button for them, and then he turned to Barbara. "And I'll call you later, if that's okay? We've got a guy here, from the FBI, a profiler, upstairs. I need to go meet with him."

"Sure."

He put out his hand to Val, gripping her hand warmly. "It was nice meeting you," he said. "Thanks again for coming down." He smiled again and stepped into the stairwell next to the elevator. Val watched him go, then turned to Barbara.

"Boy, they've sure got that Good Cop / Bad Cop thing nailed here, don't they?"

Barbara nodded. The elevator door opened, and they stepped in. Val continued talking, despite the presence of several uniformed cops on the elevator.

"And what is it about cops and great buns? Have you ever noticed? The last one had great buns. Even the short one with the attitude. Great buns."

Barbara pretended she didn't know Val as the elevator doors shut.

* * *

Ben took the stairs two at a time and reached the fourth floor, exiting the stairwell and nearly colliding with Harkness as he came through the door. Harkness didn't break his stride for a second and kept walking as Ben struggled to follow the angry cop down the hall.

"The thing is," Ben said, trying to figure out how to best broach this topic, "I think she's telling the truth."

"So do I. That's what's pissing me off," Harkness said. "Come on. O'Rourke's probably waiting for us."

O'Rourke was, in fact, waiting for them. He sat in the station's small fourth floor conference room with the case files spread out in front of him. His Bluetooth earpiece was clipped to his ear and was more visible than normal due to his closely-cropped hair. Ben was always amazed at just how much O'Rourke looked like an FBI agent. If he hadn't actually been an agent, he certainly could have played one on TV.

Harkness shut the door quietly, pointing to his ear and then gesturing to O'Rourke, so that Ben understood they weren't to disturb the federal agent while he was on the phone. O'Rourke looked up and nodded to them, still concentrating on the unheard voice in his earpiece.

They stood patiently by the door while O'Rourke silently and almost absently paged through the papers, occasionally uttering a brief "Uh huh," or "Right," or "Roger that." Finally, he pressed a button on his cell phone and pulled the earpiece from his ear. He looked up.

"Sorry about that," he said. "My ex-wife had to unload some issues. Another in a series of conversations that I'd rather not have. Some days I wish I could put myself in the Witness Relocation Program. Become a farmer named Swenson. In Wisconsin somewhere. I tell ya, I'd pay good money."

"But, anyway," he continued, holding up a file folder that was on top of the pile and handing it to Harkness. "A forensics report came in while you were gone. They're not coming right out and saying it was the same knife for both homicides, but it's pretty clear they think it was."

"Great." Harkness paged through the folder quickly. "So, did you get through much of the case file?"

O'Rourke began sorting the piles on the table, essentially straightening things up. "Yes. Just enough to realize that I'm the wrong guy for this job."

Harkness dropped the folder on the table. "How do you figure?"

O'Rourke grabbed the dropped file and added it back to the pile. Once he had the files in neat stacks, O'Rourke got up and put on his suit coat, which had been draped over a nearby chair. "This is not a typical case," he said. "It's a copycat case, and we've determined over the years that a standard profile won't work on a copycat."

"Why is that?" Harkness asked, a note of annoyance seeping into his voice.

"Because you're one step removed in a copycat case and the traditional indicators don't generally line up correctly. Don't worry, though, we're not done yet. I've found the right person for you. He's just the guy for this one."

"Great," Harkness said. "What's his name?"

O'Rourke seemed genuinely excited about the replacement he was offering. "McHugh," he said, smiling. "Henry McHugh."

Ben's smile matched O'Rourke's. "That's great," he said, then turned to Harkness. "Isn't that great?"

*　*　*

"As I was explaining to these gentlemen earlier," O'Rourke said, gesturing to Harkness and Ben, "a profile on a copycat is a tough nut."

The four of them were seated around the conference table. Harkness and Ben sat on one side; on the other side, O'Rourke sat next to McHugh, who had taken off his coat but had once again forgotten to remove his hat. With one hand he was looking through the case files and with his other hand he was digging through his pocket for his glasses.

"Made all the trickier," McHugh added without looking up, "Because we don't know exactly <u>who</u> he's copying."

O'Rourke nodded in agreement. "Precisely."

"Hold on a second," Harkness said, putting his hands down on the table top and leaning forward. "Maybe I've missed something, but isn't he copying Jack The Ripper? I mean, haven't you been saying that from the beginning? Did we switch trains here without telling me?"

"Yes, Lieutenant," McHugh explained patiently. "He is copying Jack the Ripper. The victims have the same names. The wounds are identical. That's quite clear. But what we don't know is, which Jack the Ripper is he copying?"

Harkness gave him a look that was equal parts pain and confusion. McHugh continued. "You remember the long list of suspects we gave you ..."

Harkness leaned back in his chair and waved his hands at McHugh, not wanting to go back down that path again. McHugh took out his pipe and his pouch of tobacco.

Harkness glared over at him. "You can't smoke in here."

"According to the laws of New York State, it appears I am forbidden to smoke anywhere. However, no crime is being committed, as I haven't started smoking and I didn't plan on smoking," McHugh said. "Only intended to fill my pipe. Which is, I believe, still legal." He then began to do exactly that, pinching small amounts of tobacco from the pouch and delicately pushing them into the pipe.

"Lieutenant Harkness," McHugh continued, "my point being that you take any five Ripperologists and put them in a room, you're going to come back with at least five completely different and perhaps even completely valid opinions on the identity of Jack The Ripper. In fact, you should consider yourself lucky to hear only five."

Sensing he'd get a more sympathetic ear, McHugh turned to Ben. "I can't tell you who Jack The Ripper was. No one can with any real certainty. But, with some more information, I may be able to tell you who this fellow believes was Jack The Ripper – that is to say, which suspect he's imitating so slavishly. That information may go a long way toward helping you find him."

O'Rourke leaned forward and addressed both Ben and Harkness. "Mr. McHugh – actually," he said, correcting himself, "Detective Chief Inspector McHugh –"

"Retired," McHugh added quickly.

"DCI McHugh has been a highly respected consultant to the Bureau on a number of occasions, on cases with much higher profiles than this one, I might add. I would suggest that you treat his counsel as you would my own."

O'Rourke's tone made it clear that this was much more than a suggestion. Harkness saw no way out. "All right," he said. "What do you need to know?"

"Just a few relatively mundane items," McHugh said as he flipped through the file folders. "Were there, by any chance, two murders before the first," he asked, "that you might have thought were unrelated to this case? There would have been an Emma Smith on April 3rd and a Martha Tabram or Turner on August 7th."

Harkness shrugged. "Don't know. We can look into it. Probably take a while to check that out."

"No it won't," Ben said. "I looked into that after reading your book. They didn't happen, at least not around here. Mary Ann Nichols was the first."

"Interesting." McHugh continued to page through the files.

Harkness leaned forward, starting to feel a little left out. "What does that mean? Why is it interesting that those murders didn't happen?"

"It's interesting because it means," McHugh replied, "that our killer is probably concentrating on the traditional five murders that the majority of experts agree were committed by one man, who has come to be known as Jack The Ripper."

"The canonical five," Ben added.

McHugh nodded in agreement and then stopped on a particular

page in the file. He read through it quickly and then flipped to the next page. "Did you," he asked, without looking up, "by any chance find a leather apron near the site of the second murder, the one involving Annie Chapman?"

"No, we didn't," Harkness said definitively. He was starting to be intrigued by this process. "What would it mean if we did?"

McHugh shrugged. "I can't say for sure," he said. "But as Miss Thomas and I mentioned in passing when we gave you our original list of suspects, the bloody apron found near Annie Chapman's body in 1888 led some to believe that the killer was a local shoemaker, named Jack or John Pizer. If our killer believes that Pizer was Jack The Ripper, then he might have left an apron near the scene to complete the tableau, as it were.

"He might also be taking on some of Pizer's characteristics, such as becoming a shoemaker or a shoe salesman. However, since he chose not to leave that particular clue at the crime scene, we can assume that he doesn't believe that Pizer was Jack The Ripper."

McHugh continued to page lazily through the file. The other three men watched, waiting for the next question. After a few moments it came, sounding almost like a bored afterthought.

"Does the investigating team believe that the two victims we've encountered so far were murdered somewhere else," McHugh asked. "And then brought to the locations where they were found?"

Ben was surprised by the question. "Yes, we know they were killed in locations different from where they were discovered," he said. "We haven't released that information. Why do you think it's significant?"

"It may not be," McHugh said. "But it's clear our killer went to some lengths to find two victims with the identical names as the orig-inal victims. It was very important for him to recreate the identities of the victims – more important than re-creating the specifics of the actual murders, which most experts believe took place where the bodies were found. Although why he felt the need to move the bodies to new loca-tions is still a bit of a mystery."

Harkness wasn't tracking with this. "So what does that mean?" he asked.

McHugh closed the file. "I can't say for certain what it means," he said. "It does suggest–and I must emphasize *suggest*–that our killer believes that Jack The Ripper targeted the canonical five, Nichols the first and Kelly the last, and did not just randomly kill whoever would follow him into a dark alley. That could perhaps narrow the list of classic Ripper suspects significantly, eliminating all the alleged 'crazy' suspects who we can assume were acting impulsively and disorderly, and focusing our attention on the more conspiracy-minded candidates. That is, those suspects who targeted specific women, not just any of the available prostitutes in the East End."

"So that's a good thing," Ben said, "right?"

"Well, it's certainly a place to start," McHugh agreed. "It takes our list of suspects down from seventy or so names to a more manageable twenty or so."

He realized at that moment that he was still wearing his hat. He took it off, stuffed it in his coat pocket and looked at his watch. "We have a bit of work ahead of us this afternoon, gentlemen. I think we'll have to luncheon in," he said to Harkness. "Do you have any menus? I think Thai food would be a nice change."

After a long moment, Harkness got up to find the take-out menus and McHugh turned his attention back to the files.

* * *

The phone rang in Barbara's apartment a couple times before she even registered hearing it. Once she realized it was ringing, she didn't answer it immediately.

Instead, she held up her hand in a futile "wait a sec" gesture, while she finished typing a particularly troublesome sentence on her computer. She was working, or at least trying to work, on her new novel and this one sentence had been the bane of her existence for the last ten minutes. It mixed tenses and also involved a short phrase from an unwieldy nursery rhyme. As sentences go, she had come to believe that it was a real pain in the ass.

Satisfied that she had solved that problem, at least for the moment, she saved the file and picked up the phone. It was Ben.

"Oh, hi," she said, and then realized that she had sounded for a moment like an excited high-school girl receiving a phone call from the captain of the football team. She mentally downshifted, hoping that her tone of voice would follow suit.

"Hi, it's me," he said, and then added, "Ben. Ben Black."

"Yes, I know," she said. "I remember you. You're the guy who stood by while his boss grilled my friend and me mercilessly this morning." *Was this going well or badly?* she thought. *Too soon to know for sure.* "I'm kidding, of course," she added quickly.

"Yes, I got that," Ben said, sounding distracted. "Are you okay?"

"Yes," she said, getting up and starting to pace through the apartment, moving from room to room. "I'm just in the middle of a thing with the book, the new book. Figuring some stuff out on paper. I mean, on the computer. Are you still working?"

"Yes, we're still at it," Ben said, looking over at McHugh, O'Rourke and Harkness huddled over the files. "We're narrowing down actual Ripper suspects, which is supposed to help us figure out who our suspect is copying. Apparently, we're eliminating someone named Dr. Gull because no grapes were found at the murder scenes, if that makes any sense to you."

Barbara smiled ruefully and nodded. "Sadly, yes it does."

There was a pause. Neither of them was sure if it was technically an awkward pause, but it felt like it was right on the cusp. Ben took a breath and dove in to fill the gap.

"So," he said, "I was wondering if you weren't busy later, maybe we could get a late bite to eat. Or something."

"Um, Ben," she said, hesitating and drawing out her 'Um' to almost four syllables, "are you sure that's a good idea?"

"Why not?" he asked. "I mean, are you hesitating because you're peripherally involved in a case I'm working on ... or because somehow you've learned that my past relationships with women have tended to implode disastrously?"

Barbara laughed. "I was thinking the former, but thanks for the heads up. I appreciate it."

"Not a problem," he said, and then his voice got quieter in order to keep the others in the room from hearing. "Look, Barbara, I don't see any real conflict here ... unless, of course, you've killed somebody. And, to be honest, that's actually only going to be an issue if it was one of the victims in this case. So, in a way, that gives you a certain amount of leeway."

"Well, thanks for that," she said. "I appreciate the latitude." He could hear Barbara's doorbell chime through the phone.

Barbara crossed the room and peered through the peephole, through which she could see her doorman, Hector, with his back to her, standing in the hall. "Can you hang on a second?" she said into the phone. "My doorman's here."

"No problem."

Barbara unlocked her door and opened it. Hector turned and smiled. He was holding a small box, wrapped in white paper.

"Sorry to bother you, Miss Thomas," he said. "This just came for you and the line was busy. Normally I wouldn't bother you, but it says 'perishable' on the side, so I thought I should bring it right up."

Christmas must be closer than I realized, Barbara thought. But out loud she said, "Thank you, Hector. Thanks for taking the trouble to come up."

He handed her the package and she looked around for her purse to see if she had any cash to give him a small tip. She couldn't see the damn purse anywhere. She noticed the bowl of fruit on the table by the door and, on an impulse, picked out an orange and handed it to him.

Hector took the orange and looked at it, not quite sure how pleased he should be.

"Um, thank you ..." he said as she closed the door.

Barbara stepped away, then out of habit stepped back and gave the door the necessary final shove it needed to lock shut. Still holding the phone, she took the package into the dining room and set it on the cluttered table, moving that morning's *Times* out of the way.

"Are you still there?" she said into the phone.

"Yep," Ben replied. "Everything all right?"

"Yes," she said. "My doorman just brought up a package and I didn't have anything to tip him with, so I gave him an orange. How weird is that?"

Ben was momentarily unsure how to respond to that information. So, he ignored it and plowed ahead.

"Anyway," he said, "about that going out to dinner thing ..."

Barbara looked down at the small, neatly wrapped white package.

It had a typed label with her name and address on it, but no return address. She looked at all sides of the box, but they were all blank except for the side with the label and the hand-written word 'perishable.' She cradled the phone between her ear and her shoulder and began to tear open the white paper that surrounded the box.

"Look," Ben continued, "I don't want to put you in an awkward position. How about, if this would make it easier, we could go to two separate restaurants, and then meet later to compare notes? Or the same restaurant, but different tables, and we would talk only by cell phone? Or, the same restaurant, same table, but only communicate via sign language? I'm just saying, there are a lot of different ways we can play this."

He waited for a response, a laugh, something, but there was no answer. "You've got to admit," he added, "I'm giving you options."

Still no response.

He could hear the tearing of paper. The sound of cardboard against cardboard.

And then he heard a sharp intake of breath through the phone.

"Barbara, are you all right?"

He waited for a response.

"Oh my God," was all that she said.

Thirty seconds later, Ben was off the phone and on his way to her apartment.

CHAPTER TWELVE

"It's a kidney, that much is certain."

The lab tech, Simon Breckenridge, held up the small, reddish-brown object, which had been hermetically sealed in a plastic evidence bag. There was very little emotion or interest in his voice.

"Could be human. Might be human. But it's a kidney. Most likely. But of course, we'll have to run some tests to be sure."

To Barbara, Simon looked more likely to eat the evidence as opposed to running tests on it. It took her a few moments to figure out why the large, bearded man looked so familiar, and then it hit her – Simon was the spitting image of that actor from the 1960s, Victor Buono.

He was a big man, made to appear even larger by the snug white lab coat he wore, which clung to his chunky body like a large, wet tablecloth. His face was covered by a wild, untamed beard, which started in a splotchy fashion high on his cheeks and seemed to magically disappear as it moved down his face and neck, morphing into the bits of chest hair that peeked out of the top of his sweat-stained collar.

"I'm guessing it's only a few days old," he said, placing the evidence bag on top of the pristine white counter, which constituted most of the precinct's lab space. "Like I say, we'll have to run some tests. I'll do what I can here, but this may need to go to the main lab over in Queens."

"But you're sure it's human?" Harkness asked, maneuvering in for a closer look.

It was a small room and with all the people assembled there – Barbara, McHugh, Ben and Harkness, plus the oversized Simon – it was beginning to feel like the stateroom scene from *A Night at the Opera.*

At least, that's how it felt to Ben. He was sure that at any moment there would be a knock on the door, and someone would ask, "Is my Aunt Minnie in there?" And then he'd hear Groucho's staccato reply: "Well, you can come in and prowl around if you wanna. If she isn't in here, you can probably find somebody just as good..."

He smiled at the thought and then noticed Barbara was looking at him, probably wondering why he was smiling. He stopped smiling and tried to concentrate on what Simon was saying, but he'd hit him at a momentary gap in the conversation.

Simon took a bite out of his sandwich, which looked to be a thick, wet slab of bologna or something similar. In fact, to Barbara's eye, there wasn't a great deal of difference between the look of the object in the evidence bag and the look of the meat in Simon's sandwich. It might even be liverwurst. She turned away, trying to get the comparison out of her mind, but she couldn't shake it.

"Hey, I'm not even one hundred percent sure it's a kidney," Simon protested as he chewed. "I'm just saying that's what it looks like. That's why we run tests."

Harkness held the bag up to the light. "How soon can you test for a match with the two victims?"

Simon settled back on his high stool, which creaked ominously under his girth. "Yes, well, you should know that those of us in the forensics game aren't big fans of the word 'match.' We also don't go for words like 'identical,' 'indistinguishable,' and 'duplicate.' We prefer less precise terminology."

"Really? Well, that's not the way they talk on *CSI*," Harkness shot back.

"Yes, Dale, but for those of us who live in the real world, the rules work a bit differently. Sadly, we're saddled with reality." Simon shrugged while he chewed. "I don't know," he went on. "It could take a day or so to determine any similarities."

Harkness shot him a cold look. Simon matched the intensity of Dale's gaze and upped the ante by continuing to chew slowly while staring him down.

"You could do it faster," Harkness said flatly.

"Or it could take two days," Simon replied, maintaining his gaze.

"Or it could take less," Harkness continued.

"Or it could take three days," Simon countered, biting off another mouthful of the sandwich. "Maybe a week if you don't cut out the Jedi mind tricks."

"We're gone." Harkness knew when he was beat.

He began to usher the group out of the room. Barbara turned back for one last look, just in time to see Simon wipe a stray piece of the sandwich off his upper lip. More pieces were trapped in his beard and seemed unlikely candidates for rescue. Barbara followed the others out of the overcrowded lab.

* * *

After being crammed into the tight confines of the lab space, the hallway seemed like a wide-open vista, even though it was basically just a narrow office corridor with low ceilings. As the group assembled in the hall, Barbara snuck a glance over at Ben, who was just sneaking a look at her.

They both smiled ("Caught!") and turned their attention to McHugh. He was looking closely at the letter that had been found folded up inside the white box with the kidney. The document was now sealed in a plastic evidence bag, adding an extra layer of difficulty to his examination.

"Well?" Harkness said, tapping his foot impatiently.

McHugh continued to study the sheet of paper. "Well, at first blush," he finally said. "I'd say it's pretty clearly the Lusk letter or a fair facsimile thereof."

"The lust letter?" Harkness looked around at the others, hoping for an explanation. "What the hell is that?"

Barbara shook her head. "No, not lust. It's the Lusk letter," she explained. "It was a letter that was, purportedly, sent by Jack the Ripper to the leader of a Whitechapel Vigilance Committee ..." She struggled to complete her sentence.

McHugh filled the gap without looking up. "George Lusk."

"That's right," she agreed. "It was sent to George Lusk along with a piece of what was claimed to be the kidney of one of the victims."

"I don't have a copy of the original to compare this to, but if memory serves, it does appear to be a duplicate, misspellings and all." McHugh began to read from the note. "'I send you half the Kidne I took from one woman prasarved it for you. The other piece I fried and ate, it was very nise. Signed, catch me when you can.' And, of course, the infamous return address: 'From hell.'"

McHugh handed the plastic bag to Harkness and turned to look at Barbara. "Of course, you see the problem," he said.

Barbara nodded. They both considered it for a long moment.

Ben was the first to break the silence. "I'm not sure I understand. I mean, this seems to be following the events of the original murders. I remember reading about the Lusk letter and the kidney. What's the problem?" he asked.

"It's an issue of timing," McHugh said.

Barbara nodded in agreement. "The problem is, it's too early," Barbara said. "For the first time, our killer has stopped doing things in order, in a strictly linear fashion. The Lusk letter should appear after the Double Event – the next two murders, which happened on the same night. Why is he sending it now? It doesn't make sense."

McHugh grunted in agreement. "It's like a musician, playing a song you know," he mused, "but he's playing variations on the tune. It's all the right notes, it sounds sort of familiar, he's just moving the notes around."

"Variations on a theme?" Ben asked.

"Yes, I suppose," McHugh said. "A bit like jazz. The melody is in there, buried within the notes, we simply have to find it."

He scratched his at head and realized, far later than everyone else, that he was still wearing his hat. He took it off, stuffing it into his pocket and pulled out his pipe. He glanced at Harkness before he could say anything. "Not lighting it, filling it. No need to issue a citation, Lieutenant, not just yet."

They all watched silently as he filled his pipe. When he was finished, he took a long look up at the ceiling. Ben was tempted to look there, too, but stopped himself at the last moment.

"I don't know." McHugh finally sighed. He looked at the group and then turned his attention to Barbara. "Perhaps it's me, but it's beginning to feel, more and more, as though it has something to do with you. Something personal."

He took a drag off his unlit pipe, receiving nothing for the effort, but not really noticing. Barbara felt all the eyes turn to her.

* * *

A half hour later, Harkness had assembled the majority of his staff. They were all gathered in the same conference room Barbara and McHugh had first visited, and those two naturally gravitated toward their original seats. Ben leaned against one wall and the other officers and detectives found their own perches throughout the room.

"We're going to attack this from a number of fronts, gentlemen." Harkness paced as he spoke. He glanced at Barbara and then at the two female officers in the room. "And ladies," he added as an afterthought. "First up, we'll be covering Miss Thomas, 24-7. Three shifts."

He gestured toward Barbara and all eyes turned toward her. She smiled and waved weakly. Harkness continued. "Second, we're going to run a check on every attendee at the recent 'Ripper-Thon'…"

"Ripper-Con," Ben corrected.

"Whatever," Harkness shot back. "I want background checks on all registered attendees, hotel staff, guest speakers and anyone who wandered in off the street to use the can during that convention. There seems to be a connection between these murders and the death of one William Burke, who we know spent the entire weekend at the conference."

He made his way over to the room's white board and pointed to a blow-up of the photo Big Billy had shot of the mime statue. "In particular," he continued, "we're looking for any and all information pertaining to this person, who appears to be dressed as … well, for whatever reason, dressed as a statue of a newsboy. This individual is

114

wanted for questioning and is considered to be a possible suspect in one or all of these killings."

Next, Harkness gestured toward two names that had been hastily scrawled on the white board next to the photo.

"Finally," he said, "we're going to be contacting anyone in the city with the names Elizabeth Stride and Catharine Eddowes and putting them under police protection until it's clear that ..." He paused and looked around the room. They waited for his conclusion.

"Well," he finally said, "until it's clear that they don't need to be under police protection anymore."

Several of the detectives made note of the names in their notebooks. Barbara leaned over to McHugh and spoke quietly to him. He nodded thoughtfully as he listened.

"I've posted duty assignments on the roster and we'll be suspending PTO until further notice." Harkness' tone made it clear that he was done talking and that it was time for everyone else to get to work. He glanced around the room, checking to see if there were any objections. McHugh raised his hand. Harkness nodded toward him.

"Miss Thomas raises a good point," McHugh said. He turned to Barbara, essentially handing her the floor. Barbara looked up, surprised. She had assumed that, if McHugh agreed with her thought, he would present the idea. He was, after all, the ranking expert.

"Well, one of the things that distinguished the Double Event, that is, the night when Jack the Ripper committed two murders," she said, her voice starting out quieter than she had planned, "was that not only did the Ripper commit the two brutal murders in the space of about 45 minutes, but he also managed to commit them in two separate municipalities."

"One in London, proper," McHugh added. "And the other in a square-mile section known as the City of London.

"The problem officials ran into was that each municipality had their own police force," McHugh continued. "So there was some confusion and friction between the two organizations during their respective investigations."

"Some have postulated," Barbara said, first making sure that McHugh was done talking, "that the Ripper understood this geographic distinction and used it to his advantage, playing the two police forces against each other and using the turmoil to help make his escape." She looked around the room and then at McHugh, who shrugged.

"Perhaps," McHugh said. "Personally, I think it was just a coincidence. However, whether planned or not, there is no denying that it added an unnecessary layer of chaos to an already horrific and bloody evening."

There was a pause while everyone considered the implications of this new information. Ben was the first to speak. "So you're saying our killer might attempt to commit one murder here in Manhattan," he said, "and then, after succeeding, cross the bridge to Brooklyn for the second murder?"

"Or take the tunnel," Barbara said. "The point is, anywhere he can get in 45 minutes is fair game."

Harkness sighed and shook his head. "This just gets better and better. Let's get moving, folks."

* * *

Ben took his turn guarding Barbara and was happy to discover that his first shift coincided nicely with dinner time. Although he knew he couldn't consider it a date, at least not technically, he was pleased with the situation.

Rather than go out, they'd spent a quiet evening in her apartment, with good Chinese take-out, some Stevie Wonder on the CD player and a truly spectacular view of Central Park out her living room window.

Ben finished the last of his Spicy Double Cooked Pork with Cabbage and Peppers, while Barbara picked up the bottle of wine and held it up to the light, assessing its contents.

"Are you telling me I polished off nearly this whole bottle all by myself?"

Ben gestured to his unused wine glass. "Sorry, ma'am. I'm on duty."

"You didn't have anything at dinner the other night, either."

She gave him a long look, but he didn't respond. Instead, he reached across the table with his chopsticks and picked up a bit of her Spicy Szechuan Chicken with Peanuts.

"There's this bar I used to go to in Hell's Kitchen," he said, after he finished chewing. "Back when they actually called it Hell's Kitchen, instead of Midtown West. And they had this great policy. If you turned in your pin to the bartender – your one month, your six month, your one year, any sobriety pin – they'd give you a free drink. On the house. It was quite a deal."

He extended his chopsticks across the table again, expertly snagging a peanut from her plate. "I got a lot of free drinks there over the years," he said, popping the peanut in his mouth. "I don't go there anymore."

There was a long moment between them. Barbara finally broke the silence. "I'm sure there's a longer version of that story as well."

Ben nodded. "Oh, yes. With seemingly endless chapters and frequent false endings. Highly dramatic scenes of lost nights, lost relationships, nearly lost jobs. One cliffhanger after another. You could probably turn it into a best-seller."

"Maybe. But I only do mysteries, and it sounds like this one has been solved."

"Solved? Yes, I guess so. As we say, one day at a time."

Barbara waited for a moment, still holding the nearly empty bottle of wine in her hand. And then she poured the remaining wine from the bottle into her glass.

"Well, that just means all the more for me," she said. She set down the bottle and took a sip from her glass. "So, how soon until you're off duty?"

Ben looked at his watch. "About another ... what do you have?"

He looked across the room, where Officer Klingbile sat stiffly in a chair, awkwardly holding his hat in his hands. Although Klingbile had been on the force for over two years, he still maintained a constant, nervous edge to his personality. He looked at his watch.

"Another eight minutes, sir," he said. "I'm sorry I was early. I can't help being early."

"It's a charming habit, Officer Klingbile," Ben said. "Don't ever change."

"Well, my grandmother always told us," Klingbile continued, seeming to warm to the topic, "that if you're not early, you're late."

"She's a very wise woman."

"She's dead, sir."

Ben sighed as he stood up. "My condolences to your grandfather."

"He's dead as well. Long before her. Kind of a sad tale, really." Klingbile recognized the expression on Ben's face and opted against continuing his story.

Ben turned from Klingbile back to Barbara. "I better get going," he said to her. "I'll leave you in the very capable hands of Officer Klingbile. Maybe there's more wisdom from his dead grandparents that he can share with you."

Klingbile opened his mouth to reply, and then recognized the sarcastic tone in Ben's voice and thought better of it. Barbara got up and walked Ben to the door, holding it open for him. There was an awkward pause, neither quite sure how to conclude this meeting.

"Well ...," Ben said, taking a stab at it. "Good night."

"Good night," Barbara said quietly.

"Good night, sir," Klingbile said from across the room. "See you back at the station."

The moment, if there had been a moment, was broken.

"Good night, Officer Klingbile," Ben said, tossing a smile at Barbara as he made his way to the elevator. She shut and locked the door behind him, then looked over at Klingbile.

"So, who wants dessert?" she asked.

Klingbile was not entirely certain how to respond.

* * *

Ben's cell phone began to ring just as he stepped out of the elevator into the apartment building's lobby. As he struggled to pull it out of his coat pocket, he noticed that Barbara's doorman was again seated on his straight-backed chair, his head dipped, snoring quietly.

Ben scrambled to get the phone open quickly, to silence the loud ring, in the hope of not interrupting Hector's nap. He finally succeeded in silencing the bell.

"Black here," he whispered into the phone.

Harkness' voice boomed through the phone at three to four times Ben's volume. Ben pulled it away from his ear. "Why are you whispering?"

"I'm in church," Ben said, cupping a hand around the mouthpiece. "Let me step outside."

Ben made his way silently through the lobby, stepping outside in the cool fall evening air. Once the glass door had shut behind him, he returned his attention to the cell phone.

"What's up?" he asked, now having to speak up a bit to be heard over the traffic noise.

"So far we've located three Elizabeth Strides," Harkness said. "Two in Manhattan, one in Queens. And only one Catharine Eddowes that we've found so far."

"That's pretty manageable," Ben said as he stepped to the curb and attempted to flag down a passing cab with less than successful results. Two shot by him, both carrying fares. He scanned traffic for another cab.

"I'm glad to hear you think so," Harkness replied, "because you're going to be managing it."

"No problem," Ben said as he got the attention of another cab, which cut across two lanes of traffic and screeched to a halt in front of him. He opened the back door and glanced at his watch as he climbed into the back seat. "I'm on my way in."

The cab pulled away from Barbara's apartment building, where Hector continued to sleep the sleep of the just.

CHAPTER THIRTEEN

"We've caught a lucky break," Ben said as he held the car door open for McHugh. "Turns out, our first Elizabeth Stride is already dead."

"I beg your pardon?" McHugh responded, but Ben shut the car door just as the question was leaving his lips and he had to wait to continue the conversation until Ben had come around and climbed into the driver's side of the vehicle.

"Did you say one of the Elizabeth Strides is already dead?" McHugh asked as Ben started the car and pulled away from the front of McHugh's hotel. It was a bright, sunny afternoon with just a touch of autumn in the air.

"Yes, about ten days ago." Ben skillfully navigated the car through three lanes of traffic on the crowded one-way street, positioning himself for a left turn at the next light.

"And that's a good thing?" McHugh asked, still trying to find his conversational footing.

"Well, obviously not for her," Ben replied. "However, she was ninety-seven and had, apparently, led a full and rich life."

McHugh sat silently for a few moments. "Could we start this conversation over, from the top?" he finally asked.

Ben made the left turn smoothly. "No problem. According to our research, there are three Elizabeth Strides and one Catharine Eddowes in Manhattan and the Burroughs," he said. "We've got to talk to all four and set up protection for them before the Double Event. I thought you might enjoy coming along for the interviews. You should put your seat belt on."

McHugh nodded and began to work on the belting process. "Yes, I gathered all that from your phone message. Much appreciated. However, you're saying that one of the Elizabeth Strides is already deceased?"

"Yes, Elizabeth Stride, age ninety-seven, a long-time resident of the 'We Care' Care Center in Queens. She was going to be our first stop today, but I called ahead, and it turns out that she passed away peacefully in her sleep a couple of weeks ago."

"Poor thing," McHugh mused.

"Yes. I suppose so. So, we're on to our second Elizabeth Stride." Ben grabbed a slip of paper that had been resting on the dashboard and consulted a scribbled address. "You're not allergic to dogs by any chance, are you?"

McHugh shook his head. "Not in the least. Why would it matter?"

Ben shrugged. "It probably won't," he said. "But I have this sick feeling we may be around a lot of them."

* * *

If fifteen dogs qualify as "a lot" of dogs, then Ben's prediction turned out to be correct.

He and McHugh stood in the center of the large room that served as the nerve center for Manhattan Dog Patch, a pet supply store and dog daycare center situated on the ground floor of a building at Broadway and Thirteenth.

Dogs of varying sizes and breeds caroused around the two men, while others slept quietly on blankets spread randomly around the room. McHugh was down on one knee, greeting each dog in turn as they approached. Ben stood stiffly next to him as dog after dog stopped by for a quick sniff of the new guests.

"Don't you like dogs, Detective?" McHugh asked as he scratched the head of an excessively friendly golden retriever.

"I like dogs okay," Ben replied, tentatively patting the head of a black lab. "I'm just not used to being outnumbered by them."

"Oh, don't let the numbers fool you," McHugh laughed. "Any one of them could make short work of you on their own if they wished."

Ben subtly withdrew his hand from the dog's head and pretended he needed to check his watch again. McHugh stood and brushed off his hands as the dogs scampered off to the other side of the room.

Mrs. Livingstone, a tiny woman in her forties who sported the gray hair of a much older woman, glided through the room again, shouting over the barking din. "Liz should be back in just a couple minutes," she yelled. "Walks usually take less than a quarter of an hour."

Ben nodded. "No problem."

"Who needs a bath, who needs a bath? Does Laddy need a bath?" she asked in a sing-song voice as she narrowed in on a sleeping brindle greyhound, who opened one eye lazily before slowly rising to all fours and ambling after her down a narrow hall toward what appeared to the bathing room.

"Dogs, dogs, dogs. I'd love to have a dog. That's one of the downsides of my peripatetic lifestyle," McHugh said wistfully. "I believe it was our Miss Thomas' friend, Robert Louis Stevenson, who put it best: 'You think dogs will not be in heaven? I tell you; they will be there long before any of us.'"

Ben nodded. "I suppose that's true," he said. "You know, speaking of Barbara, you never have said what you thought of her book and her theory –"

"Ah," McHugh said, cutting him off. "I would wager that this is our Miss Stride now, striding toward us as it were," he continued, gesturing to a young Asian woman walking past the large picture window at the front of the building. She skillfully managed three rowdy dogs on leashes.

Moments later she was in the main dog room, with two security gates shut tightly behind her. She released the three dogs, two beagles and a poodle, and hung the leashes on numbered hooks on the wall.

Then she grabbed a clipboard and made some notes on it as she approached the two men. She appeared to be in her late twenties, a fit and pretty woman with short-cropped black hair and a big smile. She beamed at them as she set down the clipboard.

"Are you here to see me?" she asked, brushing her hands off on her jeans.

"Yes," Ben said. "I called earlier."

"Sorry, I hope you haven't been waiting long. If we get off schedule here, then someone ends ups not getting a walk and that's never a good thing. I'm Liz Stride," she said, holding out a hand. "Detective Black?"

Ben put out his hand. "Ben Black, yes." He gestured to McHugh. "And this is Henry McHugh, who is assisting us on the case."

She finished shaking hands with Ben and tentatively put her hand out to McHugh. "I met Mr. McHugh once before," she said, almost shyly. "Although I doubt you'll remember me," she added. "I was one of about two hundred people on your Ripper walking tour in London several years ago, on a bitter cold, windy December night."

"Oh, yes, I recall. Were you the one in the hat?" McHugh asked gravely.

Liz looked surprised and began to form an answer, and then realized he was teasing her. She laughed. "Yes, I suppose that was me," she said, her smile getting even wider. "It was a terrific tour," she added.

"Thank you," McHugh said, returning the smile.

"Do you guys want to sit?" She gestured toward three plastic chairs grouped around a folding table in one corner.

Once they were settled, Ben got down to business. "As I mentioned on the phone," he said, "we're going to be assigning a security team to you. Are you familiar with the details of the case?"

She nodded seriously. "Yes, I've been following it on-line since it was announced that there was a Jack the Ripper connection to the murders."

McHugh leaned forward, resting his weight on his forearms. "And you're familiar with the details of the original Jack the Ripper case?" he asked softly. "I mean, more than just what you gleaned from my walk oh those many years ago?"

Liz shrugged. "Sort of," she said. "My old boyfriend knew about the case and thought it was really cool that I have the same name as one of the victims. That should have been a red flag right there," she said, laughing. "He's the one who dragged me kicking and screaming on your walking tour when we were in London," she said, adding quickly, "but, like I said, it was a wonderful tour."

McHugh smiled and nodded and then exchanged a quick look with Ben.

"This boyfriend," Ben said. "Do you still see him?"

Liz shook her head, laughing. "Kenny? No, and thank God for that. We dated back when I was in school in California. We broke up after he hooked up with my roommate at the time, a very skanky little number named Jocelyn, who then went on to sleep her way through the graduate English department.

"Last I heard, she moved in with her advisor and never did finish her thesis. It was on *Beowulf* and she probably did us a favor by not finishing it. Like the world needs another master's thesis on *Beowulf*, right?"

Ben waited, to make sure she was done with that portion of the story. "And what happened to the boyfriend?"

"Kenny? He still lives out there, in Pasadena," she said. "He's a bartender, I think. Probably still sleeping in his parents' basement."

"Are you still in contact with him?"

She shook her head. "No, I'm way past him now," she said, laughing.

Ben nodded. "Okay, good," he said. "So, moving on, have you had any encounters lately that you would call strange?"

"I'm a single woman living in Manhattan, Detective Black, so you're going to have to get more specific," she said, flashing her smile again. "I mean, I had a guy throw up on my shoes last Friday night at Applebee's, but that's hardly strange, just another pathetic moment in my boring life."

"Let me put it this way," McHugh said quietly "Have you had a sense in the last fortnight or so that you were being followed? Has anyone worked their way into your life recently? Or has anyone made comments connecting your name to the killings?"

Liz shook her head as she considered his questions. "No, nothing like that. Like I said, I lead a pretty boring life. Nothing out of the ordinary has occurred since," she said as she thought it over, "since forever, I guess. Now that I think back on it, the guy throwing up on my shoes has been the highlight of my year." She gave a short, self-conscious laugh.

Ben considered her response. "Okay, well obviously if that changes in any way, let us know immediately."

She nodded. "Sure. Who should I call? I still have your number on my cell phone ..."

Ben shook his head. "That won't be necessary. You'll have twenty-four-hour protection starting later today, if you approve it. I should explain, we can't make you accept this protection, but it is highly recommended."

She looked from Ben to McHugh, who nodded in agreement. "Yes, highly recommended," he echoed.

She looked back at Ben. "I guess that sounds okay, but let me ask one question," she said. "The guys who will be protecting me?"

"Yes?"

She gave an embarrassed smile. "Are any of them single?"

* * *

Their next stop took them to a restaurant on Amsterdam Avenue near Seventy-fifth Street. It was a classic old-style greasy spoon, with a long counter on the back wall and worn vinyl-padded booths set up against the windows that fronted the building. A sign right inside the front door told them, politely, to please seat themselves, so Ben and McHugh sat themselves on the stools at the counter and waited for a waitress to notice them.

After several minutes, a middle-aged waitress, looking very harried and tired, approached them from the kitchen. She was holding an order pad in one hand and balancing two plastic tumblers filled with water in the other. Her nametag identified her as 'Roxie.' She set the glasses in front of them.

"What can I get you two?" she asked in a tired rasp without looking up, her pencil poised over the pad. "Today's breakfast special is Eggs Benedict with hash browns, toast and coffee."

McHugh glanced at his watch, wondering why they were pushing breakfast so late in the afternoon.

"We're here to talk with Elizabeth Stride," Ben said.

The waitress looked up and studied Ben and then McHugh. She snuck a quick peek around the café, which held only a couple other customers.

"Oh, that's me," she said, the rasp disappearing from her voice. "I'm Beth Stride."

Ben gestured to her nametag. "Do you go by Roxie?" he asked, surprised by the sudden change in her posture, voice and attitude.

She shook her head and smiled. "No, that's my waitress name," she said. "Part of my waitress persona. We're required to behave like old-style waitresses while on duty and part of that includes having an old-fashioned name. You know, like Gladys, Rosie, Velma. They make you pick one when you start, so I picked Roxie, because I had a great-aunt named Roxie. You must be the policeman who called earlier."

Ben introduced himself and McHugh, and then quickly explained the reason for their visit.

"So, it's just because my name is Elizabeth Stride?" she asked after listening intently to his explanation. "And that's the only reason this whack job might want to kill me?"

Ben nodded. "Apparently. Are you familiar with the Jack the Ripper case or this copycat situation?"

Beth shook her head. "No, not really. I'm ashamed to admit, I don't really pay very close attention to the news anymore," she said. "It's all so bad, or sad or weird usually. Plus, I've found in the couple months I've been working here that I pick up any really important news just from talking to customers."

She reflexively reached under the counter and pulled out a plastic coffee dispenser, holding it up for them. Both men nodded and she quickly set coffee cups in front of each and poured out two cups of thin-looking but rich-smelling black coffee.

"Thanks," Ben said, taking a sip of the coffee. "So, you've only worked here for a couple months?"

Beth nodded as she placed a small metal pitcher of cream in front of them and slid a sugar holder down the counter toward the cream. "Yes, I started right after this place opened."

Ben stopped drinking his coffee in mid-sip. "This place has only been open for two months?" he asked looking around the room. "You mean it's under new ownership?"

Beth shook her head. "No, it's brand new. In fact, up until about four months ago, there used to be a Christian Science Reading Room in this space."

Ben continued to scan the small café. "I think I remember it," he said. "But, I swear, it looks like this place has been here for fifty years."

"Yes, and let me tell you, it cost a fortune to make it look that way. Talk to the owner some time. It took him forever to find all these fixtures and then even longer to age them."

Ben spun around on his stool and continued to study the restaurant space. A faded neon sign reading "Café" buzzed in the window under what appeared to be an antique pressed tin ceiling. In the center of the ceiling, a rusty fan twirled lazily. The floor was covered with black and white checkerboard linoleum, which appeared to be suitably worn and dingy.

Dull mirrors on one wall were surrounded by faded wallpaper, which was beginning to peel in a couple of places. A calendar, circa 1958, hung on another wall. McHugh had taken out his glasses and was perusing the menu.

He looked over the top of it at Beth. "And you only serve breakfast?" he asked, gesturing at the items listed on the menu and at the blackboard on the wall above her, where the daily specials were written out in different colored chalk.

Beth nodded. "Yes, we only serve breakfast. For dinner."

McHugh wrinkled his brow. "And for breakfast?"

She shook her head. "No, we're not open for breakfast. I mean, we're not open in the morning. We serve breakfast for dinner." She gestured toward the front of the menu, on which McHugh could read the name of the restaurant, 'Breakfast for Dinner.' The bright logo had a very retro look to it.

He looked down at the words, then back up at her. "So, you serve breakfast, but not at breakfast time. Only for dinner?"

She nodded. "Yep."

McHugh thought for a long moment. "Why?" he finally said.

Beth smiled and nodded at his confusion. "Remember when you were a kid and every once in a while, your mom would get tired of making dinner and she'd say, 'Kids, tonight we're having breakfast for dinner'?"

Ben and McHugh both nodded and said "Yes" in unison.

"Well," Beth continued, "this is a concept restaurant and that's the concept. We make all of your classic breakfast dishes, using only traditional ingredients and served in a perfectly restored breakfast café. But only for dinner. We open at three in the afternoon and close at midnight."

She gestured to the three customers seated in a booth across the room. "It's early now, but in about an hour this place will be packed, and it will stay that way until we close. *New York* magazine did a big story on us a couple weeks ago, naming us one of the Top Five Trendiest restaurants in Manhattan."

"In that case," Ben said, swiveling his stool around to the counter again, "before it gets too crowded, can we take a couple minutes of your time and bring you up to speed on why we're here and what's going to happen next?"

Beth looked around the room and then at the old clock on the wall. "Sure, I'm due for a break. Grab your coffee cups."

She picked up the coffee dispenser as Ben and McHugh followed her across the room to a booth.

* * *

"So, you're saying two women have already died?" Beth asked in a low voice, once they had settled into the booth and she had topped off their coffee cups to her satisfaction. Ben and McHugh nodded. Beth shook her head sadly, trying to get her mind around the facts of the case.

"And you say that in a few days, he's going to try to kill two more women, one with the same name as mine?" she continued.

"Yes," McHugh said, "we believe that's his plan. Plus, one more after that if we don't stop him."

"But we're not going to let that happen," Ben said quickly. "The plan is to have three officers assigned to you every day, working rotating eight-hour shifts. As we get a bit closer to the date of the Double Event, we may increase that coverage, but we'll keep you posted on that. Does that make sense?"

Beth nodded, looking from Ben to McHugh and then out the

window at the traffic as it passed. She sighed and wiped away what looked like a tear from the corner of her eye. Ben exchanged a glance with McHugh, who raised one eyebrow in return.

"The officers can be discreet, but they will need to be with you day and night," Ben continued. "You'll also be outfitted with a panic button, which is just a small plastic transmitter that is small enough to fit on your keychain or on a bracelet. You just press it if you feel like you're in danger at any point."

Beth turned back from looking out the window. "What's the range on this panic button?" she asked. She had lost much of the jovial attitude she'd demonstrated earlier.

"I'm not sure," Ben said. "A pretty good distance."

"Will it transmit all the way from Phoenix?"

Ben waited a moment, to see if she were kidding. She didn't look like it. "No, not that far. Only a couple of blocks." He looked at her for a few more moments. "Why Phoenix?" he finally asked.

"Because that's where I'm going to be," she said. "Starting tomorrow. My sister lives there. I've never been. So, I'm going for a visit."

"Have you been planning this trip for a while?" McHugh asked, clearly surprised by this announcement.

She shook her head and studied the tabletop, running her hand across the surface and sending a few stray crumbs to the floor. "No, but I can't think of a better time to go. I'm sure as hell not staying in this city or anywhere near this city."

She looked up at the two men and for the first time Ben could see the fear in her eyes.

"I mean," she continued, "I could put on a big front and say, 'hell no, I won't go,' but the fact is, I'm not that brave. And I'm not going to pretend that I am. You take your life in your hands in this city every day and I don't see any reason to tempt fate if I don't have to.

"Plus," she added, smiling a grim smile, "no offense to the NYPD, but I have to face the facts: the nuts got JFK and they got Bobby and King and Reagan and John Lennon, and even that little creep Lee Harvey Oswald, so what's to keep them from getting little old me? I mean, really?"

"Well, I can see your point, Beth, but we believe we've covered every contingency," Ben began, but she waved a hand and shook her head.

"Tell me honestly, Detective Black," she said. "With the officers you're assigning and the panic buttons and all your planning, can you guarantee that this guy won't somehow get to me? I mean, can you guarantee it, one hundred percent?"

She looked him dead in the eye and it was all he could do to return her stare. After a long moment, he shook his head. "No," he said quietly. "We can't guarantee it."

She nodded. "Then I'll send you a postcard. From Phoenix." She got up. "My break's over," she said as she topped off their coffees and headed back into the kitchen.

Ben and McHugh sat quietly for several minutes. "She makes a good point," Ben finally said.

McHugh nodded. "Yes, she does. Where to next?"

Ben reached into his pocket and pulled out his list of names and addresses, crossing off the third Elizabeth Stride and consulting the final name on the list.

* * *

"Yes, I'm Catharine Eddowes," the woman said, speaking loudly to be heard above the blaring music. "But everyone here calls me Cat."

Ben was trying very hard to listen to Cat, trying to focus on her face and the words coming out of her mouth, but that was difficult because she was naked. And that was throwing a wrench into everything.

Technically, of course, she wasn't completely nude. She was wearing very skimpy thong-style panties, and she had a garter around one leg that held, in addition to her leg, a large wad of bills. Ben tried looking away and scanning the room, but that didn't really help, because all the other women in the club were just as nude as Cat. He saw naked everywhere he looked. It was a sea of naked.

He glanced over at McHugh, to see if the older man had come up with his own solution to dealing with the pervasive nudity and saw that he had. McHugh was slowly, deliberately filling his pipe, seeming to focus intently on each speck of tobacco as he stuffed it into the wooden vessel.

They had realized they were in trouble the moment they stepped into The Thanatopsis Club on West Sixty-Third Street. They had assumed they were entering a typical, high-end West side nightclub, but that illusion was shattered the instant they stepped out of the foyer and into the main room. Music blared as women in various degrees of undress danced on three brightly lit stages strategically positioned throughout the large, dimly lit room.

Other women were visible entertaining male guests in booths that lined three of the four walls. Women who weren't dancing or entertaining guests roamed the room, defying gravity with every bouncing step.

A quick consultation with one of the bartenders had pointed them toward Cat Eddowes, a petite woman with long, thick auburn hair and pale smooth skin that covered her body from – evidently – head to toe and every inch in-between. She looked to be about twenty-five and moved with a studied confidence, seemingly without a trace of discomfort at her state of undress. Once introductions had been dispensed with, Ben asked where a good place would be to talk.

"It's sort of loud out here," Cat said. "Plus, it will look odd if we're just standing around, you know, talking."

"It will?" Ben asked, not grasping the inherent oddness of standing and talking.

"Oh yeah," Cat explained. "We can do it for a couple of minutes, but if I don't have you in a chair pretty quick, it will look like I don't know how to do my job."

Ben didn't doubt for a second that Cat knew how to do her job. "Where should we go then?" he asked, again doing his best to look her in the eye and nowhere else.

She glanced around the crowded club and then took him by the hand in a very practiced but surprisingly erotic move. "Why don't we talk in the dressing room," she suggested, pulling him toward a door marked 'Staff Only.'

Ben turned to McHugh and tapped his arm, signaling that they were on the move again. They made their way through a narrow gauntlet of bodies, surrounded by a seemingly endless display of bare breasts and firm buttocks, until they were released into the relative quiet of the club's drab dressing room.

* * *

Two things struck McHugh about the dressing room once he found a seat. The first was that this was apparently the only room in the club where the female performers wore clothes. Yet, at the same time, it was also the only room in the club where, in theory, male guests were not allowed. He found that ironic in the best sense of the word.

The other thing he found interesting was the large sign posted right inside the door, with the heading "The Rules" across the top of the sign. He sat and studied the ten rules detailed on the poster while Ben looked for his own place to sit as he began his interview with the still-too-nude-for-his-liking Cat Eddowes.

"This should only take a few minutes," Ben said as Cat stood in front of a long mirror and began to touch up her make-up.

He tried to find a place where he could sit that didn't offer a stellar view of her stellar body, but with all the mirrors in the room that appeared to be impossible. He finally found a spot where he could lean against the wall, keeping his eyes lowered as he pretended to intently consult his notebook.

"So, how much do you know about this Jack the Ripper copycat case?" he asked, looking up. Cat turned and faced him. Ben did his best to keep his eyes locked on hers, but the erotic pull of the rest of her body was too strong, so he gave up and returned his gaze to his notebook.

"A little, I guess," she said as she sprinkled sparkling glitter on her shoulders and then down across her breasts, brushing the extra off with one hand. Ben glanced up just in time to see her flicking one speck off her left nipple, and then buried his face back into his notebook.

"Okay then," he said. "Let's see how quickly I can get you up to speed."

* * *

McHugh couldn't tell if The Rules were listed in descending or ascending order of importance. Rule One read: 'No straddling or grinding of customer's crotch at any time.' He guessed that might be the most important rule, until he read Rule Two, which read: 'You may go down on one knee while on stage and during a table dance. One knee at a time only.' He thought this one over for several seconds and had to admit that he didn't really understand Rule Two.

He scanned down the list further, past rules about panties and tan lines and garters and accepting drinks and not smoking, and then he came to Rule Seven and it gave him pause: 'While two girls are dancing for a customer, do not touch each other. Do not touch.' He found Rule Seven to be very straightforward but was deeply puzzled by the repetition of the words 'Do not touch.'

He read Rule Seven once more and again found its meaning to be exceedingly clear without the repeated phrase. He wondered for a moment what had happened at some dark time in the club's past when it was noted that the original version of Rule Seven was not being followed to the letter. Someone, somewhere, had deemed the solution to the problem would be to repeat that three-word phrase. 'Do not touch.'

McHugh studied Rule Seven for a few more moments and then continued on to Rule Eight.

* * *

Cat had finished touching up her make-up and was making some final tweaks to her hair.

"That all sounds fine," she said, pulling a recalcitrant lock of hair out of her face. She reached for a can of hairspray and lacquered the offending strand back in place. "But I won't be able to have your guys guarding me while I'm working."

"Why not?" Ben asked, looking up in time to see Cat put one lovely leg up on a chair to adjust her garter. She pulled all the bills out, cut the stack in half, and then returned half the bills to the garter.

"Because," she said, "I'm pretty sure that the owners of the club, and probably the customers as well, are not going to look kindly on a cop sitting in a corner throughout my shift."

She moved past him and quickly spun the dial on a combination lock on one of the many old-style grey lockers that lined one wall of the dressing room. She deposited the cash in the locker, re-locked it and sashayed back to the full-length mirror.

"How about a plainclothes cop?" Ben suggested, realizing that for just a moment he had forgotten that she was naked. However, when she turned to answer him, her nudity returned in full force and he was forced to avert his eyes back to his trusty notebook.

"No offense, Detective, but I've yet to see a plainclothes cop that didn't look like a plainclothes cop. That's not going to fool anyone here."

She gave her face and figure one final check in the mirror, turning and looking over her shoulder one last time. "Here's what I can agree to, because as the only Catharine Eddowes this guy has to choose from, I don't like the odds. Your guys can stay with me 24/7, but they have to wait outside while I'm at work. Other than that, I will gladly put myself into their very capable hands. Sound fair?"

Ben considered her offer. "That sounds very fair."

"Then we've got a deal." She put out her hand and shook his hand warmly, then shot a glance at a clock on the wall. "Now I've got to get back to work. We're getting into the big earning hours and as charming as you gentleman may be, I'm not earning anything hanging out in here. Nor am I likely to."

With that she turned on her spiked high heels and headed out of the dressing room. McHugh, still studying The Rules, turned and nodded at her as she exited. Ben crossed the room toward the door and stopped, glancing at the sign which McHugh had been studying.

"Sure, spend all your time reading The Rules and leave it to me to deal with the naked woman," Ben said. "So, did you learn anything?"

McHugh shook his head. "Not only was nothing learned, but I have the distinct feeling that I know less now than when I came in. However, given the nature of this establishment, I think someone with a sense of humor is the author of Rule Ten." McHugh pushed the door open and stepped back into the club's main room.

Ben scanned down the list to the bottom and read Rule Ten. He smiled as he followed McHugh out of the room.

The Rule read: 'Give respect and you'll get respect. And remember, be a lady.'

CHAPTER FOURTEEN

A couple weeks earlier, Jack had made a similar journey to meet the four women, although he was far less open about his intentions than Ben and McHugh had been.

He was pleased and surprised to discover that he had three options for Elizabeth Stride and, consequently, wasn't overly disappointed to find that one of them was apparently ninety-seven years old. Although her age made her an unlikely candidate, he still took the time to travel to Queens, because he felt obligated to see this through on every level.

So on a warm and cloudless Saturday afternoon, Jack took the subway to the 82nd Street-Jackson Heights station in Queens. He then transferred to a bus that ran up Roosevelt Avenue to the nursing home, which was a two-story brick building situated on the corner of a sad, grey block of buildings.

The lobby was painted in a too-bright white, in vivid contrast to the gray exterior, and it took his eyes a moment to adjust to the glare in the room as he approached the front reception desk. Jack hadn't established an elaborate plan for this trip, and so when the clerk at the front desk asked his relationship to the patient, Elizabeth Stride, he said without thinking that he was her nephew, Oren.

"She doesn't get many visitors," the young woman said as she walked Jack down the sterile hall to the elevator. She also wore white, and her nametag ("Nancy") announced that she was a Medical Assistant. "It's so heartrending for some of them, they're so alone," she added as they rounded the corner and headed down another identical hall, toward the elevator at the far end.

"That's one of the reasons I moved out to this part of the country," Jack said, enjoying this off-the-cuff improvisation. "I don't want Nanna to be alone."

Nancy nodded and smiled as she pressed the call button for the elevator. "I wish more people felt that way," she said. "Some days I wish we had so many visitors in this place that we wouldn't have room for them all and we'd actually have to turn people away we had so many guests."

"From your lips to God's ear," Jack agreed. He quickly scanned his memory for an appropriate Bible verse and came up with one as they listened for the approaching elevator. "As it says in First Timothy, 'The church should care for any widow who has no one else to care for her. But those who won't care for their own relatives, such people are worse than unbelievers.'"

Nancy nodded but her smile dimmed just a bit. Jack sensed her unease, and so he added jocularly, "Of course, now that I'm here, it's going to take a court order to get me out." The elevator arrived, the door opened, and Jack stepped in, turning expectantly.

"Elizabeth is up in 309," Nancy said. "If you have any trouble finding it, the Nurses' Desk is at the North end of the building." She smiled wanly and then headed back to her desk as the elevator door closed noiselessly and began to ascend.

* * *

Jack sat in a chair by Elizabeth Stride's bed and watched her sleep. She looked very peaceful, he thought, and also very old. He wasn't sure if he had ever seen anyone this old before. Her hair was beyond gray, almost pure white, and her skin appeared to be a light shade of yellow, like a dim, dull sunflower.

The room had the cool, barren feel of a hospital and included very few personal touches. A faded but once colorful quilt lay across her on the bed. On the nightstand was a picture in a frame of a young man in an Army uniform. Jack guessed that it was a World War Two uniform, but it also might have been Korea. Ancient history, either way.

Next to the picture was a small wooden box which, when he opened the lacquered lid, played a song that he finally identified as "Edelweiss" from *The Sound of Music*.

"Great," he sighed to himself as he replaced the lid. "Now I'll have that tune stuck in my head for the rest of the day."

He sat in the stiff, straight-backed chair for a long time, listening to Elizabeth Stride's quiet but steady breathing and enjoying the peacefulness of the room. At one point she opened her eyes and turned her head, looking him directly in the eye. He cocked his head to one sided, surprised to see her awake. She blinked a couple of times, trying to get her eyes to focus.

"Who is it?" she asked in a wispy, thin voice.

Without missing a beat, Jack answered. "It's Oren, Nanna. I've come to visit."

"Oren?" she asked tentatively.

"Yes, Nanna," he said again, patiently. "It's Oren. I've come to see you."

She looked at him for a long moment. "Thank you, Oren," she said with a warm smile. "Thank you for coming to see me." She closed her eyes again and instantly drifted back into sleep.

Jack watched her for a few more minutes and then quietly got up to leave. He moved toward the door and then stopped, feeling like something was missing.

He looked down at the old woman sleeping on the bed and, without even realizing he was doing it, he bent down and gave her a tender kiss on the cheek. He smoothed her hair, pulled the pale quilt up to make sure she was warm enough, and then headed out to his next appointment.

* * *

"Are you ready to order?" Beth Stride asked the young man in the booth. He looked up from his menu.

"I think I'll just have the Eggs Benedict," Jack said. "And a small stack of the buttermilk pancakes," he added, closing the menu and handing it to her.

"Coffee?" Beth asked as she finished making note of his order on her pad.

"That would be great," he said. "With cream, please."

"No problem, hon," she said, as she moved efficiently onto the next booth and greeted those customers as warmly as she had greeted Jack.

Her nametag said Roxie, but Jack recognized her as Elizabeth Stride. He knew she went by Beth, knew she was single, knew she lived alone, and even knew her work schedule. He knew all that before he had even walked in to the café to have breakfast for dinner, but he had learned some more interesting facts since he'd sat down.

Just in chatting with her briefly, he got a sense of her personality, of her innate fear of the world, and of her vulnerability. These were all good things to know, invaluable really, particularly when it came down to making a choice about which Elizabeth Stride would be his Elizabeth Stride.

He looked around the café and smiled, recognizing the level of detail that had gone into creating this particular imitation. He respected the effort and the energy that went into such a replication. It pleased him. And it encouraged him about his own imitative work.

The food came quickly, and he did his best to eat enthusiastically, although he'd long given up enjoying such mundane pleasures as food. The serving was enormous, and the addition of the pancakes had been a mistake, wishful thinking on his part.

Consequently, he was full long before his food was finished and when Roxie returned to check up on him, there was still considerable food left on his plate.

"Who's winning, hon?" she asked. "You or the eggs?"

"I think it's a draw," he admitted, pushing the plate away.

"You want me to get you a doggy bag?" she asked, refilling his coffee cup.

He shook his head. "No, I don't have a dog," he said. "Although, lately I've been thinking about getting one."

"They can be great companions," she agreed, scooping up his plate and utensils and just as skillfully placing his check face down on the table. "You can pay that up front whenever you're ready, no rush."

"Thank you," he said, picking up his coffee cup.

"Don't be a stranger," she answered as she headed back to the kitchen with the plate.

"Oh, you probably haven't seen the last of me," he said in return as he sipped his coffee.

He watched her go and then continued to stare as the swinging door to the kitchen shut behind her.

* * *

"And what kind of dog do you have?" Liz asked as she filled in the intake form.

They were seated on plastic chairs at a small table in the corner of the main room at Manhattan Dog Patch, surrounded by yipping, yelping and sleeping dogs. Jack was wearing a nice sport coat and slacks. Liz was dressed in jeans and a white t-shirt that clung to her athletic frame perfectly.

As before, Jack had not made a specific plan of what he was going to say and do at these short interviews, so once again he simply improvised.

"He's a mix," he said. "Black lab and border collie." He watched her transcribe the information. "His name is Al," he added as a flourish.

"Great," Liz said. "And what's your current situation with Al?"

"Currently he stays home all day," Jack said. "In my apartment. That's worked fine until now, but they're changing my hours at work and I don't like the idea of him being alone that long."

"Oh, that's too bad." Liz nodded sympathetically and continued to make notes. "What do you do for a living?" she asked.

"I give tours," he said, amazed at his ability to just make this stuff up out of thin air. "I do walking historical tours of the city. For tourists. And now they're adding some nighttime tours, which is great, money-wise, but it's really putting a crimp in my schedule."

He had never in his life used the word 'crimp' before, and here it was, just tripping off his tongue. Jack smiled, proud at his new-found improvisational skills.

Liz finished with her note taking. "Well, we can help you with

139

that," she said, pulling a printed brochure out of her file folder. "Here's our current rate sheet and our schedule. We're staffed twenty-four/seven, 365 days a year, and we're the only dog day care in the city to offer such flexible scheduling."

Jack looked at the brochure, pretending to study it closely. He looked up at Liz. "How long has Manhattan Dog Patch been in business?" he asked.

"We've been here six years," Liz answered. She turned and gestured to the room. "We used to be half this big, but then the donut shop next door went out of business and we expanded and took over their space."

"And how long have you worked here?" Jack asked, folding up the rate sheet and putting it in his coat pocket. He smiled at her and she smiled back. She was a pretty girl, he thought, and the epitome of perky.

"Just about two years," she said. "And I love it. I mean, I love dogs, I love New York, so when you put the two together, it's sort of a dream job."

Jack nodded as he smiled. "Sounds like it," he said as he stood. "Well, I'm looking at a couple different places …"

"So, when do I get to meet Al?" Liz asked as she got up. She continued to smile at him warmly, and he tried to return the smile, but he couldn't match her intensity. "You should bring him by, and we'll give him a free day here, to see if he fits in."

"Oh," Jack said, reaching for the brochure in his pocket, "I didn't see that mentioned in the brochure. Is that something you typically do …?"

Liz shook her head and gave him a sly wink. "No, we don't, but I can do it off the books. I'd hate to lose you – and Al – to a competitor." She smiled again and for the first time Jack started to feel like he was losing control of this interview.

"Well, sure," he said, backing up and nearly bumping into the wall. "I'll bring him down someday and we'll see how he likes it."

"Or, if you want to learn more about how things run here, I could meet you after work for a drink. Or something." She let the last word hang in the air for a long moment as she looked him deep in his eyes.

He tried to hold her gaze for as long as he could. Mercifully, another customer entered with their dog, which sent many of the dogs in the room into a cacophony of barking.

Liz turned to shush the dogs and welcome the new customer and, in the small melee of barking and panting and tails wagging, Jack was able to slip out without further conversation with Liz. She was sorry to see that he had seemingly vanished and even sorrier to note that he hadn't gotten around to putting his phone number on his intake form.

* * *

"Do you know how 'The Thanatopsis Club' got its name?" Kat asked her new customer as she led him through the crowded strip club toward her special couch in the back.

His hand felt warm in hers and just this side of clammy. She was used to these guys, these young men in their early to mid-twenties, who came into the City with a bit of cash burning a hole in their pockets, looking for their first taste of the sins of the flesh.

This one looked no different than the others, with the exception of his eyes, which seemed to absorb rather than reflect light, making his pupils look pitch black in the dimly-lit club.

He shook his head as he did his best to follow her, clearly a little overwhelmed by the sight of the nude dancers on the stages and the barely-clad girls entertaining customers at the tables.

"It's from a poem by a guy named William Cullen Bryant," she said, instinctively increasing her volume as they passed one of the music speakers, its thumping bass vibrating the glasses on the nearby bar.

"Thanatopsis means *Meditation Upon Death*. This used to be a Goth Club, back when that was hip, and that name made more sense then, but the sign outside was so cool that they decided to keep the name when the new owner turned it into a gentlemen's club. For gentlemen like you."

Even though he nodded in reply, Cat wasn't entirely certain that he had heard her practiced speech through the din in the room. This too was typical of the new initiate to the strip club scene; they were so afraid of committing anything that might be construed a *faux pas* that they would agree to virtually anything you said.

Cat smiled, because she recognized that she earned a considerable portion of income by playing on that nervousness and naïveté.

They reached her special VIP loveseat (ten minutes for $100, although she'd found that if she actually gave them twelve minutes or so, she could score another fifty bucks for a mere two minutes of extra work).

She sat her new customer a little roughly on the red velour and began her dance, a rhythmless number that she had honed to work with any music playing while still providing the most sensuous moves that the limited space would permit.

"Do you want to hear a bit of it?" she purred seductively, whispering loudly in his ear as she let her breast graze the front of his buttoned-down shirt.

"What?" he said, leaning back away from her, enveloped in the rich smell of her sweat and perfume.

"The poem, *Thanatopsis*. Do you want to hear a bit of it?" She moved one knee and then the other onto the couch, straddling his small frame, her hair falling with a quick whoosh across his face.

"Sure," he said, both hearing and not hearing her question.

She fanned his face with her long, auburn hair again, then leaned in closely, this time whispering warmly into his other ear, her tongue quickly flicking past his earlobe.

"'So live,'" she said, repeating the poem from memory, "'That when *thy summons comes to join the innumerable caravan which moves to that mysterious realm, where each shall take his chamber in the silent halls of death, thou go not, like the quarry-slave at night ...'"

She continued reciting the poem in his ear while simultaneously and subtly grinding her pelvis up his thigh, one hand pushing against his chest, the other hand moving through his hair, grabbing and pulling small bits of it as she spoke.

"'*Scourged to his dungeon, but, sustained and soothed by an unfaltering trust,'*" she hissed, pushing her chest into his and feeling his body jolt ever so slightly from the pressure of her naked skin, "'*Approach thy grave like one who wraps the drapery of his couch about him, and lies down to pleasant dreams ...'*"

* * *

The words of the poem were lost on Jack, who found himself enveloped in an unfamiliar and forbidden cocoon of flesh and sweat and hair and skin, a combination that he found both oddly electrifying and numbing.

As she spoke to him, her words were drowned out first by the music and then by the voice in his own head, the voice that cut through the aural haze and brought forth words of comfort.

He closed his eyes and both heard and saw the words from Proverbs 7 – *The Wiles of the Harlot* – as they moved in front of his eyes and through his mind: *I discerned, among the youths, a young man, passing through the street near her corner … in the twilight, in the evening … in the time of night and darkness.*

Jack relaxed against the back of the small couch and listened to the words in his head as she continued to grind against him, the warmth of her breasts brushing his cheek quickly and then withdrawing, again, again, and once more.

He listened and he took comfort and he began to see the plan as it formed in his mind. He whispered the words as she continued to push against him.

"In the twilight. In the evening. In the time of night and darkness …"

CHAPTER FIFTEEN

Early on the evening of what he hoped would <u>not</u> be the Double Event, Henry McHugh did what he most loved to do. He went for a long walk.

McHugh loved walking and when he had the time and energy, he took as many walks as his seventy-six-year-old body would tolerate. When at home, he would step out of his small flat in Camden Town and wander the streets for hours.

And, for someone who loved walking, McHugh had come to believe that New York was a movable feast. Experience had taught him that every block in this glorious city held some surprise or treasure – a great little bodega, a small monument to a forgotten past, a beautiful and quiet church, an unlikely bit of green space between two imposing and forbidding tenements. One only had to keep one's eyes open and sport comfortable shoes.

This particular evening's walk took him South from his hotel, down Eighth Avenue. He took a right on Twenty-Eighth and headed toward Ninth Avenue, having been told by the clerk at the hotel's front desk (the nearest thing they had to a concierge) that if he continued for a couple blocks in that direction, he'd find a park.

On the way there, he passed Serenity Laser Dental, which advertised itself as providing "Laser Dentistry for Adults, Children and Great Big Babies," which gave him a chuckle.

And then he came across the Church of the Holy Apostles, a grand relic of an edifice, which dated, he guessed, from the mid-1800s. And then he crossed the street to find himself in front of Chelsea Park.

He stood for a few long minutes looking at the park's impressive World War One tribute, a doughboy statue in tarnished bronze, and then moved through the park, sitting for several minutes on a wooden bench and watching as some young men played a very spirited game of basketball.

Since the death of his wife, Cora, McHugh forced himself to get out as much as possible. This was an attempt on his part to stifle the very strong urge he'd felt in the first few months after her passing to just sit in his comfortable chair in front of the fire in their flat. Sitting was easier than going outside, and there was always something interesting to read or, if that failed, something somewhat less interesting on the telly.

However, McHugh had seen enough people his own age or older who, after the death of a spouse, sunk back into their flats and withdrew from the world. In order to fight that inevitable inertia, he forced himself to get out by accepting virtually any reasonable invitation to speak on the subject of Jack the Ripper just about anywhere in the world, as long as travel expenses were covered.

This willingness had taken him across Europe and to such United States cities as Los Angeles (a dreadful, dreadful place), Chicago (charming but bitingly cold in the winter), Las Vegas (my, what an odd idea for a city), and several small Ripper gatherings in places as far flung as Minnesota, Tennessee and New Mexico.

The love of walking had been developed in London, where he famously led two or three "Jack the Ripper" walking tours each week, even before Cora's death. He was in demand for more walks and could have worked every night of the week if he had wished, but he had found that three was about his limit; in the colder months he cut it back to twice and sometimes just once a week.

Although he'd led the walks for years, probably hundreds of times, he still found that he enjoyed them immensely and never tired of the audiences and their curiosity.

The crowds on some nights grew to nearly two hundred and were always comprised of a curious mix of die-hard Ripper fanatics, tourists who were up for anything during their fortnight's stay in London, and the occasional addled traveler who stumbled upon the tour by chance only after discovering that the Tower of London had closed for the day.

McHugh had the patter down and knew the routes to take to avoid the other, competing Ripper walks (it seemed like there were more and more sprouting up each year), while still giving his audience a good sense of the social conditions and the physical geography that defined the world of Jack the Ripper.

Unlike other tour guides, McHugh wasn't hampered by the fact that few of the murder sites bore any resemblance to the way they had looked in the fall of 1888. His knowledge of not only the facts of the case, but also the interesting minutiae, made his the most entertaining and most factual of all the tours.

To those who lived in the neighborhood, he was a familiar sight as he nearly sprinted from location to location, his large audience hurrying to keep up. In most groups he was followed closely by a handful of Ripper enthusiasts, who kept up a running stream of questions and comments about the case and their own current theories.

Then he'd reach the next spot on the walk, gather the crowd around him, and tell the story of the murder that had taken place on that location … or, in most cases, merely *near* that location. With the exception of Mitre Square, all the other sites were vastly different than they had been in 1888, but McHugh, with his ingrained sense of history, oratory and storytelling, was able to bring each location to life for his audiences.

For years he had ended his tours at the Ten Bells pub, which still stood in the same spot on Commercial Street it had occupied during the Ripper's reign in 1888. There he'd have a pint or two with some of the more fevered tourists, sell a couple of books (the owners had been kind enough to store a case behind the bar, so he didn't need to lug them along on the tour) and debate the latest and greatest theory about the identity of the ever-elusive Jack.

But he was sad to realize, times change, even in the world of Jack the Ripper. Several months before, the Ten Bells had come under new ownership, and these new owners were more interested in selling fancy vodka drinks than catering to tourists interested in the history of Whitechapel and Spitalfields.

The new owners had made it very clear to McHugh, and the other tours as well, that they could take their business elsewhere. Some did just that, finding other nearby pubs where the owners were delighted to have a steady stream of paying, thirsty customers.

McHugh, however, bucked that trend. Instead, he now ended his walking tour across the street from the pub. From this vantage point he was also able to point out the plot of land which once was home to Number 13 Miller's Court, where young Mary Kelly sadly became the last of the Ripper's victims.

Of course, the space now housed a car park, but as with the other murders, McHugh was able to bring the horror of Mary's last few hours to life for his audience. By the time he finished telling the story of the Ripper, Mary and the events that transpired in Number 13, most of the crowd would have sworn that they actually witnessed the murder site. Then, after a short wrap-up speech, he would bid farewell to the tourists before heading to his tube stop and home.

McHugh sat on the bench in Chelsea Park and watched the pick-up basketball game for a few more minutes, marveling at the speed and skill of the players (*They could be professionals,* he thought, although he had never spent more than ten minutes watching professional basketball in his life and therefore wasn't really in a position to start scouting for new recruits).

In the interest of ongoing exploration, he followed a different path back to the hotel, heading across Twenty-seventh Street, admiring the facades of some newly-renovated town homes which looked as though they had traveled, untouched, from the nineteenth century. He glanced at his watch as he passed under a streetlight, noticing that it was only a little past seven. If there was to be any activity tonight by the copycat Jack, he reasoned, it was at least a few hours away.

A loud, piercing scream ripped through the neighborhood and McHugh felt himself jump at the sound as it cut through him. He looked around quickly, trying to place the scream's location. His eyes finally settled on a group of teenagers, mostly girls, being playfully terrorized by a couple of admiring boys.

After watching them for a few moments, McHugh ascertained that one of the girls used screaming as her primary means of communication. The validity of his theory was proven as she let out another sharp, painful screech.

At the corner of Twenty-seventh Street and Eighth Avenue, he stopped to double-check his location, looking at the street signs to verify that this was in fact where he should turn left.

As he did, he noticed a bus shelter on the corner. In the center of the shelter was a large bus map, held in place by a sheet of Plexiglas. He assumed it was Plexiglas; no one used glass anymore, in this world of casual and constant vandalism. As if to prove his point, the map was covered with various graffito, most of it illegible.

However, one artist had been much clearer in his intention and execution than the others. His graffiti consisted of a large black arrow, pointed toward one spot on the map, with words above it that read "You Are Here, Asshole!"

The point of the arrow was directed at a large black star.

McHugh stood and looked at the map for a long moment. Then he stepped to the curb and hailed a cab, deciding that the rest of this evening's walk would have to wait.

* * *

"You need what?"

Ben had heard McHugh's question, but for some reason it just didn't register with his brain. Part of the problem was that there was a lot of activity in the squad room and Ben was having trouble hearing McHugh over the din. The Englishman had come into the station out of breath, holding a map and saying he needed five minutes of Ben's time.

"A map, my boy." McHugh held up a map for Ben to see. "I need a map." It was clear to McHugh that, for whatever reason, he wasn't getting through to Ben.

"But you have a map," Ben said, gesturing to the paper that McHugh held in his hand, still not understanding where he fit in this conversation.

"Yes, I do. You are entirely correct. This is a map of Whitechapel, circa 1888, drawn to the scale of one inch to one mile. See, all five of the murder sites are marked." He held the map up again for Ben, who took it out of courtesy more than anything else.

Across the top of the map was the word "Whitechapel" in a fancy scripted font and there were five red dots on the map, each apparently indicating one of Jack the Ripper's murder sites. Ben noticed that there was a name under each dot ("Nichols," "Chapman," "Stride" and so on). He handed the map back to McHugh.

"And you need another map?" he asked, signaling to Klingbile across the room.

"Yes," McHugh said. "What I'm looking for is a map of the city – the island of Manhattan – at a one-inch to one-mile scale, with the locations of the two previous murder sites indicated."

Klingbile arrived from across the room. Ben grabbed him and paired him up with McHugh.

"Klingbile," Ben said. "You know Henry McHugh. Would you get him a map of the city with the two murder sites marked on it?"

"At one-inch to one-mile scale," McHugh added, still a bit winded from his exertions.

Klingbile headed obediently toward the file room, not entirely sure that he fully understood his mission. Ben turned to McHugh and gestured toward one of the plastic chairs in the squad room's seating area.

"Why don't you just have a seat while he does that?" Ben suggested.

"Splendid. Well done. Thank you."

McHugh sat, setting his coat and hat on the empty adjoining seat. He looked up to thank Ben again, but he was already across the room, answering a ringing phone. McHugh looked across the aisle and was surprised to see Barbara seated there, suppressing a smile.

"Well, good evening," he said, reaching up to tip his hat and then realizing that he'd just set it on the chair.

"Good evening," she said.

"I'm surprised to see you here. I thought you were heavily, what's the word ... sequestered," he said.

Barbara shrugged. "Well, yes, they have three shifts of cops protecting me. But I got to thinking about it and decided these guys

149

could probably be put to better use tonight, rather than sitting in my apartment watching me while I type. So, I came down here, at least until ..."

Her voice trailed off.

McHugh nodded. "Until we see what happens."

"Yes," Barbara agreed.

They both sat quietly for a moment, on opposite sides of the waiting area. Barbara paged listlessly through a very old copy of *Readers Digest* magazine, learning more than she cared to know about 'Joe's Digestive Tract,' while McHugh sat silently, apparently studying his shoes with deep interest. Barbara soon tired of the magazine and set it aside.

"So, how are you doing?" she asked.

"Me?" McHugh said, looking up. He sighed and she thought, for the first time, that he was starting to look his age.

"Oh, well," he said. He leaned forward and she mirrored his movement. "It's an odd situation, as you doubtlessly understand," he continued. "Having spent as many years as I have on this century-old phantom, one can't help but think from time to time that it's a bloody silly way to spend one's life."

Barbara nodded, not sure how to respond.

"I can't prove who Jack the Ripper was," McHugh said. "So, I spend my life proving who he wasn't. Then, like clockwork, every two years another poppycock theory surfaces."

He stopped and smiled sheepishly at Barbara. She laughed in spite of herself.

"Beg your pardon," he continued. "But every time a new theory rises to the surface, they dredge up old McHugh to beat down the fools with their own arguments." Another quick look at her. Another sheepish grin. "Beg your pardon, again," he said.

He sat back in his chair with a long sigh. "Some nights, it seems like a bloody waste of time."

He looked around the room at all the activity and she noticed that she had been wrong. He didn't look all that old and there was a sparkle in his eyes that she rarely saw in people a third his age.

"But," he added, perking up, "Perhaps all that can be put to good use. Tonight. For once."

Barbara nodded, but before she could respond further, Officer Klingbile had returned with a map of Manhattan.

"Here you go, sir," he said, handing the oversized sheet of paper to McHugh. "One inch to one-mile scale."

"Excellent, well done, my good man, well done," McHugh said, excitedly taking the map. "Thank you, officer."

McHugh reached over to the next chair and dug through his coat, finally finding and extracting the Whitechapel map from one of the pockets. He carefully placed the Whitechapel map under the new map and then looked up, searching the room for something. Barbara looked around, too, trying to help him, but she had no idea what they were looking for.

"Aha!" he said loudly, as he jumped up and scurried across the aisle which separated them. A second later he was kneeling in the empty chair next to her, holding the two maps up against the translucent glass of a cubicle divider behind the row of chairs.

She turned and watched, fascinated, as he lined up the two stars on the Manhattan map with two red dots on the map underneath. She could see two dots on that lower map, and barely make out two names: Nichols and Chapman.

McHugh adjusted the position of first the upper map and then the lower map, and a moment later two of the dots on the lower map lined up perfectly with their counterpart stars on the Manhattan map.

"Do you have a pen?" McHugh asked her, never taking his eyes off the papers that he held pressed against the frosted glass partition. Barbara grabbed her purse from the floor and began to dig through its messy contents, pulling items out and digging further, finally finding something that might work.

"Will an eyebrow pencil do?"

"Any port in a storm, my dear. Any port in a storm."

She handed him the pencil and he began to make some fresh marks on the Manhattan map. McHugh finished his work just as Ben, followed by several other officers, made his way through the squad room.

"Just got a call," Ben said to Barbara. "Someone found a body. A woman."

McHugh stepped back from the glass divider and surveyed his

work on the map. "Somewhere around East Thirty-Ninth, would be my guess," he said. "Or thereabouts."

Ben stopped in his tracks and then turned to look at McHugh. "Between Second and Third Avenues on East Thirty-Ninth," he said. "You can tell me how you did that on the drive there."

Ben continued on toward the door, without waiting. McHugh crossed the aisle to grab his coat while Barbara scrambled to put everything back in her purse as she followed them.

* * *

The three of them crammed into a squad car, Ben in front with an officer at the wheel, and Barbara and McHugh in the back, behind the wire mesh that was designed to keep the more obstreperous backseat passengers in their place.

It wasn't a long drive, and with the lights flashing and the siren wailing, it wasn't a slow drive, either. It also wasn't a ride that involved much chit chat. Each of them sat quietly, deep in their own thoughts, not wanting to express aloud the dread that had begun to creep persistently into their bones.

Ben squinted out the windshield, trying to determine their exact location as they raced along, as if knowing where they were right at that moment would somehow increase the speed with which they reached their destination. He spoke softly yet his voice clearly cut through the roar of the siren. He was doing his best to sound positive.

"This can't be ours."

McHugh, who was still studying his two maps in the dim light of the car's interior, nodded in agreement. "Oh, I'm certain that it's not."

Ben turned and looked at him through the metal mesh that separated the front from the back. McHugh met his eyes. "All right," McHugh admitted, "I'm not entirely certain."

"I think ..." Barbara started to say, and then stopped. Both men turned their attention to her. She looked at them and then spoke again. "I think we might have made a mistake."

Ben's eyes narrowed. "How do you figure?" he asked.

Barbara bit her lower lip, trying to find a way to put the feeling into words. "I think it might have been a mistake," she said, "to assume that he would play fair."

There was a long moment while the two men considered what she had said.

"Yes, I'm afraid you may just be right," McHugh finally agreed.

* * *

Within a block from where the crime scene was supposed to be, it became very clear where the crime scene actually was. Two squad cars were parked haphazardly in front of an alley entrance, the strobes from the cruisers' light bars intermittently illuminating the area.

The alley was flanked by squat buildings that looked to be apartment houses. There were few lights on in the buildings and precious little light on the street.

A few onlookers peered from the sidewalk, but they were held back by one of the uniformed cops. Ben headed toward two officers who had stationed themselves near the mouth of the alley. No crime scene tape had been put in place yet, Ben noted. This was a very fresh site.

Barbara was three steps behind Ben and slowed to wait for McHugh to catch up. She looked down the alley, where she could see what appeared to be a body, sprawled on the ground, barely visible in the dimly lit corridor. If she hadn't been looking for it, she could have easily missed it or assumed it was a stray bag of garbage.

"What have you got?" Ben asked one of the cops.

"I don't think this is one of yours," the cop said, looking through the few notes he had already taken. "The Medical Examiner hasn't been here yet, but I can tell you that although her throat was cut, there was no mutilation like with the others."

Ben's sigh of relief was cut short by Barbara.

"There wouldn't be," she said. "The third victim, Elizabeth Stride, wasn't mutilated. The theory is that the Ripper was interrupted."

She looked to McHugh for an argument, but he merely nodded in agreement. Like Barbara, he was looking down the alley at the still, dark form on the ground. He rubbed his eyes and looked away.

The cop continued to page through his wallet-sized notebook. "Plus the name doesn't match," he said.

Ben nodded hopefully. "I don't see how it could," he said.

"Yeah," the cop continued. "The ID we found identifies her as Elizabeth Long."

Barbara took a quick intake of breath. McHugh lowered his head. Ben looked at both of them, recognizing that something was wrong but not sure what it was.

"Which means what?" he asked.

McHugh turned to Barbara. "Your notion that he wouldn't play fair was, sadly, dead on."

Barbara nodded and then turned to Ben. "Elizabeth Stride was known to many of her friends in the East End as Long Liz, because of her height," she said. "Long, Liz," she continued, gesturing with her hands as if she were physically inverting the two names. "Liz Long. We should have seen that one. We should have seen it."

"He was counting on us not to," McHugh said sadly.

Ben turned back to the cop. "Have you got anything?" he asked. "Witnesses ... a weapon ... anything?"

The cop shook his head. "Nothing yet," he said. "We're figuring that she's been here fifteen, maybe twenty minutes at the most."

A thought occurred to Ben and he turned back to McHugh. "Which gives us twenty minutes or so until the next murder is committed. Right?"

McHugh nodded in agreement. "Yes. Or until the next body is found."

Ben quickly looked at his watch. "Do you still have those maps?" he asked.

McHugh understood instantly where Ben was heading with this. He pulled both maps out of his pocket and placed one on top of the other, trying to line up the red dots and the black stars, which was difficult to do in the dim and murky light they had to work with. Ben recognized McHugh's predicament and looked around for some options.

An idea occurred to him and he gently took the older man's arm and walked him to the nearest squad car. He waved to one of the cops, who was standing on the other side of the car.

"Officer, can you turn on your flashlight?" Ben asked. The cop took his flashlight from his belt and flipped it on. Ben gestured to the car that stood between them, pointing to the driver's side window. "Shine the light so it comes through this window."

The cop, who had long ago given up asking homicide detectives any questions, quickly obeyed and shined the bright light through the front passenger window, fully illuminating the driver's side window.

McHugh stooped down and pressed the two maps against the glass, deftly lining up the red dots on the Whitechapel map with the three penciled stars on the Manhattan map. He traced his finger along the upper map, finally spotting the red dot for the fourth murder on the map below.

"Pen. Pencil. Marker. Something," he said as he firmly pressed the two maps together. Ben reached into his suit coat pocket and produced a pen, handing it to McHugh.

"Unless I'm very much mistaken," he said, marking the spot with the pen, "it looks to be the corner of Third Avenue and Fifty- First Street." He handed the Manhattan map to Ben, who noted the location as he headed back to their squad car.

"That's not far, is it?" Barbara asked.

Ben shook his head as they got into the car. "It's just uptown," he said. "But, if it's the place I'm thinking of, it's not Manhattan. In fact, it's about as far from Manhattan as you can be while still in Manhattan."

Before she could get clarification, they were in the car and roaring away from the curb with the siren blaring.

CHAPTER SIXTEEN

The British Consulate sat right in the center of midtown Manhattan, an old gothic mansion that looked to be at least a century out of place from the modern buildings on either side of it. It was constructed of massive gray brick and stood four stories high, with two turrets and three high, pointed roof peaks made of slate.

A tall, wrought-iron fence encircled the weathered structure, acting as an imposing metal moat, a visual and cultural barrier between the British government and the decidedly American traffic that roared past the building on Third Avenue.

A small, brick guard shack was positioned near the gate, providing a first line of defense against UPS trucks and other service vehicles. Once through the gate, a short circular driveway led up to the wide front door, which looked to be about four feet thick and twelve feet tall.

But to get to that door, first you had to get through that gate, which from Ben's perspective didn't look to be happening any time soon. When their car arrived across the street from the mansion, he noticed that there was already one unmarked police car in front of the building.

Two figures were standing in front of the closed gate, with two guards facing them on the other side. Ben could hear the sound of angry American voices as he opened the car door, suggesting that the ingredients for an ugly, international incident were all in place.

The lights that illuminated the grounds and the level of activity gave the distinct impression that the party had started without them. Uniformed guards were moving around the front of the mansion, and there was a cluster of figures in one area that looked to be a garden running along the east side of the building.

Ben was the first out of the car and headed toward the gate but came to a dead stop when he saw Dale Harkness coming toward him.

"Bureaucratic limey son of a bitch bastards," Harkness snarled as he approached Ben. "Black, you picked this up off the scanner, too? That was quick."

Ben shook his head. "No," he said, "McHugh –"

Ben stopped, deciding against offering up that information to Harkness just yet. "Yes, we heard it off the scanner. What's going on?"

McHugh and Barbara arrived at that moment, but Harkness did his best to ignore them as he recounted what he knew to Ben, spitting it out as he fumed in anger.

"They've found a body, pretty clearly the fourth victim," he said. "But, for diplomatic reasons too arcane and asinine to believe, we can't go in. Turns out, as New York cops, we have jurisdiction but not the right to enter. Even with a search warrant. According to Miss Manners at the gate, we have to be invited."

He turned and finally acknowledged Barbara and McHugh. "You called this one, we're in a whole different city here," he said to Barbara, then turned back and glared up at the mansion and the tall fence keeping them out. He folded his arms across his chest and set his feet in a wide stance, giving the impression that he was doing his best to open the gate with the sheer force of his will.

"So what do we do?" Ben asked no one in particular.

"We stand here holding our dicks in our hands until we read about it in the paper," Harkness replied, still glaring at the mansion.

Barbara cleared her throat before speaking. "Not to impugn your diplomatic abilities, Lieutenant Harkness, but I'm just wondering if there might be an advantage to sending someone else in. I mean, someone other than you."

Harkness shook his head derisively. "Sorry, Miss Thomas, but I don't think your position on *The New York Times'* best-seller list is going to have a lot of influence with our tea-swilling friends on the other side of that freaking gate."

"I wasn't suggesting me," she explained. "I just thought that a British citizen – with an impressive career in the British police force – might be a more welcome presence and could hold a bit more sway when it comes to getting you and your men on the other side of that gate."

McHugh looked up at the trio and then nodded slowly. "Well, as a British citizen, they will at least have to admit me. Once inside, I might be able to exert more influence with the officials, that's true," he agreed. "And it certainly can't hurt to make the attempt."

They all turned to Harkness. He thought about it for a long moment, and then mumbled, "Give it a shot." He turned back to the mansion, re-folded his arms and continued to stare at the building in a threatening manner.

With that scant permission in place, McHugh headed away from the small group and made his way toward the guard shack, reaching for his identification as he walked.

* * *

As it turned out, getting in was really not much of a problem. They were British, he was British, and the whole exchange was short, to the point and exceedingly polite.

Within moments, McHugh was standing by the man currently in charge, Gareth Shaw, Executive Assistant to Sir Timothy Bellsway, the Consul-General. Gareth was in his early twenties, exceedingly thin, with wispy blonde hair that he habitually pushed out of his eyes. Every time Gareth spoke, it was in a hushed whisper. McHugh wasn't certain, but he thought it was possible that Gareth always spoke in a whisper. He seemed to be that sort of person.

Gareth met McHugh at the gate and led him up the short driveway and across the lawn to the garden, bringing them within ten feet of the body. Around the body stood three guards. Their only function appeared to be appeasing whatever official felt that some guards needed to stand near the body. The three guards performed this role admirably.

"Nothing has been touched," Gareth said, "and I have placed an emergency phone call to Sir Timothy himself. He should be here in just a few minutes. He's at an event tonight, but he's obviously cutting his evening short." Gareth double-checked his watch, which hung perilously from his bone-thin wrist.

"Good work," McHugh said.

Then, for the first time he took a good look in the direction of the body. For a moment, it was as if he was looking at a color version of the crime scene descriptions of Catharine Eddowes. The victim lay on her back, her dressed pulled up, her trunk and torso a mass of blood, entrails and ripped clothing.

In addition to the multiple wounds to the abdomen, he couldn't help but see the slashes that had been made across her face. They had been made quickly, furiously, yet looked to be identical to Eddowes' wounds in 1888. Through the torn skin and thickening blood on her face he could see her eyes, staring lifelessly at the trees above her. It was all he could do to stop himself from bending down and gently closing them.

Gareth was doing his duty to act as a good host to McHugh, while simultaneously doing his best not to look at the body.

"Obviously, we want to cooperate with the American authorities, but I'm not empowered to do that," Gareth explained in a hushed whisper. "Sir Timothy can, of course, and he'll be here in a few minutes." Gareth again checked his watch.

"Yes, of course," McHugh said softly. He turned from the body and looked at Gareth, who was staring impatiently at the gate and the driveway, waiting for Sir Timothy to relieve him of this duty. "How long have you been at the Consulate, Gareth?"

"Just three days, sir," Gareth said, looking McHugh in the eye and adding a quick smile to cover his nerves.

"Not even a week, yet?"

"No, sir. Wednesday next."

"How do you like it so far?"

Gareth searched for the right words, but they wouldn't come. "It's warmer than I thought it would be, sir," he finally said. "I thought it would be colder here."

"Trust me, it will be. Yes, we're in the midst of what is known as Indian Summer in the States. Although given their current propensity for what they call political correctness, they may have changed the name to Native American Summer. I haven't checked lately."

McHugh surveyed the crime scene. On the ground, near the victim's feet, was a small red pocketbook. McHugh squatted down and, using his handkerchief, picked it up.

"Do you think robbery was the motive?" Gareth asked, still keeping his gaze away from the body. "If it was, how did she get in here? And how did he get in here? It's very hard to get in here," he added.

McHugh snapped open the clasp on the purse. "No, Gareth, I don't think robbery had anything to do with it. If I'm correct in my thinking, he left her purse so we could identify her more quickly."

Gareth scrunched his thin face into a sour grimace. "Why would someone do that?"

"You might well ask," McHugh said, removing a driver's license from the purse with his handkerchief. He took his glasses out of his coat pocket and held them in front of his eyes, not taking the time to put them on. He read the name on the laminated card. He looked at it for a long moment, and then set the license back into the purse.

"He left the purse because the little bastard is impatient," McHugh said. "He can't wait one moment to show us how clever he is."

He set the purse back on the ground and slowly stood up. It took longer to do this than he would have liked.

"And he is clever, I'll give him that. Bloody clever."

* * *

Outside the gates a small crowd of officials had gathered, waiting for McHugh to conclude his diplomatic mission. Several more squad cars had arrived, as well as deputies from the Mayor's office and a small team from the Medical Examiner, all waiting in an impatient pack for permission to enter the grounds.

Ben saw Isobel before she saw him and he made his way across the street to her. She flashed a wicked smile when she saw him.

"Wallace Shawn to Sean Connery is not so simple, is it my friend?" she said, shaking a scolding finger at him. "In two, I mean, to do it in two. Not so simple."

Ben smiled and shook his head. "Isobel, I don't mean to insult you, but off the top of my head I can think of two separate ways to do it. Are you telling me you couldn't even come up with one?"

"Yes, I came up with one, but is it the same method that you came up with, that's the question now, isn't it?"

"That's how we play the game. Ready to take a shot?"

She studied him intently. "How come you play games with me, you never ask me out? Why is that? Are you afraid of Jamaican women?"

Ben shook his head. "No, I'm just better at playing silly games than dating. Now, quit stalling and give me your answer."

She nodded. "All right, Mr. Game Player. Wallace Shawn to Sean Connery. I'm going to go from Wallace Shawn to Mia Farrow, by way of Mr. Woody Allen's *Radio Days*. And we go from Mia Farrow to Michael Caine by way of *Hannah and Her Sisters*. Michael Caine to Sean Connery in *The Man Who Would Be King*. That is in two."

Ben smiled. "And that's the way I did it. Well done. I think we're tied at this point."

"We are. How about I give you a hard one this time, make it more difficult for you? Make you sweat a little bit."

"I'm up for it," Ben said, smiling.

Isobel thought for a long moment. "Okay, so the last movie was *The Man Who Would Be King*. How about … Christopher Plummer. To … oh, this will be fun. To Dennis Christopher." She stared at Ben for an uncomfortably long time. "In one."

Ben let out a slow whistle. "Christopher Plummer to Dennis Christopher. In one? You're not kidding around, are you?"

"Benjamin, I'm playing for keeps. I look forward to your efforts."

With that she turned and headed back to the Medical Examiner van, where two co-workers were preparing kits to take up to the crime scene. Ben watched her go and then turned to head back, nearly colliding with Barbara. She looked from Ben to Isobel and back again.

"Kind of a sexy lady, don't you think?" Barbara asked.

"You think so?" Ben said innocently, looking back at Isobel as she conferred with her co-workers. "I don't really see it. I mean, once you get past the killer cheekbones, the eyes, the accent and that profoundly wicked sense of humor, what have you got, really?"

"Well, right now I've got a massive insecurity complex."

Ben looked her in the eye. "She's got nothing on you."

Barbara looked up at him, waiting for the punch line.

Ben smiled at her. "Seriously."

Before she could request a more thorough explanation, they were interrupted by Harkness, who roared by them on his way to the corner. "McHugh's on his way out," he growled as he sped past. They turned and followed him.

McHugh was heading down the short drive to the guardhouse and gate. The guard passed him through with a wave and before the gate had shut behind him, Ben, Barbara and Harkness were at his side.

"As we suspected, it's the fourth victim," McHugh told the small group. "The wounds look like those of the original Catharine Eddowes. However, her driver's license identifies her as Catharine Conway."

Harkness let out a short, contemptuous laugh. "So he couldn't find someone with the same last name, but he went ahead and killed someone anyway. What a dick."

McHugh was taking out his pipe and starting the slow process of filling it, so Barbara spoke up. "No, he had the right name. Or, at least, one of the right names," she said. She looked over to McHugh for support, but he simply nodded for her to continue.

"If I'm remembering this correctly," she said, "Catharine Eddowes married a man named Thomas Conway long before she moved to the East End. She didn't use his name, she always went by Eddowes, but – technically – he got the right person. We screwed that one up, too."

"He was expecting that. He was expecting it all. He anticipated that we'd put guards on the potential victims. He's been at least three moves ahead of us from the beginning." McHugh had his pipe lit and he turned to Harkness. "I've had a long and fruitful conversation with the Consul-General," he said. "I explained the nature of the case. He's agreed to full cooperation with the New York police and has requested that you consult with him immediately."

Harkness didn't need to be told twice. He turned and started toward the gate.

"His name is Sir Timothy Bellsway," McHugh called after him. "And you need to call him Sir Timothy. Not Sir Tim or Sir Timmy."

"I think I can handle it," Harkness called back over his shoulder as he broke into a trot.

McHugh watched him go, then turned to Ben. "Did I detect the beginnings of a smile on his face?" he asked.

Ben shook his head. "It's a trick of the light," he said.

"Listen, I've been thinking," Barbara said. Both men looked at Barbara, who had turned away from the old building and was looking up the street. "If he's going to play this out by the book," she continued, "our Jack has got one more spot to hit tonight and one more clue to leave behind."

"Ah, yes," McHugh agreed. "The bit of poor Miss Eddowes' apron, carelessly – or not – tossed aside as he fled the scene of the crime."

"Right," Barbara nodded. "In London, that clue was found several blocks from the murder site, on Goulston Street."

Ben looked around, a little mystified. "What are we looking for again?"

"A torn piece of fabric from the victim's dress, with her blood on it," McHugh explained. "Some have postulated that the Ripper used the scrap of cloth to clean off his hands, and then discarded it after he left the crime scene."

Ben still wasn't getting it. "But that could be anywhere," he said. "What are the odds we could find it?"

"Actually, they might be pretty good," Barbara said. "As Mr. McHugh – Henry – has demonstrated, our killer seems to be placing the crime scenes in the same locations, relative to the original murders. If he's doing that with the murders, then why not with this clue?"

She turned to McHugh. "I've visited the murder sites in London a couple of times, but you –"

He cut her off with a wave of his hand. "Hundreds of times, my dear, perhaps even thousands" he said. "I've given walking tours for years. From the Eddowes site in Mitre Square over to Goulston Street is a brisk, ten-minute walk."

"But ten minutes in which direction?" Ben asked.

They were standing at the intersection of Third Avenue and Fifty-First Street, which offered them at least four directions in which they could proceed.

McHugh reached into his coat pocket and pulled out the two maps, placing one on top of the other and lining up the matching points. He looked up from the drawing, glanced left, then right, then studied the diagram for a moment longer. He turned a hundred and eighty degrees, consulted the map, and then looked to Ben.

"Do you know which way is north, by chance?"

"North?" It took Ben a few moments to get his bearings, and then he pointed vaguely toward the direction of Central Park. "It's that way. Sort of."

McHugh considered this information and looked over at the Consulate, then back at the map. "Given the placement of the body," he said, "and if that truly is north ... then we should walk ... this way."

He turned forty-five degrees and headed away from the mansion, with Barbara and Ben right on his heels.

CHAPTER SEVENTEEN

J ack followed them. Henry McHugh, Miss Thomas and that policeman, Black.

It wasn't the first time. Since he'd spotted the trio at the Annie Chapman crime scene, he'd made a point of keeping tabs on all three of them. Nothing obsessive, of course, just the occasional peek to see what they were up to. Checking in, as it were, to see how close they might be getting.

Hanging out at the crime scene was one of the best parts of the process, he'd come to discover. Not the best part, of course. Obviously not. It was the work; it was always the work.

But he quickly realized that he got a real kick out of standing in a crowd of onlookers and gawkers, each wondering what was going on while he knew the whole story. He liked standing among them while understanding that he was, in fact, apart from them and above them.

Of course, he played it safe. He was aware that the police routinely and covertly snapped photos of the crowds at all major crime scenes, in order to spot the over-eager criminal who had returned to see the world's reaction to his or her handiwork. This didn't concern him, as he'd been properly and differently disguised each time.

Plus, even without the disguise he'd be hard to spot, because he understood that one of his gifts was that he was intrinsically part of a crowd. He didn't stand out, he never caught your eye, and he certainly wasn't memorable. Once that had bothered him; only a little, but it did. Now he thought of it as one of his greatest assets. A blessing, in its own way.

At the Chapman crime site, he had recognized Henry McHugh immediately, with his ruddy face and omnipresent tweed hat, and he'd felt a twinge of excitement. The best in the field, reviewing his handiwork. Quite an honor.

And he'd recognized Barbara Thomas, of course, the new darling of the Ripper circuit. She looked smaller in person than in the TV interviews he'd seen, but she still presented a nice package – trim, with long hair (a favorite of his), and wonderfully sad eyes. He looked forward to getting to know her better.

The cop was another story and took a bit longer to track down and identify. But you could find anything on the Internet if you were both clever and persistent. In a very short time, he had all the info on detective Benjamin Black that he could ever want. This included college scores, recent movie rentals, and even his involvement in a famous 12-step program.

And so, he followed them and watched them and made notes and identified patterns. He could tell that something was developing between the detective and Barbara Thomas. That was useful. He found that McHugh liked to take long walks and that was useful too. He discovered that Miss Thomas' publisher was a hound for publicity and that had turned out to be a good piece of information to have.

Jack knew when each of them came and went and where they shopped and what they ate and who they talked to and what they wore and it was all good. Knowledge was power.

And in that regard, he felt very powerful, because like all the best master storytellers, he knew how this story would end. And they didn't have a clue and that made it so much fun.

And so tonight he followed them as they headed away from the British Consulate toward, he assumed, his final clue of the evening. He kept in the shadows, about a half a block behind them. Following was easy and tonight it was all the easier because he knew where they were headed, knew what they would find when they got there, and knew what they just might discover if they were smart enough. All they had to do was be nearly as smart as he was.

And so they walked, heading toward his version of Goulston Street.

And Jack followed, always staying just out of sight in the dark corners of the evening.

CHAPTER EIGHTEEN

After walking for just over three minutes, McHugh halted abruptly at a corner. Ben and Barbara came to a stop a half step later, standing together behind him, waiting patiently to see where he would lead them next.

He looked around at their present location, four corners consisting of virtually identical specimens of innocuous office buildings, then studied his Manhattan map. He took that map and compared it to the Whitechapel map. Then he turned around a couple times like a dog preparing to sleep. He looked to Ben.

"North?" he asked, again.

Ben took a moment to reorient himself to get his bearings and then pointed confidently off to their left. "That's north. Well, northish," he said.

McHugh aligned this information with a quick glance at the map and then he was off and walking again. Ben and Barbara hurried to keep up.

"For a man your age, you set quite a stride," Ben called ahead to him.

"Yes, well, the faster you walk, the harder it is for Death to catch up," McHugh said, turning back to smile at Ben. "And, they say, if you walk fast enough, he may just give up and focus on someone else. At least, that's the theory."

They reached another intersection and McHugh took a sudden and sharp left, leading them down a street lined with closed shops and weathered brownstones. Lights were on in several of the brownstones and they could hear the sounds of human occupation – televisions, music, laughter and loud conversations – as they made their way down the block.

"You know, I was thinking," Barbara said, clearly a little winded from the pace McHugh was setting. "This guy, this Jack the Ripper copycat, has been scrupulous about re-creating all the best-known elements of the case. He's replicated the murders perfectly. He sent an electronic version of the Dear Boss letter; he sent the kidney with the Lusk letter. I'm guessing, if our killer is going to leave a bit of the last victim's dress as a clue, there's a very good chance that he'll also leave his own, unique version of the graffito."

"A distinct possibility," McHugh replied over his shoulder, never slowing his stride. "In fact, it would surprise me greatly if he didn't leave the graffito, in one form or another."

"The graffito? What's that?" Ben asked.

"The Goulston Street Graffito," Barbara explained. "It's one of the most ..." She struggled to find the right word. "One of the most *enigmatic* of all the Ripper clues," she finally said. "It's a phrase that was written in chalk on a wall near where the apron fragment was found. The police erased it before it could be photographed, which has only fueled the theories and controversies about it ever since."

"What was the phrase?" Ben asked.

"I knew you were going to ask that," she said, her face scrunched in thought. "'The Juwes ...'"

She increased her gait and caught up to McHugh, who was two paces of ahead of them. "I always get this part wrong. What's the exact wording, again?"

"'The Juwes are the men that will not be blamed for nothing,'" he said, without missing a beat or slowing his stride. "It's the most famous double negative in the history of serial killings."

He turned to Barbara and added, "Now that I think of it, perhaps the only one. One of the fellows at dinner during the recent convention even included it in a song parody he performed. Did you see it? It was after dinner, the first night."

Barbara shook her head. "I didn't make it to the opening night dinner."

"Oh, you missed a corker of a night," McHugh said, chuckling. "This one fellow, Dennis Connelly-Smith, he's a Gilbert and Sullivan fanatic, and he re-wrote *'I Am the Very Model of a Modern Major General,'* with all kinds of sly and obscure Ripper references. Let me see if I can remember how some of the ditty went. It was quite clever, really."

He stopped walking and scratched his chin for a moment, and then started, softly at first, to recite:

I am the very model of a modern Ripperologist,
I'm up on all the victims and could be their gynecologist,
I suspect the throne of England, and I skew the facts historical,
From Spitalfields to Miller's Court, in order categorical;
I'm very well acquainted too with matters anatomical,
I've theories on the suspects, both the likely and the comical,
About Glouston's graffito I'm teeming with a lot o' news—
With many doubtful "facts" that connect it all to the Masons'
Juwes!

McHugh laughed and continued walking, without noticing the looks that Ben and Barbara were exchanging.

"It was the highlight of the evening, and that's saying something," he said, still smiling as he resumed his mission.

* * *

Barbara fell back in step with Ben.

"Anyway," she said, "the graffito was quite controversial at the time. The Commissioner of Police, Sir Charles Warren himself, insisted that it be erased from the wall before it could be photographed, in order to prevent rioting in the Jewish quarter."

"'The Juwes are the men that will not be blamed for nothing,'"
Ben repeated slowly. "What does it mean?"

Barbara waited to see if McHugh was going to take over the explanation at this point, but he appeared to be too caught up in where they were headed. He was still quietly humming the Gilbert & Sullivan tune to himself, so she decided it was up to her to continue the lesson.

"Well," she started, "Some people at that time saw it as an indication that The Ripper was either Jewish ... or trying to turn suspicion for the crimes on someone who was a Jew. Others looked at the spelling of the word "Jews' in the graffito – J-U-W-E-S – as proof that the murders were all part of an elaborate Masonic conspiracy."

"Who are the Juwes?"

Barbara took a deep breath and continued. "The Juwes were Jubela, Jubelo and Jubelum," she explained. "According to the Masonic legend, they killed Hiram Abiff, a Mason who was in charge of the construction of King Solomon's Temple." Barbara chuckled a bit. "Wow, I'm surprised that I remember all of this."

"Well, you are a Ripperologist," Ben said.

"That depends who you ask," she said, nodding her head toward McHugh.

"Anyway, as a punishment for their heinous crime," she continued, "Jubela, Jubelo and Jubelum were all killed in a fashion that – at least to some people back in 1888 – resembled the murders that Jack the Ripper was committing. And, since many high officials in the government were Masons, people started to come up with all these wild theories as to why the government would want these five prostitutes murdered."

Ben considered the information. "Okay," he said. "So, what's your view on it? Did Jack the Ripper write the grafitto, and if so, why?"

Barbara laughed. "To be honest, I'm a rebel in this one area," she said in a *sotto voce* whisper. "I think it's all nonsense and has absolutely nothing to do with the crimes."

"Hear, hear. Good for you!"

Barbara was surprised to hear McHugh's assent. She increased her speed so that they were walking side by side.

"Henry McHugh," she said, "Am I to understand that we have finally come upon a point in the Ripper case on which we both agree?"

He smiled at her as they walked. "Stranger things have happened," he said. He turned to Ben, who was now walking on his other side.

"Miss Thomas is quite right, Benjamin," he continued. "And we are, sadly, in the minority on this point. Personally – and I've said this publicly for years and will continue to protest until I drop – I think the graffito was placed there by someone unrelated to the crime. Now, whether The Ripper chose to leave his clue near the graffito to throw us off the scent, I can't say."

They had reached another intersection. McHugh stopped and scanned the area.

"What I can say," he continued, "is that the site of the Goulston Street graffito and where they found the scrap from Catharine Eddowes' apron is – relative to our current murder sites – right there."

He raised his arm and pointed across the street at a modern, all-glass office tower, which Ben estimated to be about ten stories tall.

There was no traffic, so they ignored the flashing 'Don't Walk' sign and crossed the street, scanning the area around the base of the building for any sign of the scrap of fabric. They fanned out in front of the building, each picking a small area to search. Barbara looked up at the building and at the other buildings on the block.

"Boy, this looks nothing like the buildings on Goulston," she said.

"I would agree whole-heartedly," McHugh said. "But in this instance, a building is a building, a doorway is a doorway –"

"And a bloody scrap of fabric is a bloody scrap of fabric." Ben pointed to a small square of cloth stuffed into the corner by the building's front door. "Does that look like the same fabric you saw on the victim?"

McHugh moved in for a closer look. "Hard to be sure in this light and with the bloodstains," he said, "But since there are bloodstains, I'd hazard a guess that that's what we're looking for."

Ben removed a pair of plastic gloves and a clear plastic evidence bag from his coat pocket and squatted down to retrieve the fabric, gingerly picking it up and placing it into the bag. Barbara looked down at the piece of evidence as he put it safely into the bag, and then stepped back and turned away. The immediacy of the blood, still wet on the fabric, disturbed her.

She leaned back against the building's smooth glass exterior and tried to put the image of the bloody fabric, and by extension, the victim, out of her mind. She turned her gaze to the bus bench near the curb and tried to clear her mind by reading the advertisement on the back, but it wasn't enough to erase the images from her memory.

McHugh stood near her, looking at the building's exterior, running his hand across its shiny glass front, scanning the walls of the doorway and then craning his neck to look up across the front of the building. There was nothing but smooth glass all the way up to the roof. He stepped back and shook his head.

"Not much chance he scrawled anything with chalk on this surface," he said, continuing to survey the surrounding area. "Sidewalk appears to be clear. Nothing above the door. No skywriting, even ..."

Barbara wasn't watching him or really even listening to what he was saying. "Bagels aren't enormously popular in England, are they?" she asked.

Ben and McHugh looked at her, then at each other. McHugh walked back to her, and Ben stood up from his work, sealing the bag and putting it in his pocket. He removed the plastic gloves and tossed them into a curbside trash can.

"Bagels? No, they've never caught on in the British Isles to any great degree," McHugh said. "Although, I am pleased to report that there was, for a time, a Krispy Kreme shop in Harrods. Not sure if they're still in business. A product best purchased and consumed while they're still hot, if you want my advice." He looked back at Barbara. "Why do you ask, if I may inquire?"

Barbara pointed to the back of the bus bench. "That advertisement," she said. "It just seems ... I don't know. Kind of odd. Out of place."

Both men turned their attention to the worn and weathered print ad on the back of the bench. It was an advertisement for Behlmener Fruit Jam and showed a very British-looking young boy who had just finished writing some words in chalk on a brick wall. In the illustration he is taking a break from his work and happily eating a bagel spread, presumably, with Behlmener Fruit Jam.

The graffiti he had written on the brick wall in the ad read, *"Sweeten that hot London bagel with Behlmener Fruit Jam."*

McHugh took out a small pad and quickly jotted down some notes while Ben stepped closer to the ad, reading the tag line quietly to himself.

Barbara read it aloud. *"Sweeten that hot London bagel with Behlmener Fruit Jam."*

"We might be grasping at straws here," Ben said, stepping back from the bench. "I mean, it's an ad on a bus bench. And it looks like it's been here a while."

"Maybe," Barbara said. "Maybe we're grasping at straws."

She pointed from the bus bench to the spot where Ben had just picked up the bloody piece of fabric. "But what are the odds that on this very spot – where we were expecting to find some graffiti written in chalk – there'd be an image of someone writing graffiti on a wall with chalk? Plus, it's an ad with a very British look and feel to it. What are the odds of that?"

Ben nodded in hesitant agreement. "I agree, the odds for that ... are not good."

McHugh was still scribbling in his notebook. "And what are the odds that it would have the exact same number of letters as the Goulston Street Graffito?" McHugh asked without looking up. "Because it does."

Ben continued to nod, trying to keep an open mind. "Again," he said, "The odds are not good."

"Plus," Barbara added, "look at how he's dressed and what he's sitting on."

Ben moved closer and could see that the boy was dressed as an old-style newsboy, including the traditional cap. A stack of newspapers, tied neatly with twine, was acting as an improvised chair on which he enjoyed his bagel.

"A newsboy. That's an image we've seen before," Ben agreed, moving closer to see if any detail was visible on the stack of newspapers. "The way he's sitting, he's obscuring most of the headline. But I can make out a couple words here ..." he said, getting down on one knee in order to get closer to the advertisement.

"What are they?" Barbara asked.

"Looks like ... 'Double Event,'" Ben answered. As he stood, there was a sudden exclamation from McHugh.

"Aha," McHugh nearly shouted, as he finished his furious scribbling, "What are the odds that if you re-arranged the letters in the phrase *'Sweeten that hot London bagel with Behlmener Fruit Jam,'* you could spell *'The Juwes are the men that will not be blamed for nothing?'*"

He held up his notebook page and showed them his scribblings. "Because you can."

Ben looked from McHugh's notes to the ad on the bench, and then took out his own notebook. "Looks like I'll be making a call to the folks at –" He looked at the frame around the advertisement. "– the fine folks at All Weather Advertising."

He jotted down the phone number while McHugh and Barbara continued to look at the smiling face of the boy in the ad and the seemingly innocent words he had scrawled on the wall behind him.

CHAPTER NINETEEN

After they discovered the message on the bus bench, things got very busy on that particular corner. Several police cars and a crime lab team were there in just a few minutes – so quickly that Jack was actually impressed with their speed.

From his vantage point, he could still see Detective Black and Miss Thomas and Henry McHugh as they talked among themselves and with the newly-arrived officers. He watched them point at the bus bench and the spot where he'd left the bloody fabric and watched them point vaguely in the direction of the British Consulate. For a moment he considered joining the small crowd of on-lookers that had gathered around the site, standing among them to see what he could see and hear what he could hear.

But in the end he decided against it. It wasn't a question of taking the risk. The whole evening had been about taking risks and split-second timing and his planning had paid off – as it always did – but nevertheless he was aware that they had been right behind him every step of the way all night long.

His mind returned, as it often did, to Proverbs: *"As a dog returneth to his vomit, so a fool returneth to his folly."*

There was no reason to push his luck. Not now. Not when the end was in sight.

Plus, he had to admit, he was tired. It had been a long night with multiple stops and numerous clues and then of course there had been the bodies to contend with.

So he watched the crowd for a while and watched as Black and Miss Thomas and Henry McHugh got into a car and drove into the night. He watched the crowd slowly disperse and he watched as the street finally returned to normal.

A few moments later he crossed the street and deliberately – oh so deliberately – walked by the bus bench and the doorway where he'd put the bloody cloth. He walked by the spot as if he walked by there every night and that there was nothing special about it. Or him. He walked by and anyone watching would have thought, "Oh, there's someone walking along who doesn't even know what happened here tonight."

Jack looked innocent and felt innocent and he walked right by the spot and headed home. He had to head home. He was tired. It was late. And there was still more work to do.

Four down. One to go.

CHAPTER TWENTY

"When it comes to billboard advertising, bus bench ads are at the bottom of the food chain, if you want to know the truth."

Ben did want to know the truth, which was why he had tracked down the offices of All-Weather Advertising. Although, to call them "offices" was probably overstating it. All Weather Advertising took up two small rooms between Canal and Walker Streets on the lower East Side, accessible down a quasi-street called Cortlandt Alley.

The rooms were located up three grim and grimy flights of stairs, and were down a dark hall that needed painting, new lighting and something to get the persistent smell of rotten eggs out of the air.

One dusty room was stacked with rolls of printed ads in what appeared to be a system of square cubbies that lined one wall. The other, less dusty, office held a filing cabinet, an old rotary phone, an ancient PC, and a very old desk. Behind the desk sat the equally old owner of All-Weather Advertising, Vincent Washburn.

He sat hunched behind the desk, with several greasy strands of gray hair lacquered over the top of his otherwise bald head. His white shirt was closer to gray in color and although in its day it might have been wash and wear, it was now in desperate need of pressing. His fingers were stained with ink and tobacco, and his eyes behind his thick glasses looked red and watery. Perhaps he's allergic to dust, Ben thought.

Washburn had greeted Ben's phone call and subsequent arrival with a level of disgruntled enthusiasm not normally afforded visits from the police, especially from the officers in Homicide.

However, Ben quickly realized that Washburn undoubtedly didn't get a lot of visitors, or customers for that matter, and that he took any visit as an opportunity to hold forth on the present state of the billboard advertising world. Which he had been doing since Ben had walked into his office twenty minutes earlier.

"When I first got into this lousy business, bus bench ads were the armpit of the business and not a damn thing has changed in thirty-seven years behind this desk," Washburn continued. He took a momentary break in his seemingly non-stop tirade to sip some murky black coffee from an old mug with "Coffee is For Closers" in worn lettering across one side.

"So why, you might very well ask, have I stayed in this armpit for thirty-seven years? I'll tell you. Fads come and go. Today's brand-spanking new technology will be old by next year. There is nothing new under the sun. Yet people will always need to sit while they wait for public transport – I don't care if it's a bus, a train, an Uber, or a spaceship to Mars. And, while they sit on that bench, waiting for that ride, a good dollar can be made with an ad. You can take that to the bank."

He took another sip from his coffee and Ben saw an opportunity to cut in and get the conversation back on track.

"Yes, Mr. Washburn, and it's about one of those bench ads that I'm here today."

Washburn nodded. "So you said in your phone call, Detective. Although I have many pressing engagements this afternoon, I took the time to pull the file on that particular job you were inquiring about."

He swiveled in his chair and rolled it across the uneven wooden floor to the gray and dented four-drawer filing cabinet by the window. One drawer was already open, with a manila file folder resting on the top of the other files.

Ben was pleased to see that Washburn wasn't going to make him go through the motions of getting a court order for the information.

Perhaps, Ben thought, the old man didn't know that he wasn't required by law to divulge this information so freely.

"Now, I watch enough *Law & Order* to know that I don't have to show you anything without a court order," Washburn said, holding up the file for Ben to see. "But if this involves a murder and God forbid one of those deadbeats that I laughingly call my customers is responsible, then I don't want to stand in the way of justice. You might consider that to be an old-fashioned value, but that's the way I feel and that's an end to it."

"Thank you, Mr. Washburn," Ben said, resisting the temptation to reach over and pull the file out of the old man's hand. "It's nice to see a respect for justice in the world today."

"Tell me about it," Washburn said, rolling his chair back to his desk and setting the file down on top of a stack of similar folders. "The world's going to hell in a hand basket. Now, let me see here ..."

He began to slowly page through the five or six sheets of paper in the file. Ben quietly maneuvered himself alongside the desk, in order to look over Washburn's shoulder.

"Oh, yes, I remember this one. It was a one-off."

"What's a one-off?"

Washburn turned and looked up at him, surprised that he had moved. "A one-off is a pain in the ass, that's what it is. It's when a customer just wants to buy one lousy ad on one lousy bench. Usually, they're not very profitable. You'd much rather have them buy a ten-pack – that's ten benches – or pay for a rotation, which is when I rotate a series of ads on a limited number of benches."

Washburn leaned back in his chair and folded his hands across his chest.

"Here's the secret to this business," he intoned, looking up at Ben, "which I'm happy to pass along to a young man such as yourself: Any time we can touch the bench – to paste an ad, to replace an ad, to update an ad – we make money. Paste, replace, update, those are the three key words that I live by. Not that you'd ever get rich, God forbid, but almost anything is better than a one-off."

Washburn leaned forward and continued to look through the file. Ben jotted the words "one-off" and "Paste, Replace, Update" in his notebook, more to look busy than anything else.

"Ahh," Washburn said, tapping one sheet of paper with his stubby and stained index finger. "That's right. He wanted a specific location, which costs extra, so I did make more than a buck fifty off the bastard, good for me."

He turned back to Ben. "You see, you buy a ten pack, I promise to put your ad on ten different benches within a specified geography. But you don't get to pick which benches, unless you want to pay more. Which, apparently, this fellow did, because that's what I sold him. Good for me."

He continued to page through the papers, recreating the sale from the invoice, receipt and work order. "He provided his own artwork, which saved him some money and didn't make me a dime. How I've ever survived in this stupid business, I have to tell you, is a mystery to me."

"So you normally do the artwork?"

"Me?" Washburn laughed. "I can't draw worth a damn. You know those ads on matchbooks, 'Draw Binky the Damned Deer?' I took one of those tests when I was fifteen, sent it in, and they sent me back a signed letter saying I had no talent. And let me tell you, this was not even a form letter. It was a handwritten note from the head of the art school. 'Dear Mr. Washburn, you stink,' or something along those lines, 'thank you very much.'

"So, no, I don't do the art, God forbid. But I have people I can go to and they can do the work and I can mark it up and in the end everybody is happy. But not in this case, because he brought his own art, the cheap so-and-so."

He looked back at the papers in his hands. "And he paid in full up front, which is not so rare, being that he was a first-time customer and I would have insisted on that."

"So, it's not impossible for someone to come in, someone you don't know, like a company you've never heard of, and buy an ad on a bench?"

"Happens all the time, kid. Mostly Realtors, they love to have their big smiling mugs plastered on every bus bench from here to Brooklyn Heights. But, yeah, anyone can buy an ad on a bench. As long as it's not dirty, inflammatory, obscene or likely to incite a riot, I'll sell them the bench space. And they don't even need to come in, anymore.

Nowadays, most of them just e-mail me. Back in the day, this was a face-to-face business, but that's not how we sell today. Not by a longshot."

"And just who was it that you sold the space for the Behlmener Fruit Jam advertisement to?"

Washburn slowly sorted through the handful of papers, examining each one, until he found the invoice.

"Here," he said, pointing to the typed name and address at the top of the form. "That's the guy you're looking for."

Ben looked over Washburn's shoulder at the name he was pointing to, then looked again to make sure he was reading it correctly. He let out a low whistle. Washburn looked up at him.

"You know the schmuck?" he asked.

Ben nodded. "Sort of," he said. "I mean, I've heard of him."

Washburn shook his head. "Montague John Druitt," he said as he clucked his tongue. "I should have known there would be trouble from the name alone."

* * *

Ben crossed the coffee shop and set his cardboard coffee cup on the table by the window. After a moment, Dimitri looked up, his headphones wrapped snugly over his head. He smiled up at Ben and pulled them off. Ben listened for a moment to the tinny sound emanating from within.

"Steve Goodman?" he asked tentatively as he sat down.

"You've got that right, Detective. You're three for three. Yes, the late, great Steve Goodman. '*Somebody Else's Troubles.*'"

He pushed the spacebar on the keyboard and the music stopped. He set the headphones on the table and gestured toward Ben's cup of coffee. "Don't tell me you broke down and paid retail for a damned cup of coffee?"

Ben smiled as he sipped the coffee. "Catholic guilt. I can't keep coming in here without eventually buying something."

"Well I'm glad some cats around here are making money off you. I certainly haven't turned a profit on our relationship. Yet. So, is this strictly a social visit?"

Ben shook his head. "I've hit a brick wall and I'm hoping you can help provide a door or at the very least a window."

Dimitri shook his head sadly. "You've succumbed to metaphor. You must be desperate." He shut his laptop and sat back, giving Ben his full attention. "As we say in the business world, how can I add value?"

Ben looked around the room for a moment, then leaned in toward Dimitri. "Our killer bought an ad. On a bus bench."

"No shit?" Dimitri stifled a laugh. "Really. Well, I gotta say, you don't often see that sort of behavior in a serial killer. What exactly was the dude advertising?"

"Nothing, really. He's just playing with us, doing his version of the Goulston Street Graffito."

"The Graffito, was it? Looks like you've gone through something of a learning curve since the last time you were in here."

Ben smiled and nodded. "I'm getting there. Anyway, as you might expect, he covered his tracks pretty cleanly. Did everything on-line, set up a dummy payment account through PayPal, which had just enough money in it to pay for the ad. He provided a name, address, phone number – all phony. And since the ad company got paid in full, they had no reason to suspect anything. So we're at a dead end."

Dimitri considered this news. "How's the coffee?" he finally asked.

Ben took another sip. "It tastes okay. I mean, what do you expect? It's just coffee."

"Don't let anyone around this place hear you talking that shit. It's not coffee, man it's an experience. It's the taste of freedom."

Ben took another sip and shrugged. "Maybe I shouldn't have ordered decaf."

"Yeah, you screwed up there." Dimitri took a sip from his own coffee cup. "So, if you and the boys in blue have hit a dead end, what makes you figure I can make a difference? Or are you just grasping at straws?"

"I'm grasping at every straw I can find."

"Yeah, so would I if I was in your shoes. This dude's had four successful killings and if he stays true to the real Jack the Ripper, he'll bang out his last murder and then disappear into the history books."

"Not on my watch." Ben pulled a slip of paper out of his pocket. "We may have bought a break. The on-line form he filled out in order to buy the ad has a nice feature – it automatically grabs your e-mail address, so that they can get back to you with any questions about your order. Now, he probably knew that, but there's always a chance that he didn't. In which case, I now have an e-mail address. Which might be his."

He held out the paper for Dimitri, who took it without looking at it.

"If you have his e-mail address, why not just send him an e-mail?"

Ben shook his head. "And what exactly would I say in this e-mail?"

Dimitri considered this question and nodded in agreement. "I see your point," he finally agreed. "So, what do you want me to do with it?"

Ben shrugged. "Well, I'll admit that I don't have a detailed plan here. I was kind of counting on you to fill in that particular blank."

"'Cause I'm the computer guy, right? And us computer guys can just make things happen as if by magic, right? Thanks for the faith, man." Dimitri opened his laptop and unfolded the piece of paper.

"Maybe you could send out a mass e-mailing from the Ripper website," Ben said, taking another swallow of coffee. "I'm not sure what it would say … something that makes him want to respond. Something that grabs his attention."

Dimitri typed a few keystrokes and then looked at the slip of paper. He stopped typing and looked up at Ben. "Actually, we don't need to bother with those shenanigans," he said.

"We don't? How come?"

"'Cause fate has smiled on you, my man. One quick smile, but sometimes that's all you need." He held up the slip of paper. "I know this address. I know this dude. He's one of my guys."

"One of your guys? How do you mean?"

"I mean, on the website. The Ripper site. He's been on it from the beginning, or if not the beginning then darn close to it. He's one of my experts. His name's Malcolm Wright. I've even met him – he was at the Ripper Conference. The dude lives in Brooklyn. A quiet dude. Shit, he lives with his mother. Talk about fitting the stereotype."

"And he works on your website?"

"Damn straight. I made him a monitor very early on. He's diligent, I'll give him that. Knows his shit. He's in charge of one of the message boards."

"Which one?"

Dimitri started navigating through his files, looking for his address book. "He runs the board about the Victims. The Ripper's victims."

The two men exchanged a look. Dimitri looked back at the computer screen and started typing. "I've got his contact information right here. You got a pencil?"

Ben had his notepad open and was poised to write.

* * *

Ben arranged to meet Barbara at the Rizzoli Bookstore, on West 57th, between Fifth and Sixth avenues, where she was doing a book signing. He left a message for McHugh at his hotel to join them there.

Ben had never been in Rizzoli's before, although he had walked past it a number of times over the years. He was more of a Strand Books guy, down on Broadway, and he felt a little out of place at this fancier, Fifth Avenue shop. So, he wandered gingerly through the store, keeping one eye on the ever-shortening line in front of Barbara's signing table.

At the same time, he scanned the various titles on the shelves and leafed half-heartedly through the hefty coffee table books on display. Who buys all these books, he wondered, as he paged through a several-pound, heavily illustrated volume on Picasso that seemed to catalog and reproduce every single drawing, painting, sketch and doodle the artist had ever committed to paper? Maybe nobody did.

He set the heavy book back on the display table and looked over at Barbara again. She sat behind a small wooden table, wearing a white sweater and black slacks, and she looked great. She had a stack of her books in front of her, and she talked patiently with each customer, autographing new and old books, answering questions and generally schmoozing with her public like a pro. She turned and caught his eye, giving him a quick smile before turning her attention back to her next customer and their request.

Ben smiled and then recognized McHugh coming through the large front doors. He waved him over and soon they were both standing in the stacks, patiently waiting for the last of Barbara's fans to leave.

"Thanks for coming," Ben said quietly. There was something about the store that made him adopt his best library behavior. "She's almost done."

He gestured over toward Barbara and McHugh chuckled.

"Ah, yes," he said. "The dreaded book signing."

"I suppose that's old hat for you."

McHugh shrugged. "Well, not often in stores as nice as this one, no. But for a short while I was all the vogue at small bookstores, mystery conferences and, of course, all the Ripper events."

"Only for a short while? Why was that?"

"Oh, there's still a solid if rabid fan base, no doubt," McHugh said. "The book has stayed in print longer than it deserves and there might even be a tad bit of interest in doing a new edition. However, my mistake as an author and researcher was that I merely laid out the facts."

Ben squinted at him. "I'm not sure I understand. Isn't that the point of the book, to lay out the facts?"

McHugh chuckled. "Well, yes, I suppose so, but there's no controversy there. No, no, my boy, if you want to make a splash in the Ripper dodge, you've got to name a suspect and then spell out the key facts that prove your point and here's why, blah, blah, blah, while conveniently ignoring all facts to the contrary. And the more outlandish your claim, the better. *Habeas corpus*, as it were."

"So why didn't you do that?"

McHugh looked at Ben for a long moment before answering. "My publisher would have been much happier if I had, I can tell you that much. But I just couldn't bring myself to do it. Not with a straight face, at any length."

"Sorry to keep you waiting." Barbara had snuck up on them. The crowd around her signing table had dispersed and an assistant from the publishing house was boxing up the remaining books.

"Not a problem," McHugh said, tipping his hat. "I just got here myself."

"My right hand is just about numb from signing," she said. "I was ambidextrous when I was a kid, but the nuns in grade school wouldn't hear of that, so they forced me to only use my right hand for writing. I sure could have used the left hand today.

"So," Barbara continued, as she set her purse down and started to pull on a light jacket, "what did you learn about the bus bench?"

Ben stepped forward and helped her with the jacket. "The ad on the bus bench," he said, giving her collar a final tug into place, "was designed and paid for by an individual. I suspect you'll recognize the name. Montague Druitt."

McHugh's eyebrows shot up. "Druitt?"

"Montague John Druitt?" Barbara echoed.

"Well, that's the name he used. He covered his tracks pretty well, but he made one mistake – we were able to grab his e-mail address. Turns out, he's a guy named Malcolm Wright."

Ben started walking toward the door and the other two followed. "He lives in Brooklyn. Which is where we're headed right now."

"To see this Malcolm?" Barbara asked.

"No. We already tried to do that as soon as we figured out who he was. Apparently, Malcolm disappeared a couple of days ago."

"So why are we going to Brooklyn?" McHugh asked.

"Because I need your assistance," Ben said. "We're about to take our lives in our hands.

Barbara stopped in her tracks. "Why would that be?" she asked tentatively.

"We're going to Brooklyn," Ben answered. "To talk to his mother."

He held the door for them and pointed them toward a car waiting at the curb.

CHAPTER TWENTY-ONE

"**I**'m so sick of Jack the Flippin' Ripper, I could puke. If you'll pardon the expression."

Ben and Barbara and McHugh nodded, collectively pardoning the expression. They were seated, uncomfortably and awkwardly, in the apartment living room of Mrs. Ida Wright. The living room was a small, dark room in a small, dark apartment.

Clearly, she had lived there for years, or if that was not the case, then she had recently taken the place over from a similarly fussy old lady. Nearly every surface was covered with dust and under much of that dust were ceramic figurines of small, wide-eyed children.

The apartment, on Driggs Avenue in Brooklyn, was close enough to the river that she would have had a river view, were it not for – as she had put it, loudly and at great length – "those damned condos hadn't popped up outta friggin' nowhere!"

In the fifteen short minutes they had been there, they had learned a lot about Ida Wright and her many and varied opinions. For instance, she was suspicious of anyone who wasn't white; she was tired of being "jerked around" by the "shysters" at her HMO; she was fed up with the foreign policy of the last four sitting Presidents; and she had it on very good authority that not only had the moon landing been completely faked, but that NASA had sent manned teams to Mars on more than one occasion.

Ben hardly got a word in edgewise. Barbara and McHugh, wisely, didn't even make the attempt.

Ida was, Ben figured, somewhere in her mid-seventies. She looked shrunken, as if she had somehow withered into a miniature form of an earlier, larger self. Her wispy gray hair was cut short, which made him suspect that there may have been some chemotherapy in her recent past.

She was not, however, lacking in energy. She had welcomed them with a feisty wariness and insisted on serving them tea in mis-matched cups. Along with the tea she proudly offered stale cookies from an ancient bag of Chips Ahoy, which was so old that Ben suspected it came from an era long before "Use By" dates had been invented.

And then, once they were all seated and sipping the thin, sour tea, she held court on topics that seemingly bounced randomly through her brain, finally landing back where Ben had started the conversation: the controversial subject of Jack the Ripper.

"So, you're no fan of Jack the Ripper?" Ben interjected quickly, hoping to get her back on track.

Ida's face snapped into a scowl and she shook her head as she took a quick sip of the watery tea. "Why would a person be a fan? Some nut kills a few poor girls two hundred years ago. So why should I get into endless debates with other morons on who did what to who ... where ... on what street ... which night ... wearing what color hat? Please."

She picked up the teapot and offered it around but got no takers. She set it down on the tipsy table next to her wooden rocking chair, which creaked loudly every time she moved.

"But your son, Malcolm," Ben said. "He's interested in Jack the Ripper, right?"

"Dear, if he were just interested, it wouldn't be a problem," Ida sighed. "Just between you and me, that boy passed 'interested' a long, long time ago." She gave Barbara a sullen look, and then turned to Ben. "I recognize that one from the TV," she said, gesturing toward Barbara.

Barbara smiled weakly, not sure where this conversational tack was heading.

Ben jumped in. "As I mentioned," he said quickly, "Miss Thomas and Mr. McHugh are experts on the subject of Jack the Ripper. Both of them have graciously been assisting the investigation –"

Ida ignored him and turned back to Barbara, leaning forward and tapping her on the knee for emphasis.

"Forgive me for saying this, but my Malcolm didn't like that book of yours," she said. "And when he'd see you on the TV, he'd turn down the sound and use language that I don't care to hear in polite company. I told him so, too."

Barbara looked to McHugh for help, but for the second time since she'd met him, he appeared to be very interested in something at the bottom of his teacup.

Ben plowed forward. "So, Mrs. Wright, do you have any idea exactly when Malcolm left and where he may have gone to?" he asked.

Ida shrugged. "It's hard to say with him. Sometimes he just goes. Then he comes back. He's done that for years. Once he went away for nearly three weeks and when he came back, he picked up our conversation exactly where we'd left it.

"We'd been talking about public school vouchers, of all things, and three weeks later he walks in the door and says, 'And another thing – I think vouchers are unconstitutional.' Just like that. Like he hadn't been gone at all. You see, that's the thing about Malcolm. He always comes back."

"But normally he lives here, with you?"

Ida had just bitten into what Ben could only assume, based on his own recent experience, was a stale cookie. She shook her head and pointed toward the ceiling while she chewed and swallowed.

"No, no," she finally said, "Malcolm lives upstairs, in his own apartment. You see, we own the whole building, so we can sort of take our pick of the apartments. My father owned the building, now I own the building, someday Malcolm will own it." She finished chewing and took another sip of tea.

"But he had to get his own place," she continued, "Because we were running out of room. So, he moved upstairs. Right after the Devries' got divorced, we took back their place. Apartment 3C. It needed a lot of work, but Malcolm fixed it up nice. Or so he says; I'll have to take his word for it. I never get up there."

"Why did you need more room?" Ben asked, looking around at all the figurines that littered the living room.

"For his crap. His Ripper crap," she said. "He's got tons of Ripper crap. You can go see his apartment for yourself if you want. Trust me, it's got all the Ripper crap you'll ever want to see and then some."

She stood up stiffly and led them over to the front door, stopping to take a key from a hook by the door frame. She opened the door for them, stepped into the murky hall, and pointed a pale, bony finger up the staircase that began its ascent right outside her door.

"He's up two flights, 3C, last apartment toward the back," she said, handing the key to Ben. "I'd show you myself, but me and stairs aren't getting along so good lately. Plus, between you, me and the fence post, I'm tired of looking at his Ripper crap."

Ben nodded as he took the key and headed up the stairs. Barbara squeezed past Ida and followed him, feeling the woman's icy stare as she did. McHugh brought up the rear and Ida grabbed his arm as he walked past. She glanced up the stairs to make sure that Barbara was out of earshot, then spoke to McHugh in a dramatic whisper.

"I recognized you too," she said, "but I didn't want to say anything in front of – that one." She cocked her head up the stairs toward Barbara, who was just disappearing around the second-floor landing. "Malcolm really likes your book. He's worn it out, he reads it so much. He calls it The Ripper Bible."

McHugh smiled warmly. "Thank you. That's very kind."

"The policeman," she continued. "He mentioned, on the phone, that Malcolm was using the name Druitt ..."

"That's my understanding," McHugh said, nodding. "After Montague John Druitt, one of the Ripper suspects."

Ida tugged on her left earlobe for a moment, folding it back and forth between her thumb and forefinger. "Yeah," she said. "I know the name."

She tugged on her earlobe again and ran her bony hand through her close-cropped gray hair, scratched the top of her ear, and then leaned in closer to McHugh. He discreetly tried to step back, but he was already pressed against the doorframe.

"You see, the thing is ..." she said, haltingly, choosing her words with care. "Malcolm has always had a Top Five list. For years. His Top

Five Ripper suspects. He changes it all the time, adding people, taking names off it. Hutchinson's on, Hutchinson's off, Cohen comes and goes. Tumblety's in, Tumblety's out. He'd spend hours arguing with people on his computer about suspects. You know what I mean?"

"Yes," McHugh assured her. "It's a common practice in the field. Suspects fall in and out of favor, old evidence is looked at in a new way. Suspects move up and down – or on and off – everyone's lists continually."

She looked away from him, thinking, trying to find the best way to express her growing doubts. "Yeah, well, he used to show me that list all the time. He'd write it up and show it to me, all proud. When he started, he actually typed it and took his time with it, believe me.

"He had a laminated version for a while there that he carried around in his wallet. Then he got his computer and that made the whole damn process faster, so he'd change the list more often. Probably because it was easier."

McHugh nodded, patiently. Ida shook her head for a moment, then continued.

"Over the years, there were two things that never changed on that list," she finally said. "The first was that one suspect was always on it – he'd change the suspect's position, move him up and down, but he was always on the list. Malcolm called him 'Unknown Male.' You know that one?"

McHugh nodded gravely. "Yes, I do. 'Unknown Male' is, in my humble opinion, perhaps the best suspect we have," he said.

"There's one other thing that was always true about that list. That name, Montague Druitt, was never on it," she said with finality. "Never on his list. Not once. Not ever."

She let her words linger in the air, tapping her index finger into his chest defiantly to make her point. "What do you make of that?" she asked.

* * *

To say that Malcolm's apartment was "full of Ripper crap," as Ida had said many, many times in the short time they'd spent with her, was an understatement.

After Ben had unlocked the door and flipped on the light switch, he and Barbara stood for a long moment in the doorway, looking with growing awe and a little unease at the contents of the overcrowded apartment.

To begin with, there were bookcases, about ten of them, none of which matched and all of which were over six feet tall. They were filled with books, pamphlets, VHS tapes, DVDs, maps and manuscripts, giving the living room the look of a poorly organized library.

But on closer inspection, that wasn't really true, because although all the items on the shelves were placed haphazardly, there was an overall sense of order and purpose to the way things were filed. Books and other items about Ripper suspects took up four complete bookcases.

Another two bookcases were filled to bursting with material about the social and economic conditions of London's East End at the time of the murders.

Only one wall was free of shelves, and it was covered with a floor-to-ceiling blow-up of an historic Whitechapel map, circa 1888. Yellow sticky notes, some of which looked quite old and curled, were splattered across the photo blow-up and covered with small bird-like notes and arrows pointing to locations on the map.

In one corner of the room sat a large, weathered wooden desk with a new laptop computer on it, which looked strangely out of place among all the other items in the apartment. The rest of the desk was littered with opened books, notebooks, and single scraps of paper with short phrases scrawled on them.

Ben approached the desk, glanced down at the notes and saw sentences like "Tumblety travel documents?" and "The fence at the rear of #29 – recently repaired?" and "Maybrick Diary – check on results of paper tests!"

"Don't you need a search warrant for something like this?" Barbara asked as she made her way through the bookcases and came up behind him. Ben turned and patted his coat pocket.

"I have a search warrant. But past experience has taught me that it's more pleasant all around when the owner gives you permission."

"Oh my," McHugh said as he stepped into the room.

"It's something, isn't it?" Ben said, crossing to him and then veering left to check out a "Jack the Ripper" calendar that hung crookedly on the wall. The calendar was several years out of date and as he quickly flipped through the pages Ben noted that it contained only the months of August through November.

"In a word, yes," McHugh said as he spotted a couple of books on a nearby shelf. "Goodness. These are very rare." He continued to scan the other books on that shelf, his eyes widening as he did.

"And these are rarer still," he said, pulling one volume out for closer examination, mumbling a quiet exclamation from time to time as he flipped through the book's pages. "I've seen people offer hundreds of dollars for this particular book at on-line auctions," he commented. "And this gentleman owns three of them! Remarkable."

Ben moved out of the cramped, bookcase-filled living room down a short hall into an even smaller kitchen. Very little of the room was available for traditional kitchen pursuits. More stacks of books were piled up on the tiny kitchen table, and much of the floor space was filled with piles of back issues of magazines.

Ben squatted down and riffled through the stacks, finding assorted titles such as "The Ripperologist," "Ripperana," "Ripper Notes," "The Whitechapel Journal," and "Ripperoo," which on closer examination turned out to have been published in Australia.

As Ben got up, he noticed still another book, lying open on the kitchen counter. He picked it up to see the topic and was not too surprised to see that it was about Jack the Ripper. He was taken aback, however, to see that it was a copy of Barbara's book. He began to page through it.

Barbara leaned into the kitchen. She would have stepped in, but with Ben in there, and the stacks of magazines on the floor, there wasn't space for another person in the little room.

"Find anything interesting?" she asked.

Ben nodded as he continued to flip through the book. "His mother was right," he said. "He really didn't like your book. He's written notes on nearly every page."

He handed the copy of the book to her and she quickly began flipping through it.

"If it's any consolation, he misspelled 'claptrap,'" Ben said, looking over her shoulder as she scanned Malcolm's notes.

"Yes, that helps," Barbara said dryly. She flipped past several more pages, finding that Ben had been correct: there were notes in the margins on nearly every page.

"Next time tell your publisher not to make the margins so wide, and then maybe people won't have the space to write things like that in them," Ben suggested.

"Good thought. I'll make a note."

An idea occurred to Ben and he reached for the book. "Can I look at it again for a second?"

"Yes, I think I've seen enough," Barbara said, handing it back to him. He quickly turned to the front of the book, until he found what he was looking for.

"Well, he may have hated the book, but he did go to the trouble to get you to sign it for him."

He held the book open to the title page, where Barbara could see her flowery signature flowing across the bottom third of the page.

"Although apparently, he didn't want you to personalize it." Ben looked at the signature again. "So, it looks like you and Malcolm Wright have met in person at some point."

"We might have," Barbara said, "But keep in mind that the publisher also offers autographed copies on their website. Plus, it's possible that he bought this used on eBay or Amazon."

"I suppose there's a chance of that," Ben said, closing the book. "Given the way he felt about it, I'd hate to think he paid full price for it."

Barbara was working on the right phrasing for a snappy comeback, but Ben had already moved out of the kitchen and down the narrow hall, which was lined with large blow-ups of the autopsy photos of the Ripper victims.

She followed Ben, avoiding looking directly at the grisly photos as she moved down the hall. She came to a dead stop when she reached the doorway to the bedroom.

Ben was standing in the middle of the small room, but from Barbara's perspective it looked as if he had stepped back in time. The walls looked aged, the furniture consisted of saggy antiques, and there was even a faux fireplace on one wall and a faux window painted on the wall by the door to the room.

In addition to the bed, which was close to the door, the room held two tables and a chair. Across from the faux fireplace sat a small cupboard. Above the fireplace was a framed print of a painting of a mournful woman, looking longingly out at the ocean.

"This is an interesting decorating choice," Ben commented, looking around the room. "Something about it … it looks kind of familiar."

"It should," Barbara responded dryly. She couldn't make herself step into the room. "He's re-created Mary Kelly's room at 13 Miller's Court. The only thing missing is the body on the bed."

Ben took in this new information, scanning the room while he gave a low whistle of admiration. Before he could comment further, they heard a grunt, a short yell and a crash from the living room. Ben pushed past Barbara and raced down the narrow hall into the front room. McHugh was sprawled on the floor, with several books on top of him and one of the bookcases leaning haphazardly against the wall.

"Are you okay?" Ben asked. "What happened?"

"I'm fine. The cloth-eared git blind-sided me," McHugh said, pushing books off his chest and sitting up. "The bugger went that way," he added, pointing to the apartment's open front door.

Ben reached into his coat and unsnapped the holster on his gun, while Barbara moved to McHugh's side to help him up.

"Give him a hand," Ben said as he headed toward the door.

He glanced down the hall in the direction they had come from, and then looked in the other direction, just in time to catch a glimpse of Malcolm, in a bright red plaid shirt, disappearing in a blur down the back stairs.

Ben broke into a run and raced after him.

CHAPTER TWENTY-TWO

Ben used to run around the reservoir in Central Park three to four times a week (during good weather), almost religiously, from age nineteen until just before his thirtieth birthday. Twice around was just a tad over three miles and that had always felt like the perfect length for a run. It was just enough so that he felt like he had really exercised, but not so much that it wiped him out for the rest of the day.

He had fallen away from the practice about five years before, not because he didn't like or need the exercise, but because he had ultimately found it boring. Really boring. Running the same path every day, following or passing the same runners, none of whom looked like they were having any fun at all. And, he finally realized, neither was he.

He never achieved the legendary 'runner's high' he had heard so much about, and so one day he just stopped running. He folded his shorts and put away his running shoes and didn't give it another thought.

Today, as he raced down three flights of stairs after Malcolm Wright, he began to regret that decision for the first time.

By the time Ben made it to the back door of the building he was already winded. He recognized that as a bad sign, because when you thought about it, so far all he'd done was run down a couple flights of steps. Yet, even with a friendly assist from gravity, he was still panting and starting to sweat.

The back door was still slowly closing as he came down off the last two steps. As he pushed the door open, he could just see Malcolm – or at least his red plaid shirt – as he climbed over the battered and worn six-foot redwood fence that circled the apartment building's small backyard.

Ben headed toward that spot on the fence and then stopped, quickly scanning the yard until he found a gate. He knew he'd lose a few precious seconds if he opted for the gate, but that loss was probably minimal compared to the time he'd lose trying (and, let's face it, probably failing) to scale that fence.

He remembered a fortune cookie he had gotten once: "With age comes wisdom," it had said. That was probably true, but right now he needed speed more than he needed wisdom. He also realized that he'd probably feel more confident right now if it weren't for that twinge in his left knee that said ... what? Probably "stop running" was the primary message, but he knew that wasn't currently an option.

He pushed his way through the gate and spotted Malcolm several hundred yards ahead of him, racing down the alley, which emptied out onto Fifth Street.

Moments later, Malcolm exited the alley and turned left at Fifth Street, and when Ben came out of the mouth of the alley, he was pleased to see that he was at least keeping pace with his prey. He wasn't catching or overtaking him, that was true; but he also wasn't falling behind.

There wasn't much traffic on the street and even less on the sidewalk. The sun had finally broken through the clouds after threatening rain all day, and it had suddenly become a beautiful fall day. The few people that Ben did pass all seemed unperturbed by the foot race that was transpiring around them.

Ben didn't know this neighborhood, but he recognized that they were running parallel to the Williamsburg Bridge, which was above them on their right. The sound of the traffic overhead provided a constant white noise that meshed neatly with Ben's heartbeat, which was the only other sound he was hearing besides his occasional gasps for breath.

In front of him, about two hundred yards, was the blur of Malcolm's red plaid shirt. He was moving steadily up Fifth Street toward the old, white domed synagogue that had long ago stopped being a synagogue and was now ... Ben couldn't remember and realized that it didn't matter.

The red of Malcolm's shirt blended smoothly with the red brick buildings that he passed, the graffiti on the old brick creating a colorful, blurring mosaic for Ben.

The blare of a car horn followed by the screech of brakes and the sound of metal hitting metal signaled to Ben that Malcolm had crossed an intersection without stopping. A few short moments later he found himself at that same intersection, where the two drivers whose cars had collided were out of their vehicles and beginning the dance of anger and rage that was a familiar sight in any large city.

They yelled. They screamed. One suggested to the other that his parents had not been lawfully wed before his conception. Ben deftly zigzagged around their crushed vehicles and screaming voices and continued to run.

Ben was starting to feel the heat. He hadn't realized how hot it had gotten that afternoon, but the now clear and cloudless sky provided no break from the sun, which beat down on the concrete sidewalk and pushed up waves of hot air around his ankles. Sweat was running off his forehead into his eyes, while more sweat found its way off his scalp and down the back of his neck, where it was starting to soak his collar.

As he used his coat sleeve to quickly wipe the sweat from his face, he saw Malcolm, in the distance, swerving to the right off the sidewalk and into Fifth Street, cutting diagonally across the street. He was nimbly dodging cars and heading toward ... the ramp that led up to the bridge. The long, steep ramp.

"Dammit," Ben muttered between gasps for air. The good news was that once Malcolm got up to the bridge's pedestrian track, he'd be easier to grab, as his only escape – short of running back toward Ben – was on the Manhattan side of the bridge.

The bad news was that he had to make it up the long, nearly vertical ramp and Ben was beginning to seriously think that he might not have it in him. He made a cursory check of traffic as he cut across the street, stopping for a moment to let an aggressive car pass, and then he headed toward the base of the ramp.

Looking up as he ran, he could see quick flashes of Malcolm's red shirt up the ramp, already quite ahead of him. Ben grabbed the handrail, stopped to take a quick breath, and then realized that if he didn't keep moving, he would collapse right then and there. And how would that look? He started up the ramp, his thighs and knees throbbing as his feet slammed heavily into the concrete.

Ben continued to climb, fighting gravity with every step, deciding that as soon as he got to the top and was sure that Malcolm was headed toward the Manhattan side of the bridge, he'd stop and call for back-up. And also try to breathe again. Plus, maybe throw up.

Ben suddenly found himself in the midst of high-speed bike traffic, as bicyclists raced at him down the ramp and other bicyclists shouted from behind him as they made their way up the ramp and started to hit their full stride.

Many of the bicyclists headed toward him were already pissed off, as they'd had to swerve to avoid hitting Malcolm. He dodged his way down the bike path ahead of Ben, deftly skirting the bikes and starting to put more distance between Ben and himself on the deck's long straight-away toward the island of Manhattan.

Ben realized that if Malcolm knocked one of the bikers down and stole a bike, he'd be gone and off the bridge before back-up could arrive. So, he opted to hold off on that call for back-up and continued to run, dodging the oncoming bikes as Malcolm, the red of his shirt blending with the red chain link fence that enclosed the bikeway, adroitly side-stepped bike after bike.

For a brief moment as he ran and panted and ached, Ben remembered the controversy that had arisen when this bike path had first been put in place.

For years, pedestrians and bikers had shared the decks on either side of the bridge, with occasionally bloody and deadly results. The move to separate the paths – with pedestrians on the south side getting the view of the Brooklyn and Manhattan Bridges, while the bicyclists took the north side and its view of the river and the city skyline – had been greeted with cheers and rejoicing by both contingents.

The only bump in the plan had been, literally, bumps in the decking. These bumps proved to be no problem to pedestrians but quickly were found to be dangerous and nearly deadly to the fast- pedaling bikers. Painting the bumps a bright, eye-popping color was discovered to be no real solution, as the bumps still slowed the bike traffic and made the journey across the bridge an unpleasant and rough one.

An outcry went out, petitions were signed, a couple lawsuits were threatened, and soon the north half of the bridge deck was closed again, only to re-open several weeks later with the bumps gone and a clear path in place for bicyclists of any speed to enjoy.

Ben longed for the days of those speed bumps as he negotiated his way down the bike path toward Manhattan. He kept Malcolm in sight as he dodged the angry riders, with the sound of their yells and curses following a moment later.

Why was that, Ben wondered. Why did he see them first and hear them after they had already passed? Was that the Doppler effect he'd heard mentioned in high school science class? Before he could sink too far into that oxygen- deprived reverie, he saw a flash of red ahead and realized that Malcolm had left the bike path and was climbing up the chain link fence that separated the deck from the river below.

Ben stopped in his tracks, not quite believing the sight, as Malcolm – still a couple hundred yards ahead of him – almost effortlessly scaled the ten-foot high fence, climbing hand over hand. Once he'd reached the top of the fence, he swung his legs over and as his body passed over the top of the fence, he simply let go.

Malcolm seemed to hang in the air for a long moment, like a freeze-frame of a sporting event. All sound stopped and even the breeze that blew across the top of the bridge seemed to come to a standstill. Then, after what seemed like several long seconds, motion, sound and wind returned. And Malcolm fell, down and down, out of sight.

Ben dodged several bikes, coming from both directions, as he ran to the fence, looking down just in time to see Malcolm's body hit the river below. Ben saw a quick flash of the red plaid shirt in the water, and then another one.

And then nothing but the flowing water.

* * *

The body came to land several hours later, a few miles down the shore near Bath's Beach off the Belt Parkway. By the time Ben got the call, the Coast Guard Rescue Team was on the scene, pulling the corpse from a mooring where it had snagged and surfaced about twenty feet from shore.

Ben stood on the shore and watched them work, hands in his pockets, nervously shifting his weight from side to side. The sun was heading toward the horizon and the light was changing the water's color from a dark, emerald green to an even darker red.

Ben heard a car door slam behind him to his left and then the sound of footsteps moving across the gravel parking lot. A few moments later, Dale Harkness was standing by his side, a toothpick hanging lazily out of the corner of his mouth.

They grunted a greeting and nodded at each other and then returned their gaze to the Coast Guard boat, which had a small crane and winch on the back. Several Coast Guard workers on the boat fed the line into the water, working with a diver who floated near the surface, where he attached the line to a harness around the body.

They heard an engine fire up on the boat and a moment later the line came up out of the river, taut, pulling a water-soaked body behind it.

"They got him?" Harkness asked, never taking his eyes off the body.

Ben waited a moment until the form had been pulled out of the water. He recognized the red plaid shirt, which limply hung off the body.

"Looks like it."

They watched for a few more moments while Malcolm's body was lifted over to the boat and then lowered out of sight onto the deck. Coast Guard workers hovered over it, presumably removing the harness and wire.

"What did they find in the apartment?" Ben asked, turning to head back to his car. Harkness watched for a moment longer, then followed.

"They're still digging," he said. "The place is like a freaking Jack the Ripper museum. However, we got what looks like a suicide note ..."

He pulled a plastic evidence bag out of his coat pocket. Ben stopped walking and squinted to read the handwritten note within.

"'Since Friday I felt the best thing for me was to die,'" he read aloud, handing the bag back to Harkness. "That's pretty straight-forward."

Harkness pocketed the note again and turned to look at the Coast Guard boat. They had lowered the crane and were steering the boat away, up river to their nearest docking station. "Well, I'm sorry we didn't get him alive," he said, opening his car door, "but I sure appreciate his timing."

Ben frowned. "How do you mean?"

"Now that he's gone, we don't have to deal with the final murder in the cycle. Do you have any idea how many Mary Kellys there are in Manhattan, not to mention in the boroughs?"

Ben shook his head. "Probably a lot, right?"

"An army of them. The first count we got was nearly fifty, and that's not counting maiden names, middle names, nicknames or any other bullshit we didn't think of."

He turned and watched as the boat chugged upstream, out of sight. He spit as he climbed back into his car.

"Good riddance, you batshit bastard."

CHAPTER TWENTY-THREE

The serving of alcohol on or within the grounds of a New York City police station was strictly against the law. Everyone agreed on that point. No one could remember the exact wording of the statute, or which statute or code it was, but everyone concurred that it was a violation of some sort. They all agreed on that salient point as another champagne cork popped in the middle of the squad room and plastic glasses were held out for a second or third refill.

Barbara and McHugh had both been summoned to the station to hear the findings of the Medical Examiner's preliminary report – that the body dragged from the river was in fact Malcolm Wright and that he had died from a broken neck and bodily trauma sustained in a fatal fall from the Williamsburg Bridge. They had come expecting to hear grim news and had, instead, stumbled into a party.

The first thing Barbara noticed upon entering was that the mood in the squad room was radically different from past visits. She sensed that from the moment she walked in, when Dale Harkness, of all people, shouted her name from across the room. He pushed his way through the crowd to give her a surprisingly warm and enthusiastic hug.

She shared a mystified look with McHugh, who raised a clear plastic glass to her in a silent toast from across the room, and then fell back into what looked to be an intense and animated conversation with Officer Klingbile.

"We got the sonovabitch," Harkness said, cackling. "Dead or alive, makes no never mind to me."

He thrust a plastic glass into her hand and quickly filled it from the champagne bottle. He then handed an empty plastic cup to Ben, who had just appeared at Barbara's side.

"Black, you old so-and-so, have one with the team." Harkness filled Ben's cup sloppily and then raised his own cup to both of them, preparing to make a toast. He thought better of it and instead turned to the room at large.

"Can I have your attention, please," Harkness said, raising his voice to compete with the general clamor in the room. "Hey, shut the hell up!" he yelled, finally quieting the raucous group. Once he was sure that he had everyone's complete attention, Harkness modulated the volume of his voice down to a more socially-acceptable level.

"You can all get back to your heavy partying in a second. I just want to take a moment," he said, as he raised his cup, "to acknowledge the exceptional work of this unit. We all know that no one person is ever responsible for nailing a case of this magnitude. It's the contributions of every man – and woman – on the team. So – let's hear it for this freakin' team!"

The crowd in the room responded with a rousing "Hear, hear!" They all held up their glasses and just as quickly downed the contents. Barbara took a generous sip from her cup and looked to Ben, who was still holding the full, untouched cup of champagne that Harkness had poured for him.

He held the plastic cup up to her and she tapped her cup against his in a short, informal toast. Then, in a quick move unseen by the others, he poured the contents of his cup into hers, refilling her cup and leaving him with an empty. She smiled and took another sip.

"One of the drawbacks to hanging out with someone who doesn't drink," she said quietly, "is that it's just about doubled my intake of alcohol."

"Imagine what your world would be like if I had the same problem with chocolate," he offered.

"I'd be as big as a house," she said. "But I'd be a very contented house."

Ben was about to respond, but was interrupted by Harkness, who apparently wasn't quite finished with his speechifying.

"And I want to offer some special recognition to two members of this team," he continued, "who provided knowledge and insight that made – well, that probably made all the difference in this case. They certainly and without question saved lives. And make no mistake about it – they were and are a vital part of this team. Please join me in congratulating DCI Henry McHugh and Miss Barbara Thomas. Our Ripperologists!"

This produced a wave of spontaneous applause throughout the room. On his side of the room McHugh tipped his hat to the crowd. Across the room Barbara raised her plastic cup and toasted the group.

Harkness continued his speech. "Now, I know," he said, "that there were some in this room who, in the beginning, firmly resisted making them a part of this investigation –"

This comment was met with yelps of laughter all around, followed by cries of "Who could that have been?" and "No kidding!" Harkness smiled and waved them off with his free hand, then held his cup up to Barbara and McHugh.

"Yeah, yeah," he said. "But I want to take this chance to thank them now ... because I think you all know I'll deny it later."

This produced the biggest laugh yet, with no one finding it funnier than Harkness himself. Barbara scanned the room full of laughing people, finding only one who wasn't joining in the mirth.

McHugh, looking distracted, finally noticed her gaze. He gave her a wan smile and emptied his plastic cup in one quick gulp.

* * *

Someone, somehow, ordered a half-dozen pizzas, adding a new burst of energy to the party, which after ninety minutes had begun to wane. Harkness searched through the stack of flat pizza boxes, trying as he put it, "to find some goddamned meat" among the double cheese and vegetarian pizzas in the pile.

He grumbled and cursed as he pulled out box after box, finally giving a sharp yell of victory when he found a lone, greasy slice of sausage pizza in an otherwise empty box. He bit the end off savagely, and then searched around for something to absorb the grease that dribbled down his chin. A napkin was offered, and he took it, wiping his face and then looking up to see that the gift had come from McHugh.

"Thanks. Nothing better than cold, greasy pizza." McHugh smiled distractedly and nodded. "Indeed."

Harkness took another large bite and looked at McHugh, whose level of energy was clearly not in sync with the rest of the room.

"What's got you down?" Harkness asked as he bit and chewed, bit and chewed.

"Questions," McHugh said. "Lingering questions."

"Oh yeah? Like what?"

"Oh," McHugh sighed, as he began to recite the mental list that had been rolling inconclusively through his brain for the last few hours.

"Why does someone who adamantly believes that Montague John Druitt was not a Ripper suspect, choose that same Montague John Druitt as his alias to re-create the crimes? Why does he go to the lengths of re-staging Druitt's watery suicide, including essentially reproducing the suicide note ... but takes the dive after the fourth murder, omitting the last and most famous – the death of Mary Kelly at 13 Millers Court? Why go to all those lengths and not see it through to the end?"

Harkness shrugged. "I don't know." He chewed for a few more moments, and then stopped, as a thought occurred to him. "Try this on for size: What if he didn't think that the Ripper killed all five women, did you ever consider that? Maybe he thought this Mary Kelly murder was a separate thing, where whoever killed her was just copycatting the Ripper like our guy. So, in his mind, he was done after four."

McHugh nodded slowly. "Yes, that's possible, I suppose. There is, within the Ripper community, a small but vocal contingent who believe that Mary Kelly's murder was committed by someone other than the Ripper. So that's an outside possibility, I would have to concur."

He continued to nod, as if doing so would help to convince himself.

It was a technique he had seen sales people use. The more they nodded, went the theory, the more likely the customer was to agree with them and make the purchase. So, McHugh nodded, but his heart wasn't really in it. He wasn't buying it.

"But then, you'd have to ask," he continued, "if he felt that way about Mary Kelly's killer, why did he go to the obvious trouble and effort to re-create her room in his apartment?"

"I've found," Harkness said, finishing off the pizza in one quick bite, "that crazy people do crazy things and most times you can't make head nor tail of why. That's why we call them crazy."

"Yes," McHugh agreed. "But regardless of how crazy their actions may seem to us, they are following their own private logic, which can be as rigid as our own. I just can't get a firm grip on what he was thinking. Or why he did it the way he did it.

"And," McHugh continued, as much to himself as to Harkness, "let us not forget that he didn't play fair in the past, so we shouldn't assume that he's playing fair now."

"He's not playing anything right now," Harkness said, crumbling his napkin and tossing it into a nearby wastebasket. "Except maybe checkers in Hell."

* * *

It wasn't the liveliest party Barbara had ever attended, nor the longest, but in the end it did turn out to be a memorable couple of hours. She spent a long time chatting with Officer Klingbile, who proved to be something of an amateur gourmand and an expert on the cuisine of Southern Italy.

He offered to e-mail her a number of recipes that he'd concocted that sounded delicious and, he promised, were well within her narrow cooking skills. ("If you can cook an egg, you can make this recipe," he told her, not realizing that at age thirty-eight, she still didn't understand how much time was actually required to cook a three-minute egg.)

And she learned more about Dale Harkness and his love of hunting than she really wanted to know. This included the proper steps to

field-dressing a freshly shot deer and why it was better and more effi-
cient to hunt ducks from the middle of a cornfield than from the
middle of a lake.

After a while, the party started to wind down, and then the appearance of officers from the next shift signaled the end of the gathering.
Everyone either returned to their desks to finish paperwork or headed
home.

Ben escorted a slightly tipsy Barbara and a strangely subdued
McHugh to the front door and down the steps to the street.

"Can I give you both a lift home?" he asked, gesturing to an
unmarked squad car, which was double-parked in front of the station.
"I've got a motor pool vehicle for the night and am happy to act as the
designated driver for any and all."

"That would be nice," Barbara said. "Thank you."

Ben looked to McHugh, who took a long moment to respond.
"Thank you, Benjamin," he finally said, "but I think I'll take advantage
of this fine fall evening. I believe that the stroll will do me good."

"Are you sure?"

"Absolutely." He tipped his hat to both of them. "Good evening."

With that he turned and headed down the sidewalk into the cool,
dark night. Ben and Barbara watched him go, then Ben stepped to the
car and opened the passenger door for her. She waited a second before
turning back toward Ben.

"He keeps doing that," she said. "It seems sort of abrupt."

"I don't know," he shrugged. "Perhaps he's one of those people
who doesn't like good-byes."

Barbara looked up at him, surprise showing on her face. "Is this
good-bye?" she asked.

Ben smiled and shook his head. "No, no," he said. "Of course not.
How could it be? I'm giving you a ride home."

He held the door open for her and she got in. He shut the door and
headed to the driver's side, stopping for a moment to watch McHugh
as he disappeared down the block.

The older man was walking slower than usual, Ben thought.
McHugh reached the corner, turned right and disappeared from sight.
Ben watched for a moment longer, then got in and started the car.

* * *

They drove in silence, not because they had nothing to say, but because neither one wanted this to be their last conversation.

So, the simplest solution, as illogical as it was, seemed to be to have no conversation at all. Traffic was light and they made the trip uptown in record time, even with Ben doing his best to miss the lights and position his car behind slower moving vehicles.

Far sooner than he would have liked, Ben pulled the car to a stop in front of Barbara's apartment building. They sat quietly for a few more moments. Finally, Ben started to say something, but stopped before any sound came out. Barbara looked at him expectantly.

"What?" she asked, turning in her seat to look him in the eye.

He smiled and shook his head. "Well, I was going to ask if I could come in, but then I remembered what happened when John Travolta did that."

Barbara looked puzzled. "You're going to have to connect the dots for me on that one," she said.

He pivoted in the seat, turning his body toward her. "Remember at the end of *Saturday Night Fever*? Travolta is talking to this girl and he says that he was going to ask her if he could walk her home, and she says–"

Barbara interrupted, finishing his sentence and doing a dead-on impression of the actress's Brooklyn dialect. "'You shouldn't ask, you should just do it.'"

Ben smiled, relieved that she was tracking with him. "That's right," he said, nodding. He turned and opened his door, but Barbara reached an arm across his chest, pulling him back.

"But you're not coming in," she said, settling back into her seat as he shut the door. She smiled warmly. "I mean, not tonight. But soon."

He turned and looked at her and she impulsively leaned forward and kissed him, taking him a bit by surprise. The surprise passed quickly, though. Ben returned the kiss, wrapping one arm around her and then the other, maneuvering as much as the confined front seat would allow.

He silently cursed the recent push that had been made in the department toward smaller, more compact cars for the NYPD unmarked fleet, although he realized he had been proponent of the idea at the time. But no longer. These cars needed to be bigger and roomier and with more comfortable seats. He determined to bring that up to the first person he met in the motor pool ...

The kiss stopped for a moment and then started again, this time with greater intensity. Barbara finally pulled back, gently placing her hand on his chest.

"Soon," she said. "Very soon."

She kissed him again, more quickly this time, then pulled back and swung open her passenger door. "Dinner tomorrow night?" she asked. "My treat? Someplace dark and expensive?"

"Works for me," Ben said, finally letting go of her hand. She shut the car door, gave him a quick, sexy wave through the passenger window, and then was gone.

Ben made sure she made it safely into the building before he drove off to register a complaint with the head of the motor pool.

* * *

Barbara stopped on her way to the elevator to gather the contents of her mailbox, which proved to be hardly worth the time or the effort. With her purse in one hand, three pieces of junk mail in the other (and a song in her heart and a spring in her step, she thought), she headed across the lobby to the elevator.

She almost gave a loud, cheerful greeting to Hector, but then noticed that his hat was over his eyes as he sat slumped in his chair. She couldn't begrudge anyone a short nap from time to time, but she wondered how he ever slept at home, given how much time he spent sleeping in the lobby.

She moved quietly across the hard marble floor, doing her best to keep her heels from clicking too loudly as she made her way to the elevator and pressed the call button.

The sound the elevator bell made upon its arrival was surprisingly loud, but a quick glance back at Hector assured her that it hadn't disturbed his slumber.

She stepped into the elevator and pressed her floor button. The door closed noiselessly, and the elevator started its ascent.

A few moments later, one eye opened up under Hector's hat, and then the other.

The eyes weren't brown, they were almost black. The eyebrows were a light blonde, not dark. And the eyes themselves held an anger and an intensity that were never found in Hector's eyes.

That was probably because the eyes didn't belong to Hector.

CHAPTER TWENTY-FOUR

Doubt hung in the air around McHugh like a thick fog as he puttered around his small, tidy hotel room, sorting through the few belongings he had brought on this trip as he methodically packed his suitcase.

McHugh had become accustomed to living with a certain amount of doubt in his life. As a practicing Ripperologist ("We need to find a better term," he thought to himself for at least the hundredth time. "Something less ... silly."), he was surrounded on all sides by doubt. He was under siege. But he'd made his peace with that years ago. It was the norm. It was the price of doing business. It was a fact you learned to live with if you wanted to work seriously on the question of Jack the Ripper.

Yet the doubt he was feeling right now, the gnawing ache in his gut that said, simply, 'something is wrong,' was different. It was not the same as the usual daily dose of doubt he'd come to expect since he began researching the Ripper.

This feeling was more reminiscent of his life on the police force, a feeling that occasionally surfaced at the conclusion of a case. There was, on occasions such as this, a voice which whispered, "McHugh, this is not over. There is more to be done."

But what? What needed to be done?

He couldn't think of what it was, so he continued his packing. He double-checked drawers and triple-checked the closet, which held only his weathered raincoat, and the iron and ironing board so thoughtfully provided by the hotel. He pulled the coat out and started folding it, wondering if it would fit in the suitcase that now bulged with the addition of several weeks' worth of the small shampoo bottles the hotel provided on a daily basis.

Perhaps he should carry the coat on the plane ... which, of course, would require remembering to carry it off the plane. After several years of gallivanting from one Ripper conference to the next, he'd found that the fewer stray objects he carried, the less likely he was to leave a trail of forgotten personal effects on the various planes, trains and taxis that were part and parcel of his traveling life.

While he mused on his options for the coat, he absently ran his hands through the coat pockets, first the ones in front and then the inside pocket. He stopped, surprised to find anything in the inside pocket, but there it was, a piece of paper. No, check that, two pieces of paper.

He pulled them out and held them up, recognizing them instantly: The map of the murder sites in Whitechapel along with the Manhattan map, in the same scale, with the sites for the copycat murders marked with large black stars.

He glanced at the Whitechapel map, which he had seen a thousand times. Five murder sites, each marked with a small red dot. He set the map on his desk, in a pile of items destined to go into his briefcase.

He was about to crumble up the other map when he saw something. Or, more to the point, *didn't* see something. He was instantly reminded of Sherlock Holmes and the famous clue of the dog that didn't bark in the night. Right in front of him, he realized, was a dog that should have been barking, but wasn't.

He spread out the photocopy of the Manhattan map and looked at it intently, trying to discern what wasn't there that should have been. But nothing came. He saw the four murder sites he had carefully marked with a black star ...

And that was it, of course. He had only marked four murder sites, not the requisite five.

McHugh pulled the Whitechapel map off the desk and placed it underneath the Manhattan map. The lighting provided by the two standing lamps in the room was too dim to see anything clearly through the top map.

He looked around for a lighted surface of some kind. The night was too dark, so very little light was coming through the window. The desk lamp threw off a murky haze that wasn't sufficiently bright enough for anything.

He switched on the overhead light in the bathroom and just as quickly switched it off. His hand reached for, and then found, the other switch on the wall plate, the third switch.

The first switch was for the overhead fluorescent light, which always took a long moment to sputter on and then after several minutes grew to full brightness, or so they alleged. The second switch controlled the whiny fan, which was essentially useless. He had turned it on only once during his long stay in the hotel and that was by accident.

The third switch controlled the overhead light in the shower, and this was the one he flicked on. He walked through the dark bathroom toward the frosted glass doors of the shower. The light in the shower bounced off the shower's white walls to create the flat, lighted surface he was looking for.

McHugh kicked some towels aside and pulled the sliding translucent shower door closed with a bang. He placed the two maps against the door, lining up the four stars on the top map with the four red spots on the map beneath it. He then located the fifth red spot, dimly visible on the Whitechapel map beneath the Manhattan map.

He placed his finger on that spot and pulled the map away from the door, opening the shower door and using that light to see the spot his finger marked.

He wasn't in any sense an expert on Manhattan geography, but he didn't have to be to recognize the spot his finger indicated on the map. Its adjacency to Central Park made it instantly recognizable. Plus, it didn't hurt that he had been to the location once before.

He headed quickly back into the bedroom, where he dropped the maps on the desk and picked up the phone.

* * *

Barbara could hear the shrill ring of her phone while she was still in the hall, unlocking her apartment door. She tried to open the door faster, which somehow only served to make the process proceed even more slowly. With an exasperated gasp, she finally got the door open, tossed the mail and her purse on the table by the front door, and then went to grab the phone. Which, of course, was not in its cradle.

That's the problem with cordless phones, she thought as she scanned the room, trying to determine the location of the ringing. If she'd only learn to put it back when she was done with it, she wouldn't have this problem ... which was the same thought she had every time she searched for the phone while it rang. Well, she thought, I'm nothing if not consistent.

She finally found the phone, under some papers on her writing desk. She clicked the talk button, certain that whoever was calling was now well on their way into the seventh circle of hell, better known as voicemail.

"Hello," she said, a little out of breath.

"Hey there, girlfriend!" exclaimed a too-cheerful voice.

It was Val, her publisher. Barbara looked at her watch and then remembered that Val didn't observe the standard convention of limiting business matters to between the hours of nine a.m. to five p.m. For Val, business was a twenty-four-hour-a-day venture. Anyone in business with Val very quickly learned that there was no time of the day too early or too late for a long and dramatic phone call.

"It's me," Val continued.

Barbara could hear typing through the phone line. Val was famous for answering e-mail while on the phone. She called this multi-tasking, but to Barbara it was better known as simply being rude.

For Barbara, phone etiquette, along with other forms of etiquette, was dying a slow death. She did her best to keep it alive – with little touches, like not switching from one call to another, despite the persistence of Call Waiting – but even she knew she was fighting a lost cause. Even as she could hear Val typing, a beep in her ear told her another call was coming in. But Barbara refused to succumb to its siren song. If nothing else, she would take the higher road and be the better example.

"Are you headed out?" Val asked, as the sound of her typing continued.

"No, I just got in," Barbara said, walking back to the front door and giving it a final, necessary push until the lock latched. "What's up?"

"Remember that thing you said 'no' to, you know, that interview in that magazine that you don't like because of what that one guy said that one time?" Val asked without taking a breath or even pausing for a response from Barbara. "I want you to keep an open mind on this, as some new information has just come into my possession that will, I believe, absolutely blow your mind."

Barbara kicked off her shoes and collapsed on the couch. This was going to be a long call, she could tell, and she realized there was no point trying to fight it.

* * *

McHugh tried Barbara's number three times and got voicemail each time. He slammed the phone down and pulled out his battered brown wallet, digging through the scraps of paper and miscellanea until he finally found what he was looking for: Benjamin Black's business card.

He held the card under the dim desk lamp. Ben's office number was printed on one side, along with his name, rank and work address. Scrawled across the back of the card was Ben's cell phone number.

McHugh mentally flipped a coin as he picked up the phone and started to dial.

* * *

The quiet of the nearly-empty squad room was broken by the sound of the phone ringing on Ben Black's desk. Officer Klingbile glanced at it as he walked by, heading toward the door.

He looked at his watch, then looked at the phone, then after a long moment of consideration, continued on his way toward the door. The phone rang persistently and a moment later Klingbile doubled back to Ben's desk and reached across the stacks of files, fumbling for the receiver.

"Detective Black's phone, Officer Klingbile speaking," he said. No one responded and he realized that the call had been transferred into the voicemail system.

With a shrug he replaced the receiver in the cradle, straightened a couple of the files he had moved when he grabbed the phone, and continued on his way, heading out of the office and home for the night.

A few seconds after he left the room, another phone started ringing on Ben's desk. This ringing phone was Ben's cell phone, which sat in its charger on the corner of his desk.

The phone rang five times and then stopped.

* * *

"I thought I might find you down here," Ben said, as he walked into Isobel's small, spotless office in the basement of the precinct, which housed the Medical examiner's office, the coroner and related lab space. "Burning the midnight oil, as it were," he said, leaning against the doorframe. "So, I finally figured out how to get from Christopher Plummer to Dennis Christopher in one."

Isobel glanced up from her desk, a surprised look on her face. "Your timing is perfect. I just tried to call you. On your cell phone."

Ben padded his pockets quickly and without success. "It's...," he started to explain.

"Yes, it's sitting in the charger on your desk, which is where it was the last time I called you and the time before that and the time before that. You, my pale friend, make a mockery of the concept of mobile communications." She stood up and grabbed a file folder from a neat rack on her desk. "There is a problem with that body of yours they took out of the river."

She began to move down the narrow corridor to the exam room and Ben followed. "What sort of problem?" he asked.

"The problem is this," she said. "The man was dead before he hit the water." She stopped at the door to the exam room and held it open for Ben.

"How long before he hit the water?" Ben asked. "I mean, did he die on the way down?"

"Perhaps that is the solution. But only if he was suspended in the air for about twelve hours. Was that the case?"

Ben shook his head.

"I thought not," she said. Ben entered the large exam room and Isobel followed.

The body, which lay on the autopsy table, was covered by a thin plastic sheet. Through this thin translucent veneer, Ben could see the large reddish-black stitches that indicated that the autopsy had been completed and that the body cavity had been re-sealed. Isobel pulled back the sheet far enough to reveal Malcolm's face.

"This is Malcolm Wright," she said, putting on the reading glasses that hung on a chain around her neck. She began referring to the notes in the file folder.

"I'll have to take your word for that," Ben replied as he looked down at the pallid face on the table. "I never got close enough to him to get a good ID."

"Yes, well, he has been identified since that time. When he was pulled out of the river, the first assumption was that he had drowned."

"That's a fair assumption, when someone jumps off the Williamsburg Bridge."

"Yes, I suppose so," Isobel agreed, paging through the notes in the file. "However, leaping to that sort of conclusion can be as dangerous as ..."

"Leaping off the Williamsburg Bridge?" Ben offered.

Isobel looked at him over the top of her reading glasses without smiling. "In a way, yes." She pulled the sheet back, covering Malcolm's face again, and then placed the file folder on his chest. "Indications are that Mr. Wright suffered a massive blow to the head, which was the cause of death."

Ben thought this over. "Couldn't he had gotten that blow to the head on the way down. After he jumped? Hitting something in the river, a piling or something?"

Isobel nodded hesitantly. "Yes, but two details suggest that death occurred earlier. First is the fact there was no water in his lungs. If he had hit his head on the way down, he might have been unconscious, but he would have still been breathing. At least, until he drowned, which would have been several minutes later."

Ben nodded. "Plenty of time for the lungs to fill with water."

"Exactly. But there was no water in his lungs, which leads us to believe that he was dead before he went into the water."

"Fair enough," Ben said, as he leaned against one of the exam tables, considering what he was hearing. "What's the other detail?"

Isobel pulled a report from the file. "This is less conclusive but no less ... what is the word? Compelling."

She pointed to a paragraph on the sheet of paper. "External indicators, specifically the degree of rigor mortis, documented immediately after the body was pulled from the river, suggests that he had been dead for several hours. That, of course, was much longer than he'd actually been in the water. In reality, given the low temperature of the water, it should have slowed the rate of rigor. Which clearly was not the case."

She looked at Ben for a long moment. He shifted his weight from one leg to the other, tapping his fingers on the counter while he considered what she had just said.

"So, you believe Malcolm was dead before he jumped off the bridge?"

Isobel nodded. "Yes. We believe it was before. Well before."

Ben stepped away from the exam table and paced the room, trying to put these new facts into place. Isobel watched him as she shut the file folder and took off her reading glasses. Ben paced back and forth quietly for a few moments.

"So, you somehow solved the other mystery?" Isobel asked, breaking the silence. Ben stopped walking and looked over at her.

"Which one?" he asked distractedly.

"The one I gave to you. Christopher Plummer to Dennis Christopher. In one."

Ben smiled for a moment. "Yes. It was not as difficult as you suggested, particularly when I remembered the case I've been working on."

Isobel sat on a rolling stool next to the exam table and crossed her legs, smiling and nodding for him to continue.

"Christopher Plummer was in that Jack the Ripper movie – the good one, *Murder by Decree*. Once I remembered that, then it was just a matter of going through the rest of the cast. Pretty soon, I realize that

John Gielgud played a small part in the film, and, of course, he was in *Chariots of Fire* with Dennis Christopher. Very simple, really."

Isobel applauded lightly. Ben smiled and then immediately turned his attention back to this new, troubling information.

"So," he finally said, drawing the words out as he worked things out in his head, "if Malcolm was dead long before he went into the water, that means it couldn't have been Malcolm who I chased up to the bridge. It was someone else. Someone who killed Malcolm and put his body into the river, later, after this unknown male survived his own jump from the Williamsburg Bridge."

Ben paced for a few more seconds as he sorted out his thoughts. "This person also planted evidence, so we'd believe Malcolm was the killer. Then after Malcolm died – just like Montague John Druitt died, in the river – we'd assume that the killings would stop, just as they did after Druitt's death."

Ben stopped pacing and looked at Isobel. "Which means that whoever this person is, he's still out there. And there's still one more murder."

Ben dug through his pockets and patted his suit coat with both hands, and then remembered the current, unhelpful location of his cell phone.

He looked up from his fruitless search to see Isobel standing in front of him, holding out her own cell phone to him.

* * *

It was a long phone conversation. No, that's not true. You couldn't really call it a conversation, Barbara thought, because she did remarkably little talking.

It was, instead, a long monologue from Val that, while certainly amusing in some parts and surprisingly pornographic in others, was not how Barbara had foreseen spending the remainder of her evening. It was so entertaining that Barbara didn't bother to respond to the several beeps in her ear, telling her that others in the world were trying to call her.

She waited for Val to take a breath – because, in theory, she would have to at some point – and then when she heard that small opening, leapt in.

"Yes, Val," she said very quickly. "I think it's terrific that they want to do an interview. I think that's admirable and charming and to their credit and all those other things you said. My point is, I think they're mean-spirited and petty and not very talented and they publish a crummy little magazine for small-minded people, and I don't want to do the interview. Which, when you get right down to it, should make all the difference, don't you think?"

Val started a rebuttal, but Barbara was saved by the bell, literally, as Val's next salvo was cut off by two short bursts from the front door buzzer.

"Val, I've got to go, there's someone at the door."

"Honey, I hear everything you're saying and I understand. All I ask is this: Can we talk about this more tomorrow?"

"Sure we can," Barbara said, as she got up and headed across the room. "But I've got to warn you that the answer will still be 'no.'"

"Never say never, honey."

"I'm not saying never, I'm saying no. But, yes, of course we can talk tomorrow. Good night."

"Good night, sweetie," Val said and the phone clicked off.

Barbara set the phone on the table by the door, making a mental note to move it back to its cradle before it got lost again. She looked through the peephole and was relieved to see Hector, his back to the door, surveying the hallway while he waited for her to answer the bell. I wonder what woke him up, she thought as she unlatched the bolt and swung the door open.

"Hector, you saved my life. If you hadn't rung the bell, I would never have gotten off that phone call."

Hector turned and she was surprised to see that it wasn't Hector. Although he was wearing Hector's coat and Hector's hat.

Instead of her doorman, she saw a thin young man who was dwarfed inside the bulk of Hector's coat. He looked to be in his middle twenties and was of average height, average weight, with average sandy brown hair. His skin was pale and his lips were thin and just as colorless as his skin.

The only remarkable or memorable things about him, other than that he was wearing Hector's hat and coat, was that his eyes appeared to be almost black … and he was holding a small revolver, which was pointed directly at Barbara. In his other hand, he held a black valise, like those which doctors used to carry back in the day when house calls were a common occurrence. He moved his foot forward, and his very average brown shoe wedged the door open.

"Who are you?" she asked, although of course she knew, and he knew that she knew.

She felt a chill move up her spine and gooseflesh tingle on her arms. As a child, when she had this feeling, her grandmother would have said, "Someone must be walking on your grave."

"For tonight, you can call me Jack," he said, his voice quiet and still and nondescript as his appearance. "Mind if I come in?"

He didn't wait for her to answer as he stepped forward into the room.

Barbara reflexively stepped backward and a moment later he was in and the door to her apartment swung shut. As usual, the lock didn't click into place, but Barbara realized that this was, at the moment, the very least of her problems.

CHAPTER TWENTY-FIVE

I t was very quiet. The only sound Barbara could hear was her own breathing and the hum of traffic on the street below. Her bedroom, which had always felt so safe and warm to her, now felt cold and alien.

Jack gently placed his phone on her nightstand and hit a "play" button on his music app. Moments later she heard a scratchy recording of a woman singing in a soft, Irish lilt. Barbara didn't recognize the song and although it was a pleasing tune, it brought no feeling of peacefulness to the room.

Scenes of my childhood arise before my gaze
   Bringing recollections of bygone happy days
   When down in the meadow in childhood I would roam,
   No one's left to cheer me now within that good old home

Jack listened quietly to the song, his eyes half-closed. He then glanced over at Barbara, who was perched on the edge of her bed. Her hands were folded in her lap as she did her best not to show just how frightened she actually was.

"Do you recognize this song?"

She shook her head. He nodded as he adjusted the volume, pushing the song into the background.

"I'm not surprised," he said as he turned toward the bed and opened the black valise. "It's called *'A Violet from Mother's Grave.'* They say Mary Kelly was heard singing this song on the night she was murdered."

He removed a long knife from the case and set it on the nightstand, then looked Barbara in the eye. "How much do you want to bet that Henry McHugh would have recognized the song, pegged it dead on? I would bet you fifty dollars he'd have known it in a second."

He didn't wait for a response from her, but instead took a copy of Barbara's book, *13 Miller's Court: Robert Louis Stevenson and the Solution to The Jack The Ripper Case,* from the bag and flipped it open to a page marked with a yellow sticky note. He glanced at the page and then back at her.

"You know," he said, "I don't want to get too critical, but there's a lot in this book that's just wrong. I mean, factually wrong. Sloppy research, sloppy reporting. I don't care, I'm not a fanatic about it, I'm just saying."

There was a long quiet pause between them. Barbara, despite her terror, felt the critical sting.

"What do you want me to say?" she said. "Sure. I got some of it wrong. I'm not the smartest Ripperologist on the block."

Jack smiled and shook his head. "No need to get testy," he said in his best placating voice. "There's one area where you got it mostly right. In fact, in that section the writing was quite good. Maybe the best in the book. However, I made some minor corrections. Nothing much, just some tweaks for clarity. Start reading from the second paragraph. Where I marked it."

He handed her the book. She took it and looked down at the section he indicated. She swallowed, the blood rising to her face as a lump began to form in her throat.

She looked up at him. He gestured toward the book and she began to read, doing her best to keep her voice from trembling as she spoke.

"'Several hours later, when the police finally broke down the door to Mary Kelly's room at number 13 Miller's Court, the sight that greeted them was

horrifying beyond words. More than one constable looked into the room and was instantly ill. They had good reason to be.

Mary Jane Kelly – or what remained of her – lay on the bed, on her back. Her dress had been pulled up to her waist, the skin on her thighs peeled away, revealing the muscle and bone beneath. Her throat had been sliced all the way through to her spine. It was later determined that this wound was one of the first and it was fatal, saving her from experiencing what was undoubtedly an hour or two of slow, deliberate mutilation.'"

She stopped reading and glanced up at him. He was removing another smaller but no less deadly-looking blade from his case. He nodded in agreement with what she had read.

"It took him an hour, at the very least," he said. "Maybe two. Opinions differ. But they all agree that he took his time. They were alone. They weren't about to be disturbed. They had all night. So he took his time." He set the second blade next to the first on the nightstand. "He took his time."

Barbara pushed herself back on the bed, scanning the room, looking for an out. Jack turned to her and smiled.

"I know what you're thinking," he said. "Why me? Oh, it didn't have to be you, don't get a big head. It had to be someone, of course. We can't end this with just four. It's gotta be five, that's sort of a given. If you're going to play the game, it's got to go to five. I think we all knew that going in."

Barbara made a quick move, attempting to roll across the bed and dive toward the door. But Jack was too quick, too young and nimble and swift of foot. He leapt at her with amazing speed, grabbed her shoulder and hair and pulled her back onto the bed with a hard yank.

They tussled for a few seconds, but he quickly gained and maintained control. She finally stopped squirming. They lay there for a long moment, each breathing heavily. Their posture was surprising intimate. Still holding her firmly with one hand, he reached over to the nightstand and picked up the larger of the two blades. He pressed the blade to her throat and pushed his face toward hers.

"Shall we get started?" he asked, his breath hot against her face. And then, perhaps uneasy with their proximity, he moved away from her and stood next to the bed. Barbara sat up, shaken and still breathing hard.

"There are so many things you've yet to comprehend," he said, changing his demeanor, now acting like a college professor beginning a well-practiced lecture.

"Let me take a moment to explain."

* * *

McHugh hurried through the building's lobby, not recognizing or registering the fact that this door-manned apartment building was currently minus one doorman. His worn shoes squeaked across the tiled floor and he brushed aside a bead of sweat that had started to form on his forehead.

He punched the call button impatiently, hitting it twice more to ensure the speedy arrival of the ancient elevator. When it finally arrived, its doors had barely opened before he barreled his way into the box, jabbing the floor indicator and quietly cursing the slowness of all things mechanical.

Years later, or so it seemed to McHugh, the elevator finally reached Barbara's floor. He turned right upon exiting the elevator and then remembered his first trip to this location and made a sharp u-turn. He headed down the hall in the other direction.

Upon approaching her apartment door, he raised his hand to knock but then noticed that the door was not shut completely. A small gap was visible through the doorjamb. He gave the door a push and it slid open silently as he stepped into the dark apartment.

It was as he remembered it from his first visit. Untidy but not dirty, cluttered but not disorderly. He scanned the living room, found it empty and, without hesitation, headed down the hall toward the bedroom.

As he approached, he heard an unfamiliar male voice. McHugh realized that he could be, if his instincts had failed him, stepping into a rather embarrassing situation. It was entirely possible, he admitted to himself, that Miss Thomas was in the midst of an assignation, entertaining a gentleman caller. That she was not in danger. That the killer was not still alive and very much fulfilling his plan.

McHugh was fully prepared to be wrong as he crept closer to the bedroom door, which stood ajar at the end of the dim hall, a shaft of light falling on the thick, beige carpet in front of him. And then the voice, the male voice, became clearer and McHugh realized that he was right. Dead right.

"You may be thinking that murder is not an art form," the voice was saying. "But you'd be wrong. Let's not forget Ezekiel 21: *'I will hand you over to artisans of destruction. You shall be fuel for the fire, your blood shall flow throughout the land.'*"

* * *

Barbara sat on the center of the bed, her legs folded under her, her weight resting on her hands as she leaned backwards. She was trying to keep as much physical distance between herself and Jack as she could manage without being too obvious about it. He didn't seem to notice, or if he did, he didn't care. He paced in front of the bed, tapping the knife blade on his palm for emphasis as he spoke.

"I mean, as I see it," he said, "the real problem for the artist is that it's all been done. It's all been created. Look around. Everything's been done and done to death and now imitation, reproduction, replication – these are the only art forms left to us.

"The geniuses have come and gone and all we can do is attempt, in our own meager way, to pay our respects by re-creating – and, thereby, honoring – their greatest creations."

He stopped pacing and pointed to a framed print on the wall of her bedroom. "For example, that's a Matisse, right?"

Barbara nodded. "Blue Pot and Lemon," she said. "It's not an original, if that's what you think –"

"Of course, it's not," he said, cutting her off like an officious professor barely tolerating an annoying student. "That's my point. It's a copy, a print, a reproduction. It's beautiful, one of a kind. There's no need for new art, that's what I'm saying, it's all been done and it's been done better than any of us could ever hope to do. The geniuses have all come before us. People are slowly coming to the realization that we, as a culture, are done creating. The art form of the twenty-first century is re-creation and imitation.

"Andy Warhol was the first to see it coming," he continued. "Think about it: he created a world wherein people would pay thousands, no millions, for a painting of a can of soup. A can of soup. He saw where we were heading.

"But it didn't stop there. It moved to publishing. They don't write new books. They hire people to re-create existing books in a new form. So we get new versions of *The Godfather*, sequels to *Gone With the Wind*, new Robert Ludlum books for God's sake, and he's been dead for years.

"And we can't forget motion pictures, where this concept has been a well-regarded notion from the inception of the nickelodeon. They don't create new movies, they re-create the old ones – they make re-makes and sequels and take bad television shows and make them into even worse movies. Do you know *The Maltese Falcon*, with Humphrey Bogart and Peter Lorre?"

Barbara was taken aback, as his monologue suddenly became a dialogue. She nodded weakly. "Yes, I've seen it."

He laughed. "Well, did you know that version was actually the third time they had shot that story? It was the third remake and that's the one we remember."

Barbara almost said something but then thought better of it.

However, he had seen the look on her face.

"Yes?" he asked.

"Well," she said hesitantly, "I was just thinking. Wouldn't the third time it was shot make it the second remake?"

There was a long moment of silence and then a burst of laughter exploded from him, taking Barbara entirely by surprise.

"Yes," he said, still smiling, "I believe you are correct, Barbara. Thank you for that grammatical correction."

He continued to pace in front of the bed, making a wider arc each time he turned, continuing to tap the blade of the knife against his open palm.

"But *The Maltese Falcon* is just one of hundreds of examples. They even re-made *Psycho*, for goodness sake, and why would anyone need to do that? And then, did you hear about those teenagers, the kids who filmed a shot-for-shot reproduction of *Raiders of the Lost Ark* a few years ago? Shot for shot, every single shot in the movie, it took them *years*. But they understood, they got it, they were ahead of the curve."

He stopped pacing and sat on the edge of the bed, a couple beads of sweat running down his temple. His eyes blazed with excitement.

"It's all been done, Barbara," he said. "That's the sad fact that we artists need to face. Those of us who want to create can only sit at the feet of the masters and re-create their best works in a vain attempt to match and honor and – for however brief a moment – touch their genius."

He wiped the sweat away from his forehead and looked at the moisture on his fingertips before continuing. "It was first written in Ecclesiastics, let's not forget: 'The thing that hath been, it is that which shall be; and that which is done is that which shall be done; and there is no new thing under the sun.'"

Barbara's head was spinning and she could tell by her shallow breathing that she was beginning to hyperventilate.

"So, this is your art form," she said, flatly. "Murder."

"Yes," he said, standing and gesturing to the room and, by extension, the city beyond. "This is my canvas, and on it I have re- created – slavishly and minutely, if I do say so myself – the work of the greatest serial killer of all time. The canonical five, as McHugh would say, Nichols the first and Kelly the last."

"But," Barbara stammered, "But ... my name isn't Kelly," she finally said, trying to make sense of what she was hearing.

"Well, you've got me there," he said, with a quick, sharp laugh. "I did make a couple minor concessions to originality. Like sending the Lusk letter a tad early. Playing fast and loose with a couple of the victims' names. Drowning my Druitt before his time. And making you my Mary Kelly.

"You know," he continued, "I had considered legally changing your name to Mary Kelly. It's really quite easy to do, you'd be surprised. But in the end, I decided that this would be my one original stroke. My own touch. A little bit of me, as it were. It's not like I'm painting a mustache on the Mona Lisa, after all. I mean, I've got the date and time right. And the location, which – relative to the other murders – makes this Number 13 Miller's Court.

"Granted, we're about 16 stories higher than we need to be, but that's nitpicking. But when it comes to the crime itself," he said, running the blade of the knife along his fingertips, "I promise you that it will be an exact reproduction. Jack himself wouldn't know the difference."

He laughed self-consciously, looking up from the knife, his eyes clearing and his breath slowing as he shifted his mood, getting himself ready for the next phase.

"As you can see," he said, smiling a little sheepishly, "This is a subject I feel passionately about."

He headed back toward the valise and as he passed the bedroom door, Barbara caught a glimpse, just a flash, of what appeared to be McHugh's face in the dim light of the hall. She involuntarily gasped. Jack looked to her, bemused.

"It's starting to settle in, isn't it," he said. "The weight of what we're doing here tonight. The gravity. It's almost a religious experience, I think you'll see. And you should be honored to be taking part in such an historic reproduction."

"They'll catch you," Barbara said, straining to not look at the door, not look to see if it really was McHugh's face and not just a trick of the light. She couldn't look, she didn't want to have that rug pulled out from under her. And so she focused her attention on Jack. "They'll find you and they'll catch you."

"You think so?" he said as he gently, reverently, took another blade from the bag, followed by a neatly folded red plaid shirt, which he placed on a chair next to the nightstand. "Don't count on it. All they'll know for sure is that it wasn't Malcolm Wright. They'll figure that out – that police detective friend of yours, Mr. Black, will put those pieces together. He'll figure out that Malcolm didn't place that ad, didn't run across that bridge. He'll realize that Malcolm was dead long before I took that long leap into the river for him.

"They'll realize that he had no water in his lungs. Other than that, what do they have? Nothing. No, all they'll have is one more reproduction, a precise, exact copy of the greatest denouements of any serial killing in the history of mankind."

He headed around the bed, looking for the best angle from which to start his work.

"Plus, in the highly unlikely event they do manage to track me down and put me away, there will always be someone else out there to pick up where I left off. To create new reproductions. I'm not the only one who's seen the writing on the wall. This is a revolution and trust me – it's not a revolution of one. Others will copy me just as I copied Jack. There is, quite literally, nothing new under the sun."

He strolled back to his original position, and then took a step backward, assessing the whole room. He cocked his head to one side, looked at a lamp across the room and headed toward it.

"We'll need a bit more light," he said. "The original Jack worked by the light of Mary's fire, with a candle or two for assistance, but to get this right I need to see what I'm doing."

McHugh, peering through the crack between the door and the frame, saw Jack clearly in the mirror across the room. He watched as the young man made his way across the room. Just as he came near the door, McHugh threw his full weight against it, slamming the door into Jack and knocking him backward, sending him sprawling to the floor.

McHugh pulled back the door and headed toward the fallen man, but the blow had not been as severe as he thought. Jack was up a moment later, barreling toward McHugh with full speed. They collided with a heavy thud and McHugh tumbled backward with Jack on top of him, the weight of the younger man momentarily knocking the wind out of him.

They rolled on the floor while McHugh flung his free arm at Jack with little effect. Jack got up, putting one knee squarely into McHugh's chest, then cocked his right arm back and slammed his fist cleanly into McHugh's face.

The punch succeeded in hammering McHugh's head into the solid wood floor with a sickening thwack. He weakly raised his head again, only to be met with another, harder punch from Jack. This one did the trick and McHugh's head hit the floor again, his eyes closed, a trickle of blood beginning to form at the corner of his mouth.

Flush with adrenaline, Jack jumped up from the floor and turned to see Barbara, still on the bed but now brandishing one of his knives with both hands.

He smiled, wiping spit from his lips with his shirt sleeve. Barbara, her arms beginning to tremble, attempted to hold him at bay with the blade. They looked at each other for a long moment, neither blinking, as he glanced from her eyes to the knife and back to her eyes.

And then he was on her, slapping the knife away with one strong hand while his other hand went for her throat. He held her with one hand for what seemed like a full minute, before releasing her, pushing her backward onto the bed with a violent shove.

Jack reached across the wide bed for the knife, grabbing it and holding it almost casually at his side. A cough followed by a wheeze from across the room took his attention away from Barbara, who was massaging the deep red mark across the front of her throat. She gasped for air as she rubbed the skin, using her other hand to pull her hair back out of her eyes.

On the floor, McHugh was attempting to prop himself up on one arm, a struggle that he appeared to be losing. Jack looked at him with a mock stern expression, clucking his tongue with annoyance.

"Mr. McHugh, how nice of you to join us," he said as he ran his free hand through his hair, which had become disheveled in the tussle. "I thought after our little run-in at Malcolm Wright's apartment, that we were unlikely to meet again. However, as nice as it may be to see you, this really won't do. When I leave, there can only be one body in this room, and it has to be hers."

McHugh coughed again and rubbed his eyes, still trying to get himself up on one elbow. "I suppose that's true," he said, shaking his head to clear his brain. He wiped the blood away from his mouth with the back of his hand.

Jack got off the bed, glancing at Barbara before taking two steps toward McHugh. "I'll need to find a way to get rid of your body. We don't want the police thinking they've stumbled onto a lovers' suicide pact. It would ruin the symmetry."

"And we wouldn't want to be asymmetrical, would we?" McHugh asked with a slight wheeze. He was finally able to sit halfway up, leaning over onto his left side for leverage.

"No, not after I've gone to all this trouble to get the details right. And I did get them right, didn't I?" He waited expectantly for McHugh's answer.

McHugh nodded in agreement. "Yes you did," he said. "You got the details right."

Jack's face broke into a wide grin as he took a moment to savor the response. "I'm not fishing for compliments," he said, leaning down toward McHugh, "but I figured you, of all people, would appreciate the details. The identical wounds, the placement of the bodies, the graffito, all the touchstones of that series of murders that have, essentially, defined your life for the last twenty years. I can't begin to imagine how excited you must be to witness all of this. Think of it: after all these years, you are finally face-to-face with Jack the Ripper. Essentially."

McHugh shook his head, massaging his sore hip with his right arm. "I'm afraid I don't share your enthusiasm for your crimes. They are unoriginal. Without vision or poetry or … panache. The way I see it," he said dryly, "you have only one thing in common with Jack the Ripper that I can attest to with any real certainty."

Jack stood up, affronted, his arms at his sides, almost in a pout. "Oh?" he said. "And what would that be?"

"That you're both dead."

McHugh had stopped massaging his hip and had pulled a small caliber revolver from his pocket. He fired three shots in quick succession, directly into Jack's chest. The sound echoed in the room for several seconds.

Jack looked down at his chest, where the three small holes were starting to turn red. The knife dropped from his hand as he took a step forward, wavered, stepped backward and then collapsed like a rag doll onto the floor.

The room was quiet, with just the faint echo of the shots still reverberating. McHugh looked over at Barbara, who was now sitting up in the center of the bed, her hair disheveled, her hand still massaging her throat.

She looked down at him, still sprawled on the floor, his coat sleeve torn and a few small blood stains on his wrinkled blue shirt.

"Your front door doesn't lock properly," he said finally.

"Yes, you have to push it shut. Until it clicks," she said, nodding slowly. "I've been meaning to get that fixed."

They sat there quietly for a few more moments, as their breathing began to return to normal. Barbara looked at the revolver, which McHugh was still holding in his right hand.

"I thought you didn't carry a gun," she said, a note of surprise hanging in her voice. "I mean, I heard that you didn't ever carry a gun."

McHugh nodded. "Well, not when I was on the force, no. None of us did. But, my dear," he said, a look of bemusement slowly developing on his face. "Consider my situation. I'm in America. I'm in New York City. And there's a serial killer on the loose. How many more reasons does a person need to carry a gun?"

"I can see that," she agreed, and then another thought occurred to her. "But," she said, "if you were carrying a gun the whole time, why did you wait so long to use it?"

McHugh nodded sheepishly. "Yes, you have me there. I was just hoping you wouldn't follow that train of logic quite as far as you did, to its somewhat embarrassing conclusion," he said. "The simple fact is, I forgot I was carrying the bloody thing until that ruffian threw me to the ground. When I slammed into the floor, the gun jammed into my hip and a little light bulb went off, as it were. Chalk it up to old age, if you must."

Barbara smiled, but before she could respond there was a flurry of footsteps in the hall and the bedroom door was kicked open with such force that the top hinges came loose from the frame.

Two police officers, in full SWAT gear, burst in, their high-powered rifles scanning the room before settling on McHugh and Barbara. Behind them, gun in hand, was Ben, who quickly surveyed the scene and gave them the visual cue to stand down.

He looked at Barbara, made a rapid assessment that she was unharmed, then glanced down at McHugh, who was just starting to sit up.

"I got your message," Ben said.

"So I see," McHugh said.

Then all was quiet again as they looked at the body on the floor.

"Who's that?" Ben finally asked.

"An unknown male. Beyond that, we may never know," McHugh said, as Ben helped him to his feet.

He brushed off his pants and adjusted his suit coat, looking down at his torn sleeve then back at the body.

"But I can tell you this much: I, for one, am glad he's dead."

CHAPTER TWENTY-SIX

Ben walked into the Starbucks at Worth and Lafayette and looked around the surprisingly crowded space, unable to spot his intended prey. He scanned the room one more time and was about to leave when he finally discovered that Dimitri was, in fact, seated in his regular spot by the window.

With a second look, Ben realized immediately why he had failed to notice him. Dimitri was dressed in jeans and a Giants t-shirt, instead of his traditional suit, tie and starched white shirt.

"I nearly didn't recognize you," Ben said as he approached the table. "What's up? Are you going to a funeral?"

Dimitri looked up and came very close to cracking a smile. "You're a funny man, detective. This police thing doesn't work out, maybe they can find a spot for you at Caroline's down in Times Square."

Ben pulled up a chair and gestured at Dimitri's laptop. "No music today?"

Dimitri shook his head. "I'm not technically working," he said. "I just stopped in to answer a couple e-mails."

"So, I suppose you're basking in the reflected glow. Your Ripper site has gotten a lot of publicity since all this broke."

Dimitri shook his head. "It ain't my site anymore," he said. "I sold it. Sold them all." He looked over at Ben who appeared stunned at the announcement. "You better close that mouth of yours, detective. You let it hang open like that, you're going to start catching flies, as my grandmother used to say."

Ben shook his head, still mystified. "You sold your serial killer websites? All of them? Why?"

Dimitri shrugged. "Well, you could say it was because some dudes backed a truck up and started pouring money on me. That sounds like a valid reason that I suspect would sway just about anyone. But I don't think that's it, not really."

He closed the lid on his laptop and sat back, taking a sip from his coffee cup. He looked out the window at the passing traffic and then back at Ben. "I just sort of lost my taste for it, I guess," he said. "So, what brings you here? Don't tell me you've now got a jones for the Third Place?"

Ben shook his head. "No, I'll stick with precinct coffee. I just thought you might be interested in the identity of our killer."

Dimitri raised an eyebrow. "You guys finally got a name for your John Doe? Or should I say, Jack Doe?"

"Yes, with the help of the FBI we finally got a positive ID. His name was Oliver Penn and he hailed all the way from Columbus, Ohio."

Dimitri clucked his tongue and shook his head. "You lay the name Oliver on me, I just might become a serial killer, too."

"Well, that's as good a reason as we've come up with so far. He was twenty-six years old and worked for an electronics store as one of their computer repair people. We've talked to his parents, his friends, his relatives, his co-workers.

He'd been a model student in high school, captain of the swim team, went to college for a while and then dropped out and got a job. He was the classic quiet guy next door who no one ever suspected would be a killer."

"Well, as they say, stereotypes exist because there are enough people out there who fit them."

Ben nodded. "I suppose that's true. The FBI in Columbus went through his computer for us and found all the evidence we'd need. He'd been very thorough in his planning. And he'd spent a lot of time on your website," Ben added. "He had the user name FAMOUS_JACK."

"I don't recognize the name," Dimitri said, "But we've got a lot of fools who use our message boards."

"Actually, you probably wouldn't recognize the name," Ben said. "That's the thing, he hardly ever posted. However, according to the computer history, he read just about everything everyone else posted."

"Ah, a lurker," Dimitri said. "God only knows how many of those we have. Or, I guess I should say, how many <u>they</u> have, 'cause it ain't mine anymore. So, that's how he found Malcolm Wright?"

"Yes, we think so. He got to know Malcolm via e-mail and then when he came to town, he set things up to make Malcolm the fall guy."

"Literally."

Ben shrugged. "I guess so. He left a manifesto of sorts on his computer, not too different from what he told Barbara at her apartment."

Dimitri smiled. "Yeah, I read some of that nonsense in the paper, 'bout how everything's been created and how the latest trend is all about the art of imitation."

"Even murder."

"Well, if you ask me, that's just lazy," Dimitri said, shaking his head. "People have been finding new ways to kill each other since the dawn of time. I think your pal Oliver just lacked imagination."

Ben nodded as he sat back in his chair. "He lacked something, that's for sure." Ben turned and looked at the people seated in the coffee shop and the long line of people waiting at the counter.

Dimitri studied at him and followed his gaze. "Here's the thing about a cat like that," he said. Ben turned to look at him and Dimitri leaned forward. "I've seen this a lot on the sites. You'll read some crazy-ass idea that some fool has come up with, and then a bunch of people will shout him down. But sure as I'm looking at you, there's always someone else who chimes in that they agree with the crazy fool."

Ben looked at Dimitri for a long moment. "So what are you saying?" he finally asked.

"I'm just saying that senseless ideas like his are just like that Whack-a-Mole game out on Coney Island. You know the one I mean? As soon as you whack one mole, another one just as fanatical pops up somewhere else, with his own crazy-ass ideas. At least, that's been my experience."

He picked up his laptop and began putting it into its carrying case. "You whacked one mole, I'll give you that, but keep an eye out, my friend. There are always other crazy moles out there, waiting to pop up."

"So, if you're selling the serial killer web sites, what's next for you?" Ben asked.

"Well, if I wanted, I could do nothing for a good long time. You know that truck I told you about? The one they backed up filled with money?"

Ben nodded.

"Did I mention that it was a big truck? Like a semi-trailer?"

Ben smiled. "Good for you."

Dimitri shrugged. "I guess so. So, I could live a life of leisure, but that doesn't really suit me. Instead, I'm thinking I might ..." His voice trailed off.

"What?" Ben asked, leaning forward. "Let me guess. You're opening a restaurant that only serves breakfast, but their gimmick is they only serve it for dinner."

Dimitri gave him a long quizzical look and then shook his head. "No, sadly the ship's already sailed on that brainstorm," he said with a smile as he finished zipping up the carrying case. "But you're not too far off. You're going to think I'm crazy, but I'm looking into buying myself a coffee shop."

Ben's smile started small but grew quickly. "A coffee shop?"

Dimitri shrugged. "Why not? I spent half my time in a coffee shop. Might as well be making some money in the process. Plus," he added, "I've got some ideas on how to give these Starbucks folks a run for their money."

"If anyone can do it, I'd put my money on you," Ben agreed, glancing at his watch. "Oh, I've got to go. I've got to drive someone to the airport," he said as he got up.

"Hey, I've got a tip for you," Dimitri said. "You might not be hip to this, but they have vehicles that will do that now. Take someone right to the airport and drop them smack dab at the door. They'll take you home from the airport, too. It's called an Uber. Unless you want to go old-world and call yourself a cab."

Ben smiled. "Yes, I know."

Dimitri smiled right back at him. "It's a lady, isn't it?"

Ben held up his hand. "The New York Police Department doesn't comment on domestic affairs."

"Yeah, right. Well, here's my advice to you: If you keep driving a lady to the airport, before long she's going to come to expect it. And at that point, you might as well be married."

"That's the plan," Ben replied, and before Dimitri could comment further, Ben had made his way through the crowded coffee shop and out the door.

CHAPTER TWENTY-SEVEN

L ike most airports, JFK has a very strict policy about vehicles loitering while they drop off passengers in front of the terminals. As a result, the area is policed 24 hours a day to keep cars moving and traffic flowing.

So it's safe to say that if Ben hadn't had an NYC police detective badge, he would have been told to leave by each of the five airport traffic cops that knocked on his window during the forty minutes that his car sat parked in front of Terminal Four. But with badge in hand, he kept the law at bay while he and Barbara said their good-byes.

"You've got my cell number and the number at the hotel and I brought my laptop, so I'll be checking e-mail as well," Barbara said, running down the mental list she'd been carrying around in her head all day.

"Yes, I know," Ben said. "I've got all your numbers. And I've got my cell phone and I promise to keep it on my person at all times." He patted his coat pocket. "At least, I thought I had my cell phone ..." He patted his other pockets quickly and came up empty.

Barbara reached past him and picked up his cell phone, which he had placed on the dashboard earlier.

"Thanks," he said, and then looked at his watch. "So, do you really have to go to this thing?"

"It's only for three days," Barbara reminded him. "Plus, with all the press I've been getting this week, it will be nice to get away from it all. Val's not too thrilled with me disappearing, but she'll just have to live with it."

"I understand," he said. "I just think that it's hard to build a relationship when one of us isn't here."

"Hey, for some relationships, that's a plus. My aunt Jean and uncle Morris only saw each other for half a day a week and they were happily married for over forty years."

Ben rolled his eyes. "That's a sterling example."

"Look," she said, reaching out her hand to touch the side of his face, "you drove me to the airport. In some cultures, that would make us married."

This produced a smile and then a laugh from him. She leaned in to give him a quick kiss, then reached for the door handle. She opened the door a crack, pulled it shut again, and turned back for another, longer kiss. This was followed by two shorter kisses, and then one quick peck.

"Have fun," he said.

"Hey, it's a Jack the Ripper conference. How can I not?"

She opened the door and got out, heading straight into the terminal with her overnight bag over her arm. She gave him a final wave over her shoulder without looking back, before disappearing through the automatic glass doors.

Ben watched her go and continued to stare for a few more moments, before a knock on the driver's side window from another airport traffic cop brought him back to reality. He gave the cop a wave, put the car in gear and pulled into traffic.

* * *

Even after the long goodbye with Ben and a longer-than-usual wait in the security line, Barbara still had plenty of time to kill before her flight boarded. So, she headed to her favorite spot in the airport: the large Hudson's bookstore in Terminal Four. She had already brought along plenty of reading material for the flight, but like most writers (and readers) she was drawn to bookstores in airports by the irrational fear that she might be missing just the right book for this particular flight.

She was not disappointed in her search. Within the first few moments she found a paperback of one of Lawrence Block's *Burglar* books that she had never read, along with a *Thursday Next* novel from Jasper Fforde that she had somehow missed.

With these books in hand, she realized that she now, officially, had too many books for this trip. That knowledge provided her with the sense of completion she needed.

With that work out of the way, she wandered over to the non-fiction section and casually, oh so casually, checked to see if this particular bookstore stocked a copy or two of *13 Miller's Court: Robert Louis Stevenson and the Solution to The Jack The Ripper Case*.

She was pleased to see that they had four copies, arranged in a place of prominence on the shelf with the cover facing out. The recent news reports had clearly resulted in a flurry of renewed interest in Jack the Ripper books.

Barbara scanned the other books on the shelves, then looked around to make sure that none of her fellow shopper/travelers was watching. Assured that her actions would go unnoticed, she pulled her four books from the shelf and turned them so just the spines faced out, and then put them back on the shelf.

With a decent-sized gap now available, she pushed some books down the row. Then she took the only copy of another book on that shelf and turned it so that its cover was facing out. The book was McHugh's *The Jack the Ripper Omnibus*.

She stepped backed, pleased with the results of her handiwork. A voice from behind her broke the quiet in the bookstore.

"Thank you, my dear, but I believe in my heart of hearts there's enough space on that shelf for the both of us."

Barbara turned to see Henry McHugh, dressed for travel with a small weathered satchel in his hand, his raincoat over his arm and his ever-present hat sitting slightly askew atop his head.

She smiled and realized just at that moment how genuinely pleased she was to see him. "Are you on your way to Cincinnati?"

McHugh nodded. "It wouldn't be a Jack the Ripper conference

without dragging out old McHugh," he said as they walked to the cash register. "In fact, I believe we may be on a panel or two together."

Barbara laughed nervously as she gave the clerk her credit card. "Terrific," she said. "Another opportunity for you to tear me and my theory apart in public."

"On the contrary, my dear," he said, reaching into his satchel. "I've looked your book over and I must say, you have some genuinely fascinating ideas. Robert Louis Stevenson as the Ripper. Quite interesting."

He pulled out his copy of her book and held it up to prove his statement, and then squirreled it away back in his case.

"You're just being polite," she said, signing the receipt and taking back her credit card. "If I'm really going to be honest, I'd admit that my theory's riddled with holes. It always has been. I was just never willing to admit it."

"Holes?" he said with well-feigned astonishment. "Really? I don't believe I noticed a one ..."

Barbara took the plastic bag proffered by the clerk and then turned to McHugh. "Well, for starters," she said, "All eye-witnesses have put Jack the Ripper's height at between five-foot seven and five-foot nine, right?"

McHugh nodded. "Yes, I believe so."

"Well, Robert Louis Stevenson was well over six feet. And that's a fact." She headed toward the store's door and McHugh followed.

"Plus," she continued, "all the experts agree that the murders required a detailed knowledge of the back streets and alleys of Whitechapel, an area of town Stevenson was not known to frequent. That's also a fact. And, most damning of all, would be his whereabouts during the fall of 1888."

McHugh raised a hand in objection as they made their way toward the gate. "Now, now, no one can prove that Stevenson wasn't in London in the autumn of 1888..."

Barbara cut him off. "No, but they can prove that he was in the South Pacific – Samoa, to be exact – from 1887 until early 1890. And I think we'd both agree that Polynesia is more than just a short carriage ride from the East End."

McHugh put out a hand and stopped Barbara, taking a moment to consider her argument. "Barbara, Barbara," he said earnestly, "those are minor details to be sure. You've named the killer, and a celebrity at that."

He looked her in the eye and held up a finger to silence any possible response. "Let me tell you, entire careers have been based on evidence far shakier than yours."

Barbara considered a verbal response but smiled instead.

"Now, come along my dear," he continued, taking her by the arm and directing her toward their gate and their plane. "We've got to get to Cincinnati and put on a show. Our fans and our fanatics await us."

CHAPTER TWENTY-EIGHT

I t was not much later when another traveler approached the same clerk in the same bookstore. The clerk, a second-year freshman at NYU, had become accustomed to serving a varied number of customers during each of her eight-hour shifts at the airport. Just as soon as she got one taken care of, another one would pop up and need her assistance. And as soon as that one was done, another one would pop up.

She looked up from her most recent customer to see a middle- aged man approaching with a single book in his hands. He was thin and balding and wore a plain brown suit. There was nothing exceptional about him. Just another guy, traveling from point A to point B. Except for the eyes. There was something, she couldn't figure out just what, behind those eyes.

"Did you find what you were looking for?" she asked as she took the book he had placed on the counter and ran it under the scanner.

"Yes, I did," he said, as he smiled at her and looked intently at her nametag. "In fact, Beth, I found exactly what I was looking for."

She smiled back at him and then glanced down at the book as she slid it into a plastic bag. *Helter Skelter.*

Wasn't that a Beatles song? she thought. "Where are you headed

....?" she asked for what was probably the seventy-fifth time today, as she took the cash he held out for her.

"Charlie," he answered. "You can call me Charlie."

"Okay. Where are you headed today, Charlie?"

"Los Angeles," he said. "The Hollywood Hills, actually."

"That sounds like fun," she said, handing him his change. "Have a great trip."

"I hope to," he said. "I think it's going to be very ... productive."

And then he stepped away and another customer stepped forward, setting a small stack of magazines and a couple packs of gum in front of her.

Beth smiled at this new customer, looked at the cash register and noticed she had forgotten to give the *Helter Skelter* guy – Charlie – his receipt.

"Sir, wait, you forgot your –"

But he was gone. He had stepped through the door and had already disappeared, absorbed into the never-ending flow of people moving through the terminal.

Charlie was on his way.

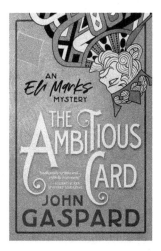

THE AMBITIOUS CARD

An Eli Marks Mystery (#1)

The life of a magician isn't all kiddie shows and card tricks. Sometimes it's murder. Especially when magician Eli Marks very publicly debunks a famed psychic, and said psychic ends up dead. The evidence, including a bloody King of Diamonds playing card (one from Eli's own Ambitious Card routine), directs the police right to Eli.

As more psychics are slain, and more King cards rise to the top, Eli can't escape suspicion. Things get really complicated when romance blooms with a beautiful psychic, and Eli discovers she's the next target for murder, and he's scheduled to die with her. Now Eli must use every trick he knows to keep them both alive and reveal the true killer.

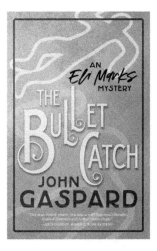

THE BULLET CATCH

An Eli Marks Mystery (#2)

Newly-single magician Eli Marks reluctantly attends his high school reunion against his better judgment, only to become entangled in two deadly encounters with his former classmates. The first is the fatal mugging of an old crush's husband, followed by the suspicious deaths of the victim's business associates.

At the same time, Eli also comes to the aid of a classmate-turned-movie-star who fears that attempting The Bullet Catch in an upcoming movie may be his last performance. As the bodies begin to pile up, Eli comes to the realization that juggling these murderous situations – while saving his own neck – may be the greatest trick he's ever performed.

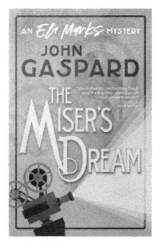

THE MISER'S DREAM

An Eli Marks Mystery (#3)

A casual glance out his apartment window turns magician Eli Marks' life upside down. After spotting a dead body in the projection booth of the movie theater next door, Eli is pulled into the hunt for the killer. As he attempts to puzzle out a solution to this classic locked room mystery, he must deal with a crisis of a more personal nature: the appearance of a rival magician who threatens not only Eli's faith in himself as a performer, but his relationship with his girlfriend.

But the killer won't wait and starts taking homicidal steps to bring Eli's investigation to a quick and decisive end. Things get even worse when his magician rival offers his own plausible solution to the mystery. With all the oddball suspects gathered together, Eli must unveil the secrets to this movie-geek whodunit or find himself at the wrong end of the trick.

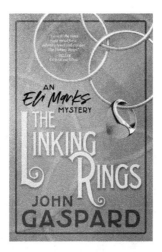

THE LINKING RINGS

An Eli Marks Mystery (#4)

Eli's trip to London with his uncle Harry quickly turns homicidal when the older magician finds himself accused of murder. A second slaying does little to take the spotlight off Harry. Instead it's clear someone is knocking off Harry's elderly peers in bizarrely effective ways. But who? The odd gets odder when the prime suspect appears to be a bitter performer with a grudge...who committed suicide over thirty years before. While Eli struggles to prove his uncle's innocence--and keep them both alive--he finds himself embroiled in a battle of his own: a favorite magic routine of his has been ripped off by another hugely popular magician.

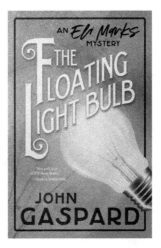

THE FLOATING LIGHT BULB

An Eli Marks Mystery (#5)

When a magician is murdered in the midst of his act at the Mall of America, Eli Marks is asked to step in and take over the daily shows--while also keeping his eyes and ears open for clues about this bizarre homicide.

As Eli combs the maze-like corridors beneath the Mall of America's massive amusement park looking for leads, he also struggles to learn and perform an entirely new magic act. Meanwhile, the long-time watering hole for Uncle Harry and his Mystics pals is closing. So in addition to the murder investigation and the new act, Eli must help the grumpy (and picky) seniors find a suitable new hang out.

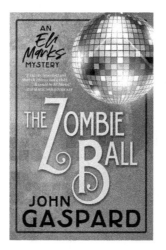

THE ZOMBIE BALL

An Eli Marks Mystery (#6)

Eli's asked to perform his magic act at a swanky charity gala, *The Zombie Ball* – a former zombie pub crawl which has grown into an annual high-class social event. What begins as a typical stage show for Eli turns deadly when two of the evening's sponsors are found murdered under truly unusual circumstances.

Compounding this drama is the presence of Eli's ex-wife and her new husband, Homicide Detective Fred Hutton. Under pressure to solve the crime before the 800 guests depart, Eli and his detective nemesis go head-to-head to uncover the bizarre clues that will unravel this macabre mystery.

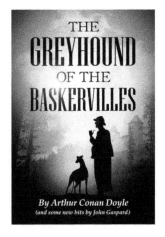

THE GREYHOUND OF THE BASKERVILLES

This is new edition of Arthur Conan Doyle's classic mystery, "The Hound of the Baskervilles." It's the same story. Mostly.

That is, it contains the same characters, the same action, and much of the same dialogue. What's different?

Well, it's a little shorter, a little leaner, a little less verbose in some sections. But the chief difference is that it's now narrated by a dog. A greyhound, in fact, named Septimus.

In this new edition, he tells his story of how he became "The Greyhound of the Baskervilles." Same story, new tail.

ABOUT THE AUTHOR

John is the author of the Eli Marks Mystery Series, which follows magician Eli Marks and the murders he finds himself embroiled in.

In real life, John's not a magician, but he has directed a bunch of low-budget features that cost very little and made even less – and that's no small trick. He's also written multiple books on the subject of low-budget filmmaking. Ironically, they've made more than the films.

He's also written for TV and the stage.

John lives in Minnesota and shares his home with his lovely wife, one or more greyhounds, a few cats and a handful of pet allergies.

Find out more at: https://www.elimarksmysteries.com

 facebook.com/JohnGaspardAuthorPage

 twitter.com/johngaspard

CPSIA information can be obtained
at www.ICGtesting.com
Printed in the USA
FSHW021944220819
61343FS